FORMAL ARRANGEMENT

KYLIE GILMORE

Formal Arrangement: © 2017 by Kylie Gilmore

Cover design by Sweet 'N Spicy Designs

Published by: Extra Fancy Books

ISBN-13: 978-1-942238-30-0

To hardworking parents everywhere…

1

Alex Campbell was cursed with a two-year-old demon from hell. He'd thought Viv's first year had been difficult. No-o-o-o, that had been a cakewalk compared to this. Two-year molars were going to kill him. Three weeks with no end in sight. He'd taken her to the pediatrician, scoured the Internet, asked his very experienced dad, and THERE WAS NO CURE.

Her fresh wails threatened to rupture his eardrums. He set her down in the kitchen, pulled an ice cube from the freezer, and wrapped it in a washcloth. Then he scooped her up and pressed it to her lips. "This'll make your gums feel better. Put it where it hurts."

She sucked on the washcloth and dropped it, wailing again.

He stared at it on the kitchen floor. Five-second rule. He snagged it and offered it again. "Here. Put it in the back where your molars are coming in."

Her gums were swollen, the tiniest bit of white showing in the upper gums. The lower molars had come in with no problem. He helped her get the ice in the right place on the side with the most swelling and she quieted. He relaxed a tiny bit, taking in her chubby cheeks now red from so much snot and tears, her light brown hair messy and probably tangled, another struggle he was not up to dealing with, her big brown eyes sleepy.

He sank to a kitchen chair with Viv on his lap and glanced at the time on the microwave. Only six p.m. He was *not* looking forward to another long sleepless night, up every two hours, trying to comfort a crying, cranky spawn of Satan. Wait, that would make him Satan. He was a damn saint in this scenario.

The doorbell rang. Yes! He'd asked his older brother Josh to stop by with takeout from the restaurant he managed, Garner's Sports Bar & Grill. Alex didn't have the energy to make dinner. He was running on fumes, so behind on work, hopeless and desperate for relief for both his little girl and him.

"Dinner's here," he told Viv, rushing to the front door with her in his arms. She had to be held constantly or she tantrumed. He'd never known a true tantrum until the two-year molars turned his little sunshine into baby Chuckie.

She dropped the washcloth on the way, her outraged cry so loud his ears rang for a moment. He opened the door where Josh stood, same height as Alex, six feet, similar build, but Josh's dark brown hair was fashionably rumpled, no dark circles under his brown eyes, his jaw was clean-shaven, and his black T-shirt and faded jeans stain-free. Alex noticed these things now that he'd reached the hell zone where looking presentable was a luxury. Most important, Josh looked well rested and stable. A life jacket to a drowning man.

"Come in!" Alex exclaimed loud enough to be heard over the wailing. "Thank you so much for coming."

Josh stepped inside, took in Viv, Alex, and the messy house and declared, "You party hard around here."

Alex barked out a laugh and quickly explained the two-year molar situation.

"I brought your favorite, Viv," Josh said, ruffling her hair and holding up the take-out bag.

She turned red-rimmed eyes to her uncle, quieting for a blessed moment of peace. "Worms?"

Josh chuckled. "Yeah, worms and dirt balls." Spaghetti

and meatballs. He gave her a high five and headed to their small square kitchen table.

A delirious spark of hope ignited. Maybe spaghetti and meatballs would work. He'd requested them in desperation, she hadn't eaten his version of the meal, but this was Garner's much better food. And this was Uncle Josh, who Viv adored. Probably because Josh was mellow and laid-back, like Alex used to be before he knew the immense responsibility of caring for another human being totally dependent on him for everything. Viv's mom, Tammy, had died during the C-section having her. Alex was it for Viv, a parent with zero experience with babies, thrown into the deep end.

He put her in her high chair, added a bib, and served her a plate full of dinner along with a plastic fork. He hadn't even finished filling his plate when the fork bounced on the table followed by a frustrated scream. Heart-wrenching sobs followed. His head throbbed and his chest ached for her. He understood. It wasn't just the pain, it was that she couldn't enjoy her favorite food. Her mouth was wide open, bits of noodle stuck to her lips and chin. He quickly cleaned her up with the bib, ready to cry right along with her. But he didn't have time for a breakdown. Instead he stared at her, trying to think of what he could do to make it better.

Josh spoke up. "Did you give her the baby medicine?"

"She throws it up. I have this numbing gel, but the doctor said to use it sparingly. I save it for bedtime so she can try to get some sleep."

Alex dug around in the cabinets. Maybe he had some old jars of baby food. That stuff tasted terrible, but she wouldn't have to chew. Nope. He needed a blender. He added it to his mental to-do list, hoping he'd remember later. He turned to the refrigerator, got out the milk, and poured some in her favorite pink and green cup with the straw. She took it, slurped, and coughed a bunch.

He lifted her hands in the air. "Touchdown." She kept her hands up while he patted her back. That settled, she started drinking again.

He sank to his chair, too tired to even bother with dinner.

He'd have to stop eating in a few minutes anyway when Viv finished her drink.

Josh stared at him. "You're a mess."

Alex scrubbed a hand over his scruffy face. "I know." He hadn't shaved, he had dark circles and bags under his eyes, his last shower was…he wasn't sure. When was his dad last here?

"How much sleep are you getting?"

"She's up every two hours. It's worse than when she was a baby. Everything upsets her—all day and all night."

"What did Dad say?"

"Mom dealt with it."

Josh's lips formed a flat line. Their mom was a sore subject. "What did Dad do with Mad?" Their dad had been a solo parent with their younger sister, Mad, since she was one. That was when their mom left her six kids, suffering from severe postpartum depression. And then she never came back. Alex hated his mom for that, but lately he'd had an inkling of understanding of the total black despair that could make a parent want to escape. Not that he'd ever leave Viv. She was his everything and he was hers.

"Mad never cried over teething," Alex said.

"Eat something," Josh ordered.

Alex shoveled some food in, figuring he should try to keep up his energy. A few minutes later, he heard his name.

"Daddy," Viv said, reaching for him.

He took off her bib and lifted her out of the high chair, pacing with her in the small kitchen and rubbing her back like he did when she was an infant. Viv rested her head on his chest and then lifted it, putting her hand to her cheek and crying again. He bounced her a little.

"Ice?" Josh asked.

"She spits it out."

"Ice cream?" Josh asked.

"Ice cream!" Viv hollered.

"No, you had some already," he told her.

Viv screwed up her face, but before she could get out a

good wail, Josh interrupted. "Popsicles! The kind that's just fruit juice."

Viv reached for Josh and Alex gladly handed her over. Josh pushed his chair back from the table and Viv knelt on his lap, putting both hands on Josh's cheeks and staring into his eyes. "I want popthithe."

Josh smiled. "Okay. Uncle Josh will get you popsicles." He turned to Alex. "I'll run to the store."

"We'll go with you," Alex said, not eager to be left alone with Viv so soon.

Josh winced.

"She'll nap in the car," Alex said. "It's my only chance for peace."

Josh lifted Viv off his lap and set her on the floor. "All right, let's go."

Viv rushed Alex's legs and grabbed tight, making his knees buckle. He pried her off and lifted her into his arms. "Can you drive?" he asked Josh. "Keys are on the table by the front door. I haven't slept through the night in three weeks. I don't think I'm safe behind the wheel."

Josh's eyes widened. "So you've been home the past three weeks?"

Alex gestured to head out. "Yeah, Dad drove me a couple times to the store and the pediatrician, but otherwise, home." He worked from home as a graphic designer with a variety of projects—book covers, picture book illustrations, logos, and website design.

Josh shook his head and snagged the keys from the skinny cedar wood table that served as a holder for keys and miscellaneous crap. The bottom shelf held Viv's shoes—rain boots, snow boots, and sneakers. Today she wore her white sandals since it was a warm June day.

Josh opened the door. "That's not healthy. You're like a shut-in."

Alex followed him out the door. "My life is not my own."

They headed to Alex's car, a silver Honda CR-V, chosen not because he liked it all that much, aesthetically speaking it was blah, but it was safe and reliable. That was his goal in life ever since Viv had been born. He buckled her into her booster seat and got into the passenger seat.

It was a ten-minute trip to the supermarket. Viv whined and cried and then conked out five minutes into the drive.

The sudden silence should've been welcome, but, as often happened in quiet moments, Alex fell into a dark place of self-recrimination. He'd actually thought of Viv as a demon. She wasn't. She was his little sunshine. The light in his dark life. Guilt over Tammy's death burned in his gut like it always did when he felt overwhelmed as a single parent.

Alex had been careless; Tammy had gotten pregnant. His fault.

She didn't want the baby; he did. He'd promised to marry her, to take over the bulk of child care, and then she died having the baby she never wanted. His fault.

Viv had a rough start in life and deserved everything Alex could give her. Somehow it was never enough. His little girl was miserable. He was miserable. His fault.

All of it, his fault.

All my fault, all my fault, all my fault. The thought looped through his brain in endless torment until the car stopped in the supermarket parking lot and Viv woke with a harsh wail. Alex's head throbbed, his ears ringing.

"I'll take her in with me," Josh said. "Stay here and rest."

He couldn't. Viv needed him. "It's okay. I'll get her." Alex quickly exited the car and tried to unbuckle her. Viv was kicking, so it was tough. She was mad to be awake after such a short nap. He had to hold her legs with one hand and reach across her to undo the car seat belt. He carried his wailing daughter, stiff in his arms, through the parking lot.

Josh shut the car door for him and caught up with them. "Hey, Viv, you want to drive a car cart?"

She quieted. Josh pointed to one of the huge carts with a plastic toy car attached to the front. It had a tiny steering wheel. There were only two of them available, ever, and Alex had never let her drive one because he knew she'd want to do it every time and there was no guarantee there'd be a car cart every time. Nothing worse than a tantruming toddler in the supermarket, except maybe one in the throes of two-year molar hell at home.

Viv nodded through her tears. Josh took her and put her in one, buckling her in. She slapped the squeaky horn in the middle of the steering wheel.

Josh started pushing her toward the entrance in a zigzag pattern. "Whoa! Make sure you steer or we'll crash!"

Viv squealed in delight. Maybe Josh should be the one to take care of Viv, Alex thought darkly. Why didn't he think of a fun distraction like that? Because he couldn't think clearly at all. He felt like he'd been run over by a truck coming and going.

By the time they made it to the register with two boxes of popsicles, Viv was happily "driving" the cart with one hand and sucking on a strawberry popsicle. Alex went ahead of the cart to pay. He peeked down at Viv. Red strawberry juice and drool ran down her chin, ruining her light yellow shirt, but he didn't care because it was working. The popsicle was long enough to numb her gums a bit and she seemed, for the moment, like the sweet sunshine he remembered from long, long ago. The sunshine he feared had deserted him forever.

He paid and they headed back to the car, Viv still enjoying her popsicle. "Let her finish in the parking lot," he told Josh. "Otherwise it'll get all over her car seat."

Josh dipped his head and put the bag in the back of the car, where Alex kept an insulated cooler. Having Viv taught him right quick the value of being prepared. He also had a complete change of clothes for both of them and extra diapers in an emergency diaper bag in there. Learned that one the hard way miles from home, both of them covered in barf. Good times.

He rested his elbows on the cart handle, hanging his head, too tired to hold himself up.

"You can't keep doing this," Josh said. "You need full-time help."

Alex lifted his head. "We're fine."

"Are you behind on work?"

He didn't answer. He had to turn in a new series of

fantasy book covers in two weeks for the children's publisher he freelanced for. He'd completed one of the three and it was garbage. He was an artist who couldn't create. The well had run dry. He should just focus on the website-design side of his business. It paid well, though it was soulless. Who cared about his soul when he was already in hell?

Josh tsked. "When's your deadline?"

"Two weeks."

"I repeat, you need full-time help."

He peeked at Viv finishing up her popsicle, her eyes bright and happy again. His heart squeezed painfully in his chest. He never thought he could love another person as much as he loved Viv. Not even her mother had gotten this deep into his heart. All he wanted was Viv's happiness.

He turned to Josh. "She goes to full-day preschool in September. Nine to three. I can make it that long." Though now he was thinking of canceling the whole preschool thing. Viv still needed him so much. He'd registered her for a Montessori preschool that gave the kids a lot of freedom to explore their own interests and a lot of outdoor time too. She'd be two and a half, was already so smart, and he'd thought she'd be ready for more learning. But who else was going to get her through her day after the hellish night?

"That's more than three months away," Josh said. "Hire another nanny."

"It's a waste of time. Viv hates them or I hate them. Besides, who would want to be around either of us right now?"

"That's why you need someone even more. You're a wreck."

He let out a long breath, knowing Josh was right, but also knowing he didn't have the energy for another nanny hunt. "I can't make any decisions right now."

"I'll find someone for you."

He leaned against the cart again, resting his head in his hand and closing his eyes. "Whatever." He must've dozed off because the next thing he knew, Josh was hollering at him to get in the car as he put a crying Viv in her booster seat.

Alex checked that Viv was buckled in correctly. Yup, Josh managed it. He took his seat and buckled himself in. Viv conked out the minute Josh pulled onto the main road. Alex conked out a minute later.

He woke when Josh poked him. They were in his driveway and Viv was thankfully still sleeping. "Thanks for your help, you're the best," Alex said and meant it. Big brother to the rescue.

"I'll have someone by Friday," Josh said. "I'll take care of everything."

Alex was so out of it he couldn't recall what exactly Josh was taking care of. He wasn't even sure what day it was. "Okay."

He collected his daughter and let himself back in the house, looking forward to a few hours of sleep.

Josh followed behind a moment later. "You forgot the popsicles."

"Shit. That would've been bad. I'm going to tuck her in." He headed down the hall to Viv's room and gently set her down, covering her with a light blanket. He gazed down at her for a moment. Her lips parted in sleep, the little bow in her top lip and the cleft in her chin were pure Tammy. Even her name, Vivian, had been Tammy's idea. Of course he'd honored Tammy's wishes under the tragic circumstances. The hard truth was he would always be reminded of Tammy when he looked at their daughter. And he could never forget what Viv had lost.

He turned, crossed to his room, and flopped on the bed, too tired to bother getting under the blanket. He heard the front door shut. Wait, who was happening on Friday? Or what?

2

Lauren Bishop tucked her long light brown hair behind her ears and worked for an interested, curious expression as Hailey began her dramatic reading of *The Matchmaker's Daughter* at the Happy Endings Book Club meeting. Lauren had secretly read ahead, as usual. The sweet romance had one very hot sex scene. No book passed muster with the Happy Endings Book Club without at least one steamy scene. Even the classics they'd read—*Pride and Prejudice*, *The Princess Bride*, *Gone with the Wind*—had been supplemented with new *gorgeous* sex scenes provided by a former book club member, Julia Marino, who happened to be a famous erotic romance author. The scenes were always told from the heroine's point of view and, at least for Lauren, colored the rest of the story with an undercurrent of erotic tension that had been sorely lacking before.

Hailey Adams, leader of the book club as well as a matchmaking wedding planner, shot Lauren a significant look right in the middle of chapter one.

Lauren gave Hailey a smile in return that said, *yes, I've noted your subtle nod to my life in the story you chose for just this purpose* (but with less sarcasm, she tried to always speak kindly to people she knew had good intentions, even in her head).

She'd grown up with Hailey in Clover Park, Connecticut, though they'd only recently become friends. Throughout most of school, and especially in high school, Hailey had been the most popular, beautiful, poised and polished girl, way more sophisticated than most teen girls thanks to her beauty pageant training. And Lauren had played flute in the marching band. (Which was awesome and she made the best friends there, just not Hailey.) Their paths hadn't crossed socially until Lauren returned to town much later and saw the flyer advertising a singles book club. Lauren had discovered that under Hailey's somewhat intimidating polished exterior was a generous loving person, which was why Lauren had recently signed up for Hailey's Make Love Bloom (TM) plan. (The trademark was pending, but it was important to include it.)

After turning twenty-seven a few weeks ago, Lauren had decided to stop wasting time on relationships that were going nowhere. Three of her friends from book club—Claire, Mad, and Charlotte—were all happily matched to their forever mate. And when Charlotte announced recently that she was pregnant, well, Lauren had to admit to a twinge of envy. Maybe more than a twinge, a full-on *pang* of longing. She was ready for marriage and kids of her own. And that, as they say, was that.

She continued listening serenely as the matchmaker's daughter went on a date with a very unsuitable man. The story had not only highlighted some parallels to Lauren's life —girl next door fumbles through dating until the matchmaker takes charge—but also applied directly to Hailey's life. Her friend was a matchmaker without a match. Shocking! A self-professed love junkie and happy-ending facilitator should definitely have love in her life. Lauren planned to screen every candidate Hailey tossed her way, first for a spark for herself, as she was supposed to do, and if that didn't happen, she'd put on her analytical glasses (metaphorically, her vision was 20/20) and consider them as a candidate for her friend. A twofer.

Boy, if this worked out for both her and Hailey, Lauren

would definitely urge the remaining single ladies in book club—Carrie, Ally, Missy, Sabrina, and Lexi—to sign up for Make Love Bloom (TM). Hailey could make a mint. Lauren was her first client and, as such, was a freebie, being the guinea pig and all.

Hailey finished chapter one and the women erupted with questions.

"Is it a series?" Carrie, a sweet blonde nurse with glasses, asked. Lauren liked her a lot. She adored nice people.

"Please tell me there's some hot scenes," Mad said, crossing her black work boots over each other. Mad was not nice. She was tough, brash, and in your face. Lauren used to be a little jumpy around her, but as she got to know her situation, the youngest and only girl in a houseful of Campbell brothers and a cop dad, she understood Mad (and secretly sympathized with her). Lauren only had one much younger sister. If she'd grown up with all those loud athletic brothers, plus their honorary brothers who hung around the house all the time, she'd probably have turned out the same way. Well, a couple of the Campbell men were nice and not too loud, specifically Alex and Logan.

Hailey flicked her strawberry blond hair over her shoulder. "Yes, it's a series, and yes, there are hot scenes. Would I steer you wrong?"

Mad grumbled something about *The Princess Bride*.

"Don't forget Julia's barn scene in the hayloft," Lauren reminded her. That was the bonus sex scene they'd all read from their erotic romance author friend.

The women tittered. Mad flushed. "Yeah, that was pretty good. I should reread that."

Hailey stood in her designer short-sleeve pink dress with matching pumps. She always dressed up. The rest of them were dressed casually in T-shirts, leggings, and shorts. "Everyone up for drinks at Garner's?"

"Yeah," the women chorused, except Mad, who said, "You have to ask?" It was their Thursday night tradition.

"It never hurts to ask," Hailey said. "If someone wasn't up to it, I'd like to hug them and chat to make sure they're okay."

"We're good," Mad said. "Let's roll, bitches."

Mad led the way out the door of Something's Brewing Café. Garner's was right across the street. Lauren went to follow when Hailey snagged her by the elbow and pulled her to the back of the group. Mad's gaze followed them and Hailey gestured for her to go on.

Mad rolled her eyes and kept going.

Hailey nearly vibrated with excitement at Lauren's side. "I've set up a dinner date for Saturday night with a promising candidate from eLoveMatch.com. His name is Patrick McGee."

"Okay." Hailey had enrolled Lauren in the online dating service and also planned to organize some group functions to efficiently ferret out sparks with eligible single men. This was her first date since putting Hailey in charge. She felt more relaxed than she ever had about dating, knowing her love life was in Hailey's capable hands.

"That's it?" Hailey asked. "Just okay?"

"Sounds good," Lauren added.

"Don't you want to know anything about him?"

"I trust you." She smiled, glad to have Hailey as a buffer to smooth out all the edges. No more vague texts or waiting for the phone to ring or, worse, getting stood up for a second date.

Hailey beamed. "Wonderful. I'll just tell you this, he's cute and loves animals."

"Great. I love animals too." She had two cats, a girl and a boy, that hated each other but loved her.

Hailey squeezed Lauren's arm. "I'm so excited for you!"

Lauren smiled. "Me too. I'll call you after and give you all the details."

"Unless you're out late," Hailey said, bumping Lauren with her hip. "Maybe if things go well, you'll stay for drinks or dancing."

"I don't think so. Dinner is plenty long enough to know if there's a spark. And if there is, I'm sure he'll follow up for a second date. Everything will happen in its own time."

She'd always believed that it if it was meant to be, it

would happen. She'd had two serious relationships that unfolded naturally with no real effort on her part. Her senior year of high school she'd fallen for Drew and backpacked across Europe with him after graduation. They broke up two weeks in, and then, on her own in the south of France, she met sweet gorgeous Lucas, a local, five years older with his own place. She'd ended up living with Lucas all summer. That breakup had been even more difficult than with Drew because Drew had cheated on her, so he was obviously scum, but with Lucas, sweet Lucas, she'd thought she'd met her soul mate. He'd confessed, as the time for her return home drew near, that he was gay. He'd hoped because of how close they'd become that he might be wrong, but he finally had to admit the truth to himself and everyone else in his life. Later, her friends back home, in a postmortem of the Lucas-Lauren relationship, had commented on their lack of a sex life (mostly they cuddled, held hands, and kissed; Lucas hadn't wanted to rush her), and the fact that they spent all their time cooking, shopping, and taking long walks along the Riviera. She'd been too obliviously happy to notice anything was wrong at all.

She suddenly realized Hailey was studying her curiously. "If it's meant to be, it will be," Lauren elaborated.

"So philosophical!" Hailey exclaimed.

"I guess."

"I'm so glad you're taking this leap into getting your own happy ending!" Hailey exclaimed with a big bright smile. "He said he'll be wearing a pink shirt. You really have to appreciate a guy with the confidence to wear pink!"

"Mmm-hmm." At Hailey's frown, she tried to put more enthusiasm into her voice. "Looking forward to it." And then with real enthusiasm, she shared, "It's a big relief to let you worry about dating stuff instead of me."

Hailey smiled. "And I'm happy to do it."

They were the last of the group to arrive at Garner's because Hailey stopped to chat with the woman who ran the bookstore connected to the café. Lauren knew her too, so she had joined in. Mad gestured them over to a couple of seats she'd saved for them at the bar.

Josh Campbell, the bartender and manager of Garner's (also Mad's older brother), appeared in front of them. He was, by any measure, a handsome man. Thirtyish with dark brown hair that curled a bit, tall and muscular, charming, and effortlessly sexy. Well, all of the Campbell men were sexy. It was an aura they had, a confidence that rolled off them that announced they had "it" and knew what to do with it. That was just a fact that any intuitive woman would pick up. Lauren had always been drawn to Josh's laid-back nature. Unfortunately, Lauren knew he wasn't right for her because what really got him going, like it or not, was Hailey.

Also unfortunately, but most entertaining, Hailey had become embroiled in a frenemy one-upmanship with Josh. Their squabble had begun with hard feelings after Josh quit as Hailey's paid escort for the many weddings she planned, and had escalated into spicy peppers slipped into nachos (Josh's move), rumors of an affliction that caused impotency (Hailey's move), to running out of Hailey's favored mojito ingredients *forever* (Josh's move).

Josh smiled at Lauren with his usual charming smile, and she smiled back, quickly averting her eyes. Josh had dark old-soul eyes with hidden pain. She always felt a twinge of sympathy for him when their eyes met. The only time she could sustain eye contact with Josh was when he and Hailey were doing their frenemy thing because that was the only time the pain in his eyes receded. He set a glass of her favorite chardonnay in front of her.

"Thank you," Lauren said.

Josh inclined his head and bent to retrieve something behind the bar. Lauren glanced around. Everyone else had their wine already. Mad had a beer; Charlotte had water with lemon since she was pregnant. This next drink must be for Hailey, which was significant because Josh had denied her any drink at all ever since Hailey squashed the impotency rumor (at Josh's urging) by implying the issue was simply a tiny banana.

Hailey eyed him. Unexpectedly, Josh began preparing Hailey's favorite mojito. The first hint was the glass. She and Hailey exchanged a surprised look. By the time Josh added the mint leaf, Hailey was grinning ear to ear. All of their friends were whispering and watching. This was history in the making. An olive leaf of peace in the form of a mojito.

"Thank you, Josh!" Hailey exclaimed as he set the glass in front of her.

He kept his hand on the glass and lowered his voice. "I need a favor."

Hailey put her hand on the glass above his and whispered hopefully, "Is this a truce?" She looked around to make sure all of their friends were watching.

Lauren caught Josh's eye, clear of pain, his face an expression of exasperation. He let out a heavy sigh and focused on Hailey again. "It's an arrangement, princess. You get a mojito; I get a favor."

Hailey dropped her hand from the glass. "What kind of favor?"

Josh jerked his chin. "You know a lot of women."

Hailey lifted her hands in a double stop sign. "Oh, no, I'm not setting you up. It's bad enough you've been telling everyone we used to date."

Josh chuckled. Hailey glared.

Lauren stifled a laugh, secretly applauding Josh's move to counter the tiny banana rumor by implying it was Hailey's sour grapes. Fruity warfare at its best!

Hmm, maybe Lauren should intervene and make peace between the pair. If they'd stop squabbling long enough, they might actually appreciate what each had to offer. They were yin and yang, opposites in nearly every way, but that could work. Hailey was light and bright, ambitious and driven, dressed for success. Josh was dark and low key, laid-back and casual, dressed like he'd just rolled out of bed and grabbed whatever old T-shirt and jeans were handy. But underneath all that, they both loved a challenge; they both felt passionately about their chosen professions. Hailey loved being a wedding planner so much she sacrificed her own love life to put all her energy into building her business. Josh was saving to open his own bar with awesome food one day. He managed Garner's for now, but he had ambition for more.

Plus it was hard to miss the crackling chemistry between them.

Josh smirked. "I only told Maggie we used to date because she kept harping about the sex therapist she sent over here to help me out with a *nonexistent* problem." That had been an unfortunate side effect of Hailey's impotency rumor. Maggie O'Hare, an elderly grandmother who lived nearby and cared deeply about any and all people in Clover Park, had taken Josh's matter into her own hands, so to speak.

Hailey scowled. "That's the same as telling the entire town and you know it."

Josh got serious. "I need a favor for Alex."

Lauren leaned in, drawn both by his serious tone and the mention of his brother. Alex was one of the few men she'd felt an instant spark with every time she saw him. And by spark she meant raging lust. Like all of Mad's brothers, he was tall with a muscular athletic build—wide shoulders and a broad chest tapering to a narrow waist. Dark hair, dark eyes, sensuous lips, etc. She tried not to dwell on it. Long tapered fingers, artist's fingers. Skilled. Masterful. She imagined his fingers were masterful, not that she knew on a personal… ahem. It wasn't just his looks, though, he also had the purest most endearing love for his daughter, Viv. For Lauren, who loved kids, it was an intoxicating combination. She hadn't told anyone of her secret lust because she was looking for a relationship and he clearly wasn't. His dark old-soul eyes were full of pain and sorrow over the loss of his fiancée, Tammy. Plus he was extremely busy as a single dad. Viv had taken a nap on Lauren once at a wedding reception and called her "thuper." Lauren had been sure she meant super.

Hailey brightened. "Ooh, Alex wants me to set him up? Hot single dad will be a snap."

Lauren found it hard to believe that Alex wanted to be set up. Everyone knew he hadn't dated at all since Tammy died.

"No, princess," Josh said between his teeth. "Not a setup.

He needs full-time help with Viv this summer. She starts preschool in the fall, so then he'll be okay."

Hailey was uncharacteristically quiet. Lauren fidgeted. She had the summer off as a teacher and could step in, but she knew Alex worked from home (she'd asked him once about his work situation). If she volunteered, she'd be close to Alex all summer, secretly lusting when she was supposed to be searching in earnest for Mr. Right. How could she truly be open to finding love if she was longing/lusting/craving her unavailable employer?

She kept her mouth shut. Hailey had lots of connections in the community. Surely there would be someone appropriate. Maybe a grandmother, who would be immune to Alex's appeal.

"What?" Josh asked when Hailey still had no response. "You won't help?"

Hailey grimaced. "No offense, but Mad says Viv's a handful. Alex has been through a ridiculous amount of nannies."

"Twelve in twelve months," Mad chimed in.

"Offense taken," Josh snapped. "She's no different than Mad at this age."

Hailey raised her brows. "I rest my case."

"Hey!" Mad exclaimed. "I happened to be an awesome kid. So's Viv."

"There you go," Josh said not all that convincingly.

Lauren could only imagine Mad as a toddler. She would've been very active, for sure, and fearless. Mad was a total badass.

"I'd help," Mad told Hailey, "but I'm working double shifts here this summer to cover my college tuition."

"Come on," Josh said to Hailey. "You know tons of people."

"Okay," Hailey said. "I'll *try* to help you find someone."

Josh relinquished her drink and Hailey eagerly sipped it through the skinny straw. "Ah. I've so missed my mojitos." Hailey gazed at him adoringly. "Thank you." She sipped some more.

"I need someone right away," Josh said urgently.

The hair on the back of Lauren's neck stood up, her heart pumping hard at what she knew was the right thing to do. Alex must be in dire need. Josh never sounded urgent about anything. She could help Alex—she'd been a nanny all through high school and college before she was a teacher—and, with some effort, could ignore all her stupid one-sided longing/lusting/craving sparks.

"I'll do it," she told Josh firmly. "I'm a teacher, so I have the summer off."

"Thank you, Lauren," Josh said and snagged Hailey's mojito, dumping it in the sink behind the bar.

"Josh!" Hailey protested. "I thought we had an arrangement."

Josh's smile was wicked. "Turns out I don't need a favor."

Hailey's mouth moved, but no sound came out. Her face and neck were flushed pink. Finally she announced, "Excuse me, I need to powder my nose."

Josh snorted. Hailey turned away stiffly and marched to the ladies' room. Lauren followed on shaky legs, both needing a distraction and hoping to smooth things over for her friend. "Wait up, Hailey, you know we go in pairs."

Hailey laughed and they walked down the hallway to the restrooms together. Once inside, Hailey opened her purse and actually did powder her nose. The rest of her face too and then she moved on to touching up her pink lipstick.

"Hailey," Lauren said gently.

"Mmm-hmm," she said, rubbing her lips together and then smiling at herself in the mirror, probably checking for lipstick on her super shiny white teeth.

"I have an idea for you and Josh."

Hailey's pale blue eyes narrowed at Lauren in the mirror. "There is no me and Josh."

Lauren rushed on. "I think if you're the bigger person, you know, be extra nice, he'll reciprocate."

"Ha! You don't understand Josh at all. He's devious. You did just see him take back my drink?" She tossed her lipstick in her purse. "Excuse me. I'll see you out there." She went into one of the stalls.

Lauren headed back to the bar, where her nice glass of chardonnay waited next to Hailey's empty space of no drink ever. "Josh?" she called.

He came over right away. "Yes, ma'am," he said with a wink and a smile. He was being extra charming because she'd volunteered to help Alex.

"I have an idea for you and Hailey."

"Save your breath," he muttered.

She went on, determined to smooth things over before someone got hurt. "I think if you're the bigger person, be extra nice, she'll reciprocate."

His dark brown eyes lit up. "Or she won't know what hit her. She'll go nuts trying to figure out what I'm up to. You're brilliant!"

She held up a hand. "No, I actually think—"

"Brilliant," Josh mumbled, smiling to himself as he fetched another mojito glass.

Oh dear. Lauren sipped her wine, uneasy at what she might've unleashed. She glanced over to see if anyone else heard, but her friends were chattering away oblivious. Well, there was nothing to do but watch and run interference if needed.

Hailey returned to her seat. Josh immediately served her the freshly made mojito.

Hailey's eyes widened. "What's this?"

Josh grinned. "I'm being the bigger person. This mojito is on the house." He said that last part loud enough for all of their friends to hear.

The women watched curiously at this surprisingly kind gesture on Josh's part. Lauren modestly congratulated herself on at least beginning the path to peace.

Hailey glanced around at all the curious eyes and then turned back to Josh. "I'll pay double so you have a large tip."

Josh snort-laughed.

Hailey frowned. "An extra-large tip."

"That's what she said," Mad quipped. Josh and Mad cracked up.

Hailey's head whipped toward Mad. "Whose side are you on?"

Lauren jumped into the fray. "There's no more sides. Everyone is all made up. Now let's enjoy the peace and harmony." She lifted her glass in a toast. Everyone clinked glasses with her.

Hailey refused. "You should've been a hippie."

Lauren gave Hailey's shoulder a gentle squeeze. "I like it better when everyone gets along. Isn't this so much better?"

Hailey harrumphed.

"It is better when we all get along," Josh said in a silky tone.

Hailey eyed Josh suspiciously. He chuckled most deviously before turning to Lauren. "Can you meet Alex for a lunch interview on Saturday?"

"That should work." She didn't have anything on her schedule until her dinner date.

"An interview?" Hailey exclaimed. "He'd be lucky to have her. She's an elementary school teacher with the patience of a saint."

"I don't mind," Lauren said. "It's smart to get to know the person watching your child."

Josh gestured to Lauren, like *what she said.* "Lauren, once again you've proven your brilliance."

Lauren's cheeks heated and she tucked her long hair behind her ears. "Thanks."

Hailey looked between the two suspiciously and then moved to mingle at the other end of the bar.

Josh leaned across the bar toward Lauren and lowered his voice. "Don't let Alex's appearance alarm you. I'm not sure he's even getting regular showers, but he'll get it together soon."

Her heart squeezed. Alex must be in desperate circumstances. He *needed* her. Viv needed her too.

"Don't worry," she said confidently. "I'll make sure he gets regular showers." She felt herself flush, suddenly picturing a naked Alex in the steamy shower. Maybe he'd have a tattoo. He had an edgy vibe to him when he wasn't focused on Viv.

"Good," Josh said with a smile in his voice.

She rushed to explain. "I mean, I won't be *with* him when he does it, like—" she wagged her finger "—get in that shower, Alex!" *Omigod, shut up.*

Josh just stared at her, so she kept explaining what she *really* meant to say before she started picturing Alex in the shower.

"I mean, I'll be watching Viv, so he can get naked alone—to get clean, I mean! Not for..." She stopped herself because now Josh was grinning at her. "I need a drink," she muttered and drained her wine.

"Oh-kay," Josh said, shaking his head and then pouring her another glass.

She took a sip of wine and told herself to pull it together. Alex needed a professional and that was exactly what he'd get. She could so do this.

Josh crooked his finger at her and she debated for a moment if she should lean in. He had a devilish look in his eye and she wasn't sure if she could handle any more embarrassment. He didn't give her a chance to waffle any further, instead leaning close to whisper, "Alex has been celibate for two years."

She jumped back. "I can't imagine why you're telling me this. That's private." She reached for her wine and promptly knocked it over. "Ah! Sorry!"

"That's why," Josh replied, grabbing some paper towels and sopping up the mess.

"Thanks for cleaning that up," she said, turning away from him in her embarrassment. A small happy feeling came over her that she really tried to squash down. She should *not* be happy that Alex was celibate. It was his pain and sorrow that made him that way. He needed time to heal. Yes, that was her job. Her mission this summer was to take care of Viv so Alex had the space he needed to deal with his stuff.

She quickly decided she was *thankful*, not happy he was celibate because it made it easier for her to be open to Hailey's Make Love Bloom (TM) plan with eligible single men. And that was that. Most definitely.

3

―――――

Lauren wore her favorite dark blue and white polka-dot sundress with skinny straps that tied over her shoulders and headed down the sidewalk of Main Street to meet Alex for lunch at Something's Brewing Café. It was a sunny June day, not too hot, with a light breeze that felt wonderful on her bare shoulders and back. She spotted him sitting in the outdoor area at a wrought-iron table with a patio umbrella.

She gave him a little wave. He stood, wearing a T-shirt in the same shade of blue as her dress, black basketball shorts, and sneakers. *Spark!* She took a deep calming breath as she approached, taking in his appearance in an objective manner merely to see if he was in as bad a shape as Josh had said. His dark brown hair was clipped super short on the sides, only slightly longer on top. He hadn't shaved and, given a few more days, would probably have a full beard. She quickly decided Josh's warning had been unwarranted. He didn't seem all that bad, just a little scruffy. His eyes were hidden by aviator sunglasses and for that she was immensely relieved. His dark old-soul eyes always gave her a twinge of sympathy for the pain she read there and she wanted to keep things upbeat during their interview.

She reached the table and smiled. "Hello."

"Hi, Lauren. Thanks for meeting me." He crossed to her side and held out her chair for her. She was a little surprised at the gentlemanly manners. Most guys didn't bother. Bonus, he smelled great. Fresh from the shower was her absolute favorite scent.

"Thank you," she said, taking the offered seat. He helped push her chair in.

"No problem," he murmured before taking his seat across from her.

"We match," she said, gesturing between her dress and his shirt.

He gave her a small smile. "Did you call Viv to find out what I was wearing?" His two-year-old daughter carried around a cell phone toy to be like her dad.

"Yes, she said you'd be in blue and it was important I wore the blue dress to make a good impression."

He chuckled. "She's savvy that way." He gestured to the menu in front of her. "Take a look, let me know what you want, and I'll go order it for you." The café was strictly counter service. They didn't have waiters.

She took a quick peek at the menu and put it down. "I always get the chicken and sun-dried tomato wrap."

He stood. "Drink?"

"Lemonade."

"No coffee?"

She shook her head. "I already had some this morning. I'm good."

"Lucky you. I need it all day long. Be right back."

Lauren waited, people-watching the steady stream of people enjoying the beautiful summer day at the local shops and restaurants. Across the street was Shane's Scoops with the best ice cream on earth and further down Garner's Sports Bar & Grill, where she hung out with her friends. Next door to the café was Book It, where she tried to buy all of her books, including books for her second-grade classroom. It was important to support locally owned businesses if they were going to stay around. She'd grown up in Clover Park and loved it. In fact, her colleague, third-grade teacher Liz

O'Hare, had been her babysitter. Now they were good friends, frequently having lunch together in the teachers' lounge. It was Liz that put in the recommendation for Lauren to get the teaching job.

Alex appeared a short while later, his arms full with two wraps, a large bag of potato chips, her lemonade, and an iced coffee.

She leaped out of her seat, taking the drinks from him. "I would've helped you carry all this."

"That's okay," he said. "I'm used to juggling a bunch of stuff."

She helped him set out lunch and they dug in, chatting about the people they both knew. She'd met most of his family, except for a few of what Mad called her blood brothers, the guys her father had mentored and taken under his wing when they were kids.

"Hard to believe we've got so much of our family involved in show business now," Alex said.

"I know, right? I mean, okay, Claire Jordan was always big-time Hollywood, but now Jake, Ty, and Park." Jake Campbell was Claire's husband and the producer of a reality TV show featuring Ty and Park fixing up and selling classic cars. Ty was also a Campbell; Park, an honorary Campbell.

Alex shuddered. "I would hate it."

"Me too. It looks glam, but it's super boring. Me and my friends were extras in Claire's movie *Fierce Longing*." She made a face. "So repetitive. Hours and hours of doing the same thing to get the perfect shot."

He nodded. "Kind of like being a parent, hours and hours of the same thing. Except you don't know how it's going to turn out until your kid is all grown up and by then it's too late."

She sensed he was worried, so she rushed to reassure him. "Viv's great."

He flashed a brilliant smile at the mention of Viv. "Yeah, she's pretty great. Not sure how much of that is because of me."

"I've seen you with her. You're doing a fantastic job."

He dropped his gaze to his lunch, mumbled a quick thanks, and went back to eating.

Once they finished lunch, Alex took off his sunglasses, setting them on the table. "Okay if I ask you some questions?" He met her gaze directly. He had dark circles under his dark brown eyes, and those eyes—her heart squeezed—so tragic. In his shoes, she would be devastated. She longed to make everything better for him or at least take some of the burden off by helping with Viv. She wanted to hug him too, but she didn't know him well enough for that.

"Lauren?"

"Oh. Sorry." She smiled. "Of course, ask away."

"So why don't we start with you telling me about your experience with kids?"

She held up a finger, snagging her purse from the sidewalk by her feet. "I love kids." She opened her purse and took out her résumé, folded neatly in quarters, and handed it over. She spoke as he read, giving him the relevant highlights. "I'm a second-grade teacher at Clover Park Elementary, I babysat my little sister growing up, she's ten years younger than me, and I've spent summers as a nanny for local families all through high school and college."

Alex read out loud from her résumé. "Master of education, coursework in child psychology, certified in pediatric first aid and CPR." He met her eyes. "You're overqualified for this job. What do you normally do in the summer since you graduated college?"

"I was working on graduate school, but that's done. I decided to take it easy this summer."

His brows drew together. "Working for me wouldn't be taking it easy. Why would you want this job?"

"You need me."

He cocked his head quizzically. "I do need some help."

"No, you need *me*. I'll help with Viv, which will give you the time you need to deal with your life."

He set the résumé down, studying her. "What do you mean deal with my life?"

Your eyes, she thought. So much pain and sorrow. She

spoke carefully, not wanting to upset him at this first meeting. They'd never really sat down and talked before, just the two of them. "I mean, well, you've had a lot happen in a short time and maybe you need a breather."

He leaned back in his seat. "You know about Tammy." It wasn't a question, so she remained quiet, giving him the time he needed to deal with his grief. He looked off in the distance. "I'm fine. It's been two years. My main issue is sleep deprivation."

She didn't agree that was the main issue, though she was sure the sleep deprivation didn't help. "Okay."

He was silent, his jaw clenched tight.

"I've overstepped," she blurted. "I'm sorry. I'm just a very empathetic person and I can sense feelings in people's eyes. Not everyone. Just some people have what I call old-soul eyes. Like Josh. Sometimes it hurts me to look at him because I feel his pain so deeply."

Alex was quiet for so long she feared she'd blurt her take on his old-soul eyes, so she busied herself, taking a sip of lemonade through her straw. Alex stared at her lips as she sucked the straw before he finally spoke. "Josh struggled with PTSD for a while, but he's doing great now." He met her eyes —pain, sorrow, and fatigue hit her all at once. Her heart ached for him.

She set her drink down. "Mad mentioned he was a paratrooper in the army."

"Yeah. Hard-core front lines stuff. Hand-to-hand combat." He stared at her for another long moment before asking, "Do I have old-soul eyes?"

She nodded.

"Are they like Josh's?"

"No." She thought about telling him she saw fatigue in his eyes, something he could easily push away as temporary, but that wouldn't help him in the long term. "Your eyes reflect pain and sorrow," she said solemnly.

He snatched his sunglasses and shoved them on. "Anyone might guess that if they knew about Tammy."

She swallowed down all the sympathy she had for him.

"You're right. Absolutely. Anyway, I want to help and it would be wonderful to spend more time with Viv. She's an angel." She knew the mention of Viv would improve his mood.

His lips quirked to the side. "She's not an angel. I feel compelled to warn you the two-year molars have spawned a devil."

She waved that away. "Temporary! She is definitely still an angel. Remember how she napped on me at Claire and Jake's wedding reception?"

"That's sleeping Viv." He was quiet for a long moment. "Are you sure you want this job? I completely understand if you want the summer free."

He was giving her an out, yet she'd already made up her mind. She was going to help him and that would help Viv in the long term. Any woman with eyes in her head could see that, despite Alex's admittedly handsome face and fit physique, he was emotionally unavailable. It was all clear as day in his old-soul eyes. And his daughter would need more from him as she grew older.

"I wouldn't waste your time if I wasn't sure," she said. "I like to help people. I'm good at it."

He dipped his head. "Okay, when are you available?"

"I'm flexible. School ended yesterday. When do you need me?"

"All day and all night."

She laughed.

He grinned. "You think I'm kidding? It's been hell—all day and all night. Viv is a two-person job, maybe three or four."

She lifted her palms. "I'm only one person."

He got serious. "I'll take nights. Can you do nine to five Monday through Friday?" He mentioned an hourly wage that was fine with her. She would've done it for free. This was her sole mission this summer—to help him and Viv. (Also, find Mr. Right, but that was Hailey's mission now.)

"Yes to everything. I can start this Monday and I'm free

until the last week of August. That's when I have to go back to work."

"Sounds good to me." He flipped her résumé over. "Let's make it official. You have a pen?"

She dug around in her purse and handed him one. Alex wrote quickly, in neat all capital letters, before sliding it over to her. She read the terms of her employment—dates, times, location (his house), and pay.

"So formal," she teased.

He crossed his arms. "I find it's best to have the arrangement all spelled out."

Of course that immediately made her wonder what had happened with all of those other nannies that hadn't worked out. Maybe without the formal arrangement things had gone to heck in a basket full of hungry puppies. Everyone snapping and barking at each other.

"Should I sign it?" she asked.

"Sure."

She took the pen from the table and signed with a flourish. He folded her résumé, now their formal contract, and tucked it into his shorts pocket. Then he offered his hand.

She shook it, enjoying the strength and warmth of it. Only because he was good people and she adored good people. "Can I ask you a question?"

He kept her hand for some reason, staring at it. "What?"

She tugged her hand out of his grip.

He shook his head. "Sorry. I'm really sleep deprived and…what did you want to ask?"

"Why have you had so much trouble keeping a nanny?" He didn't answer right away, so she rushed on. "I've heard you had twelve in twelve months. I only ask so I can avoid that mistake." She wrapped her long hair around her hand before admitting, "Also, I'm curious."

"It's not Viv's fault."

"Oh no, I'd never blame a child."

He frowned. "It's not my fault either."

"So you just pick terrible nannies all the time?"

He barked out a laugh. "No. Well, some of them. I took a year off for Viv's first year. I wanted to give her that after..." He swallowed and took a deep breath. "The next year, after she turned one, I needed to work. Jake had financed the first year and put us in the house we're in. He took care of the down payment, I pay the mortgage. I didn't want to mooch off him anymore—"

"It's not mooching when it's family who cares about you." Jake was his older brother, wealthy from his tech company and now married to a wealthy movie star.

"I needed to earn my own keep," he said evenly. "Anyway, Viv and I bonded. She doesn't like nannies. She flat out ignores them. I work from home—I'm a graphic designer—so I know what goes down. Some of them quit in a snit."

"And the others?"

"I fired them for not caring enough to try to reach her. Those nannies just watched TV or played around on their phones while Viv got herself into mischief. They should have tried to connect. She got a bum deal just having me."

"I doubt she sees it that way. She's crazy about you."

He said nothing, seeming lost in thought.

She broke the silence. "So you've been through more than a dozen nannies in a year and no one was up to the task?"

"Two of them were okay, but then they hit on me, so I fired them."

"Oh! Ha!" she blurted, her cheeks burning. Had she given away her lusty feelings for him? Was he warning her off?

He stiffened. "You don't think anyone would hit on me?"

"No, not that." She sipped her lemonade, trying to regain her cool. "Sorry. I was just surprised because you don't give off an 'I'm available' vibe."

He frowned. "That's because I'm not available. I'm not interested in being with anyone right now. They made it weird. I let them go."

If that wasn't a clear signal to remain professional, she didn't know what was. Still, her mouth kept going. "Were they your age? Hoping for a child?"

"It wasn't Viv they were after…" He stopped himself. "How old do you think I am?"

She guessed thirty-five, but kept it to herself in case she was too high. No reason to insult him, though she feared she already had.

She shrugged. "Younger than Josh." She knew Josh and Jake, twins, were the oldest Campbells. She had no idea how old Josh was, though. Thirtysomething.

"I'm thirty," Alex said tightly.

Good thing I didn't guess!

He went on. "Anyway one of the nannies that hit on me was eighteen."

Lauren hissed out a long breath. That was much too young to be making an advance on an older man.

"Yeah," he said. "That was pretty much my reaction."

"And the other?"

"Fifty-five."

How odd to attract women on both ends of the age spectrum. Of course, she didn't know their history. Perhaps the women saw, as she did, that Alex was extremely attractive, which completely obscured his emotional unavailability. Or maybe they just wanted him for baser needs. She was above that. She was on a *mission*.

He seemed to be waiting for her to say something.

She quickly put his mind at ease. "You certainly don't have to worry about any untoward advances from me."

"Untoward," he echoed, a small smile playing over his lips. He took off his shades and his eyes were warm on hers. Thank goodness. It was extremely difficult for her to feel his pain and not do anything about it. Like hug him.

She twirled a lock of hair. "Mmm-hmm. I'm officially off the untoward advance market."

Alex leaned across the table toward her, still smiling a little. "So you have a serious boyfriend?"

"Oh!" She waved airily. "Ha! Sounded like that, huh? But no. I mean, not yet."

He gazed at her steadily, so she kept explaining.

"I mean, probably soon I will." She laughed a little. "That's the plan."

He arched a brow. "You have a plan?"

Her cheeks burned. Why did she say she had a plan? She did *not* want to explain Hailey's plan for Lauren's summer. "It's not *my* plan."

He smiled, big and bright and white against the dark whiskers on his jaw. It made him look younger and seriously hot. "Whose plan is it?"

"Oh, gosh." *Look away, look away.* She couldn't look away. She had to soak in the hotness even as she tried not to talk about dating other men. She swallowed. "I'm not supposed to be talking about this."

He chuckled. "I'm guessing Hailey has something to do with your plan?"

"How did you know?"

"Because she was all over Mad, trying to help her and Park get together. And she herded all of you to a romance quiz night with the guys." That night was Hailey's attempt at understanding romance and the bachelor man while also mingling single people. Alex had been there with the guys, but had refused to comment on romance. No one disturbed him, knowing he was grieving.

She lowered her voice and leaned close to whisper, "Hailey has an end-of-summer guarantee. I'm letting her handle my love life."

He leaned in to huskily whisper his next question, their faces inches from each other. "And how does she do that?" His voice was deep velvet that brought a rush of warmth to her cheeks and neck and several points further south. It was like warm chocolate melting on her tongue while her body was surrounded by a soft blanket. Deliciously sensual.

She straightened abruptly. "Oh, it's very complicated. She's extremely thorough. I filled out a bunch of questions on personality, romantic expectations, stuff like that. She signed me up for an online dating service that she screens for me and I'm also going to some group functions with single men. But it's not awkward at all. That's the important thing." She frowned, thinking on that. Hailey had promised it would be comfortable and easy, but Lauren didn't know for sure since she hadn't gone on any dates yet. "All I have to do is show up and then report to Hailey if there's a spark." She flashed a smile and concluded, "It's all very simple and civilized. It takes the angst out of dating and for that I'm grateful."

He seemed to be smirking. Not quite a smile. Just one corner of his lip curled up. She squirmed a little, hoping that hadn't sounded too weird. She truly was happy not to have to worry about all that awkward messy dating stuff anymore.

"What?" she finally asked.

He shook his head, still half smirking, half smiling. "How's it going so far?"

"My first date from the online service is tonight. Next Saturday night is the group event."

"Uh-huh. And what does Hailey get out of it? Are you paying her?"

"Oh, no. It's completely free. All I have to do is give a testimonial for her Make Love Bloom service—" She stopped and narrowed her eyes. Was he laughing? He held a napkin in front of his mouth, but his shoulders were shaking suspiciously. "She's applied for a trademark," she huffed. "It's a real thing."

He dropped the napkin and pressed his lips together for a long moment. "Please continue." He wasn't smiling, but his eyes held a hint of amusement.

"And I agreed to appear in all of her marketing materials as a happy bride," she finished, a little miffed at his barely restrained humor at her expense. This was serious stuff.

He must've realized that because he got serious, staring at her hair, then her eyes, nose, mouth, and neck, his gaze drifting to her bare shoulder, where it stayed. His voice was deep and smooth again. "But you're not a bride."

"Not yet," she said. Her voice sounded strangely foreign to her ears like another person was sitting here babbling about her future as a bride while she was lost in the deep velvet of his voice. "It'll happen soon," she added, though he hadn't challenged her on it. "The bride thing, I mean."

"I still don't get why you'd let her pick for you." His voice turned hard. "Have you had a bad experience? Someone hurt you?"

She rushed to reassure him. "I wouldn't say that." She knew all of the Campbell brothers could be protective. Mad was the baby sister and complained about it plenty. "Just a lot of the usual guy stuff. You know, they're not that into me, but they don't come out and say that, so I'm left hanging, trying to understand what the heck just happened with weird texts or late night phone calls that go nowhere."

"You mean like a booty call?"

She felt a flutter low in her belly that meant straight-up lust because "booty call" and Alex together was all it took for her mind to go there. Two years of celibacy. He'd be *ravenous*. All of her boyfriends were of the nonravenous variety. Step by plodding step to completion. Which was fine. Who would want to feel out of control, overwhelmed by a ravenous man?

Could she handle ravenous?

Omigod, calm down. He's given you zero indication he wants to change that situation.

He was smirk-smiling at her again. Why was that so sexy?

She looked at the table. "It's not very flattering when a guy calls just for that." Especially after standing you up for a date. For real. These were the kind of losers she was meeting in the dating pool.

His lips curled up in a slow sexy smile. "Guess it depends."

"On what?"

His voice dropped low and smooth. "What the guy can do for you."

Her stomach took another dip. Was he flirting?

"And if that's the arrangement," he added with a shrug, "works for some people."

"Not me."

He dipped his head, drank some iced coffee, then leaned back in his seat, staring at her for reasons unknown. This was why she needed Hailey. Men were so confusing.

Back to the mission.

She worked for a casual breezy tone. "Anyway, it won't interfere with Viv's care. Make Love Bloom (TM) is a strictly weekend endeavor."

He was smirk-smiling again, which would've put her on edge, but his eyes were tender, and his velvet voice flowed over her in a warm sensual rush. "Sounds like a plan."

4

That night Lauren met her date at Lombardi's, a nice Italian restaurant in nearby Eastman. She'd taken the time to make a good first impression, wearing her prettiest green embroidered sundress that matched her eyes, full makeup, and deep conditioned her long light brown hair, which had some nice highlights in it from the summer sun. She'd even sprung for a rare treat—new shoes—sexy strappy black heels. She had high hopes for her summer Make Love Bloom (TM) venture. Nothing had ever been so easy with Hailey on her side. She'd been instructed to look for a man in his thirties with black hair, wearing a pink shirt.

She spotted him right away, sitting in the outdoor seating area. She also spotted a huge yellow snake draped around his neck. An involuntary squeak escaped her lips. She stopped dead in her tracks, her heart racing. It wasn't that she was afraid of snakes, but, okay, yes, she was afraid of snakes. And psycho men who showed up on first dates with them.

He stood. "Lauren?"

She moved toward him on wooden legs, forcing herself to get close enough to politely bail. Her heart slowed as she realized it was a stuffed animal snake. Not real. Still, what the heck?

"Patrick?"

He smiled what appeared to be a genuine smile. "That's me." He had dimples. Also thick, jet-black hair with piercing blue eyes that were definitely not old soul. They reflected nothing. A complete blank. Definitely handsome, as Hailey had promised, but everything else was wrong, wrong, wrong. No spark for sure. She wouldn't even wish snake man on Hailey, though the woman would be getting a *serious* talking to. Clearly they needed a tougher screening process.

"I'm Lauren," she said as she tried to think of the fastest way to bail with no hard feelings.

"I know. You look just like your picture. That doesn't happen often."

She hadn't seen his picture, merely trusted Hailey to screen men for her. *Massive* error in judgment.

She cleared her throat. "Yes, well, I knew it was you from your, um, pink shirt." *Should I ask about the snake?* She stared at it. It was long, wrapped once around his neck and the ends hung down his chest. She glanced around the busy outdoor seating area to see if anyone else noticed the odd sight in front of her. They did.

"Please have a seat," Patrick said. "I thought we could talk over drinks outside before going in for dinner."

She immediately felt like she was getting the brush-off. He didn't want to spring for dinner if they didn't hit it off, though she was not unhappy about it. She sat, feeling the need to politely explain she had somewhere else to be.

"Do you like snakes, Lauren?" he asked right away.

"Not especially."

"Ah."

"Is that why you have a snake around your neck? Was this a test?"

He inclined his head and then rubbed his cheek against the snake. "Very astute. Yes. Your profile said you loved animals."

She focused on his empty cold blue eyes. Like a snake. "I love animals with fur like cats and dogs."

He brightened. "Oh, I do have some animals with fur—rats. To feed Jeffrey. That's my Burmese python. He's ten feet, but could grow as large as twenty. Obviously whoever might work as a partner for me would have to be comfortable having Jeffrey as part of the family."

Her stomach rolled. Rats. Python. No, no, no. Case closed! Strangely, she was glad he'd gotten right to the point with his weird snake obsession. If she'd met him sans stuffed snake, she might've been taken in by his good looks and then, if she ever went to his place, been absolutely terrified to find a python eying her. Zero chance of that now.

She stood and decided to be as honest and forthright as he'd been. "It was nice to meet you, Patrick. Sorry, I don't do snakes or rats." She suppressed a shudder.

He dipped his head. "It's good to know this right away."

"Yes." She backed away. "Enjoy your snake, I mean, dinner."

"I certainly will." He gestured to the waiter.

She took off, speedwalking toward the parking lot behind the restaurant. She got into her ancient red Toyota, turned it on, and yanked out her cell phone. She had to call Hailey right away. That was a freaky date by any measure. Not just to someone sensitive like herself. As soon as Hailey picked up, Lauren barked, "No spark! He has a pet snake and rats!"

"Lauren?"

"Who else?" She turned the air-conditioning vent toward her, belatedly upset and overheated by the bizarre experience.

"Why aren't you at dinner?"

"Patrick showed up with a stuffed-animal snake around his neck. It was huge and yellow and he cuddled with it! I failed the test, Hailey! I'm not Patrick girlfriend material. He told me so, but believe me, *nothing* was ever more clear from the moment I spotted him."

"Was he cute?"

"Yes, he was cute! He was also psycho! If this is going to work, we need much stricter screening standards. Did you talk to him at all or just look at his profile?"

"Err…"

"Never mind!" She gestured wildly though Hailey

couldn't see her. "I know you didn't or he wouldn't have brought up Jeffrey. That's his python, by the way!"

"Now, Lauren, please calm down."

"Part of his family!"

"I don't want you to be put off by this one date. You have to kiss a lot of frogs to find your prince."

"Did I mention the rats?" Her voice cracked in her freak-out. "He feeds them to the snake!"

Hailey went on in a soothing tone. "With my help the numbers are on your side."

"I don't want numbers! I want someone that doesn't make me go *eww* the very first time I meet him."

"Next Saturday will be a big improvement. A group function with eligible single guys at Marcus's bar in the city. You'll have me there to back you up and we'll do a sort of speed round for sparks, okay? And if no one sparks, you'll still have me."

"Anyone else?" Oops. She hadn't meant to let the snark out. It was just…snake and rats. She shuddered thinking of how many rats he kept. Probably the house was swarming with them. And the snake swallowing them whole.

Hailey remained unperturbed. "Yes, I've invited some single book club members too. It'll be like a casual girls' night out with the potential for more."

She calmed down a little. "Yeah, that sounds okay."

"It will be. Marcus is happy to host us. He's nice and nice looking."

The woman was devious. She knew Lauren adored nice people. Marcus was one of Mad's honorary brothers. Lauren had never said more than a brief hello to him at Claire's wedding and at that romance quiz night. Ty was the only guy at quiz night who was into romance and guess what? He swept jaded, tough Charlotte right off her feet. Lauren wanted to be swept off her feet too.

She took a deep breath, ready to give it another go if there was a chance of sweeping or at least stumbling into strong arms. "Have I met the other men already?" She didn't have very high hopes if Hailey was pulling from the same pool of men from quiz night who could care less about romance.

"It's Ethan, Ben, and Marcus. The other guys were busy."

Those were definitely from the same pool of nonromantic men. The honorary brothers who grew up close to the Campbell family. She hadn't spent very much time with any of them. She only knew that Ethan was a cop and Marcus owned the bar. She knew nothing about Ben and didn't ask. Her hopes for Make Love Bloom (TM) were rapidly wilting.

"Okay?" Hailey asked. "We're in this together and I won't let you down."

Lauren sighed. "Do the guys know why they're there?"

"I told them it was for my birthday."

"Hailey! That's a month away." And the funny thing was Lauren and her friends had planned a surprise birthday party for her. That must be why only a few of the guys were showing up. Everyone had been invited to Hailey's party, so they must know something was up with this early get-together at Marcus's bar. They probably suspected it was another one of Hailey's matchmaking efforts. And they were right.

"Close enough," Hailey said. "One month difference is nothing."

"What did they say about your birthday? Were they surprised?"

"Of course they were surprised. They don't know when my birthday is."

"What if they get you presents?"

"Then I'll say thank you."

She grinned, sort of happy to have a secret on Hailey since it was a good one that she'd like when she found out. "Okay. I look forward to it." Lauren put on her stern teacher voice. "But, from now on, no more one-on-one dates without a thorough screening. You have to eliminate the weirdos before they get to me."

"I solemnly swear no more weirdos. Sorry, Laur."

She instantly forgave her, given the sincerity of her words. "It's okay."

"How'd your interview go with Alex?"

"Great. I start on Monday."

"He's cute."

"He looks a lot like Josh, don't you think?" she asked with a wicked smile. Luckily Hailey couldn't see her.

"I'd better go. Very busy. Bye!"

"Bye." She hung up, smiling to herself. Wouldn't it be fun to set Hailey up with Josh? Especially if neither of them knew they were being set up. All she had to do was take Hailey's best practices for setting Lauren up and reverse engineer them. What would Make Love Bloom (TM) be in reverse? Maybe the Exploding Love Making plan. Oh my! That would be an embarrassing trademark to file. She'd have to keep it under wraps.

5

______

Alex still couldn't believe the overly qualified sweet Lauren was willing to commit to the entire summer with Viv so quickly. He figured she didn't fully comprehend how bad it was at his house, so he called her on Sunday and told her the first day could be a trial run before making her final decision. Her response: "I don't mind observing for the first day so I can learn your routine, but I already know I'll love her to pieces, so let's just say I'm all yours through the end of August."

An angel of mercy sent to rescue him from his personal hell.

Of course, he remembered Lauren from Jake and Claire's wedding. She'd swooped in like an angel then too, offering to hold a sleeping Viv so he could relax and enjoy the reception.

He almost wished he'd asked her to move in and be a full-time nanny around the clock. But, of course, that wasn't practical. His three-bedroom ranch home wasn't large enough. He and Viv each had their own bedroom and the third bedroom was his art studio. Besides, he couldn't have Viv getting too attached only to say goodbye at the end of the summer. He was just so damn grateful for Lauren's calm sweet demeanor in their lives. And she hadn't even started yet.

On Monday morning, he was determined not to scare her

off. He'd borrowed his dad's blender and made Viv a banana smoothie for breakfast. It was the second day for smoothies and so far, so good. They filled her belly without hurting her swollen gums. After breakfast, he put Viv in her favorite blue dinosaur T-shirt with blue and red striped leggings. Then he brushed her teeth and rubbed the numbing gel on her gums so she'd at least be civil for an hour or so in the beginning. She stood on her plastic step stool at the bathroom sink.

"Miss Lauren is coming to play with you today," he told her as he grabbed the brush and brushed out her light brown wavy hair. It just reached her shoulders. He'd washed it last night and combed it out with the baby conditioner, so it was an easy brush today. "She might even play with you all summer."

Viv looked curious and interested. "Old lady?" She was fascinated with old ladies because of a picture book she loved with a white-haired grandmom. Every white-haired lady she saw she was sure was a grandmom. She didn't have a grandmom of her own. Tammy's parents had disowned their daughter—serious mismatch there—Tammy a defiant wild girl, her parents Puritanical hardasses. Alex had showed Tammy's parents a picture of newborn Viv at the funeral. They'd sent a large sum of money for Viv's care and wanted nothing more to do with their granddaughter. The card that accompanied the check read: "Our debt is now paid. Don't expect another cent." Hell yeah, he took it. He figured Viv deserved it, whether it paid for child care, art classes, or college. He kept it in a separate account just for her needs. Between that and his savings from website work for some major companies, they were doing fine, even with the recent interruption to his work schedule. His own mom was permanently out of their lives since she'd walked out on her six kids.

"Not an old lady," he said. "Aunt Mad's age probably. Twenty-six or so. That's not old. Hold still." He parted her hair down the middle and brushed half of it into a high pigtail on one side. She looked extra cute with pigtails. They needed all the help they could get.

Viv scowled. "Nanny?" Smart girl. She knew not many people came over to play with her that weren't nannies. Just family usually. His social life had been nonexistent since she was born. By choice. He'd had offers, but he didn't have the desire or energy for a relationship.

He wrapped the hair band around the pigtail then twirled the hair so it made a corkscrew curl. "She's better than a nanny. She's like an angel."

Viv's eyes widened. Shit. She'd recently learned about angels and heaven. "It's just an expression," he said. "She's not an angel. She's a very nice *person*."

She shifted, done with standing still and ready to bolt when he caught her. "Hold on. One more pigtail to go." He quickly gathered her hair up, not bothering with the brush, and wrapped the band around it. She moved before he finished the second wrap around, pulling her own hair.

"Ow!" she cried, shooting him an accusing look.

"I told you to hold on." He finished with the band and managed half a corkscrew curl before she took off. Close enough.

Viv ran to her room and returned wearing her Frankenstein mask. Great. That was her *stay away, I'm scary* tactic.

"Put the mask away," he said. "You'll like her."

Viv shook her head. Her pigtails flew around from where they stuck out the top of the mask. Still pretty cute. It was one of those plastic masks with a thin rubber band in the back. She'd fallen in love with it last Halloween.

The doorbell rang. He took a deep breath and went to answer it. Lauren stood there looking freshly rested and young; her long light brown hair fell over her shoulders, her green eyes bright, her lips pink and sweet. No, not sweet, just pink. His eyes followed more pink to her tank top that showed some cleavage with white shorts that ended high on her thigh. Her legs were long, toned, and tan. His gaze took the return trip back up those beautiful legs before he realized she was speaking.

He jumped back. "Hi, come in."

Lauren smiled, her eyes only for Viv, who was now

holding onto his jeans, peeking around his leg at Lauren. "Hi, Frankenstein," Lauren said. "Great to see you today."

Viv growled.

"Viv," he warned, "say hi to Miss Lauren."

Viv let go of his jeans and got closer to Lauren, her hands in claws, growling ferociously.

He sighed. Really, she knew better. He was about to tell her to be nice when Lauren crouched in front of Viv, bringing them eye to eye. "Tomorrow I'll have to bring my Frankenstein mask, though yours is much more scary."

Viv turned and ran, leaping on the wood coffee table and doing a stomping dance in her bare feet. An accident waiting to happen.

"Get off the table!" Alex yelled.

Viv leaped to the sofa and jumped the length of it.

"No jumping on the sofa!" Alex rushed over to grab her, but before he could, Viv climbed on top of it, assuming a corpse pose, her hands folded over her stomach. Alex grimaced and backed away.

Lauren appeared at his side and asked loudly, "Is that Sleeping Beauty?"

Viv shook her head and resumed her pose.

Alex leaned close to Lauren and whispered, "She's playing dead."

She whipped her head toward him. "Why?"

He inclined his head for her to follow a distance away. Viv kept on pretending to be dead. Finally at the edge of the room, he lowered his voice and explained, "She noticed I'm the only dad on the playground with a bunch of moms. You know, during the work day. So I had to explain where her mom was. I said she died and is sleeping forever in heaven with the angels." He stared at his Frankenstein daughter. "I know it's morbid, but I figure she's connecting in her way and for a few minutes at least I don't have to worry what she's getting into."

"It's okay," Lauren said sweetly. "Whatever works for her." Her voice was melodic, patient, and understanding. She smelled like flowers and spice. *Sugar and spice and everything nice.* Not his type at all—he'd liked edgy and wild back when he actually cared about getting with a woman—but she was perfect for Viv.

"Wake up!" Viv shouted, rolling down and dropping onto the cushions below.

He and Lauren rushed forward at the same time in case Viv rolled off onto the hardwood floor or hit the coffee table. Instead Viv sat up, holding her cheek under the mask, and started crying.

"Are you hurt?" Lauren asked. Viv kept crying, more like wailing.

"It's her teething." He scooped her up and rubbed her back. "She's getting her two-year molars in on top. The gums are swollen." He tried to pull the mask off, figuring it was soaked with tears, but Viv pulled it back down.

"Have you tried kids' ibuprofen?" Lauren asked. "It should help with the pain and swelling."

"She throws it up."

"What flavor?"

"I don't know. Red."

Lauren stuck out her tongue. "Red is gross. Let's try grape or bubble gum." He hadn't even noticed there were other flavors. Of course, he'd been at the drugstore with a cranky Viv right after the pediatrician appointment, where she'd been less than cooperative, and in a hurry to get out of there.

Viv wiggled to get down and he set her on the floor. She raced away, arms straight out in front of her, making Franken-stein noises. "Err, err, err."

Lauren moved the coffee table further away from the sofa. "Just seems safer."

"I know," he said. "She pushes it back. She has ideas about where things are supposed to go."

Viv raced in circles and then started spinning—arms spread wide—until she lost her balance and landed on her big diapered butt.

"Have you tried potty training yet?" Lauren asked.

He let out a breath. Lauren seemed to notice everything and it wouldn't be long before she realized just how much work Viv was. "I tried off and on the past couple of months. We read the potty book. I got the potty that plays a song when you go and she could care less."

Lauren nodded. "I'll have her trained by the end of the summer. It'll be easier when she goes to preschool."

His brows shot up in surprise. "You could try." He lowered his voice. "The main problem is she wants to stand and be like me. And she doesn't have the patience to sit for long."

Viv stood and took off toward her room. He and Lauren followed, watching Viv dig through her basket of toys.

Lauren spoke confidently. "I helped potty train my sister and a couple of the kids I nannied for. You just need the right motivation. I'll find what works for her. Consider it done."

He liked the confidence, but had serious doubts. She had no idea how stubborn Viv could be. "Okay, thanks."

Lauren turned, looking up at him, and he realized he was standing too close because the air suddenly felt charged like he was about to kiss her sweet pink lips, which was *ridiculous*. He stepped sideways and focused on Viv. He'd have to be careful to keep an appropriate distance. Lauren was only a few inches shorter than him.

A stuffed cat and a doll with chopped-off yellow hair flew out of the toy basket, joining the assortment of toys on the floor. Viv was searching for something special.

"When do you work?" Lauren asked.

He spared her a quick glance. "When Viv's sleeping."

"Does she take long naps?"

"No, she stopped napping right after she turned two, except for short naps in the car. I meant at night."

"So you watch her all day and then you stay up all night working?"

"Pretty much, like half the night. Well, I used to. The past few weeks she's been up crying every couple hours from teething, so I haven't been working at all."

"Oh, Alex, that's not healthy," Lauren said with so much sympathy he got a lump in his throat. It did suck and having someone acknowledge it made him emotional for some reason. Like he wasn't alone in this private hell.

"Yeah," he managed.

"Okay, how about this? Since I'll be here nine to five, we'll gradually shift your work hours to the daytime."

"That would work if I could get some shut-eye in."

She nodded once. "I'll see what I can do about that."

Viv emerged from her toy basket, rubber snake in hand. She rushed over and shook it at Lauren.

Lauren squatted down to Viv's level. "Ooh, snakes are my favorite. Did you know snakes smell with their tongue?" She stuck her tongue out and wiggled it. Alex quickly averted his eyes, focusing on Viv instead.

Surprisingly, Viv took off her Frankenstein mask, tossing it behind her, and imitated Lauren, sticking her tongue out and moving it around.

"That's right," Lauren said. "You'd make a very good snake. Let's put these toys back in the basket; then we'll slither like snakes."

Alex watched in amazement as Lauren sang an "It's time to put the toys away" song that ended with "so we can be snakes" that had Viv eagerly helping. Lauren looked up at him, smiling as she sang, a halo practically hovering over her head. She shooed him out of the room with one hand.

He left, overwhelmed with gratitude. Lauren reached out to Viv in a way no nanny ever had. He wiped under his eyes at the wetness there; the fatigue must really be getting to him. He was too tired to work, so he went to the living room sofa in case he was needed. He closed his stinging eyes, sending a silent prayer of gratitude to whoever upstairs had sent him and Viv an angel.

～

Alex must've nodded off because when he woke, Viv had moved onto blocks, dropping them with a clatter on the wooden coffee table.

"We're building pyramids with blocks," Lauren said. "She wanted to show you and I figured you'd had a decent nap."

Viv got right to work.

He straightened and checked the time on his cell, surprised to see it was eleven thirty. He was shocked Lauren had been able to keep Viv entertained all morning without Viv waking him up to show him something.

Viv worked quickly on her pyramid. He went to take a picture with his cell. Too late—she swept the entire bottom layer out and blocks went flying.

"I was thinking of taking her to the playground after lunch," Lauren said after she and Viv put the blocks away.

"Swing!" Viv exclaimed.

"She's not used to separating from me," he said. "She's only ever been comfortable alone with my dad."

"I just thought I could keep her busy while you get some work done or maybe just rest. What playground do you usually go to?"

He wasn't willing to let Viv go out on her own yet. "After lunch, we'll all go."

Halfway through lunch, Viv started wailing. Even chewing strawberries hurt her gums.

"Ooh, I see one of the little points poking through up top," Lauren said. Hard to miss with Viv's wide open mouth. "Let's take her to Baldwin Park over in Clover Park. It's a little further drive from here, but it has a fenced-in playground and the drugstore is within walking distance. We can get some medicine in her and then take her over."

"Okay, let me change her and then we'll go."

She gave him a strange look. "I can do it. That's what I'm here for."

"I got it." He knew Viv would be difficult in her current state. He scooped her out of her high chair, took her to her room and did a quick change on her bed, distracting her with her teddy bear, making it kiss her neck. She giggled, momentarily forgetting her pain. He finished, pulled up Viv's leggings, and slipped on her socks while she punched her teddy bear in the belly.

"Okay," he said. "You just need shoes."

Viv ran out of the room. He followed her to the kitchen, where she jumped up and down next to Lauren, saying, "Swing! Swing!"

He washed his hands at the kitchen sink, dried them, and turned. Lauren hadn't finished her lunch. "We can let you finish," he said over Viv's chatter about the playground.

Lauren put the lid on her salad container and spoke to Viv. "I'll eat later once we've gotten some medicine into you and you're feeling all better." She turned to him. "Ready to go?"

Angel. She put Viv's needs first. He nodded once, filled with gratitude again.

Viv ran to the front door. He got her sneakers on her, scooped her up, and turned to Lauren. "You mind driving my car? I thought it would be good for you to get the feel of it in case you need to drive her somewhere."

"Sure thing."

He handed her the keys and followed her out the door.

"Your car is easier to fit the booster seat anyway," Lauren said when they got to his car. "My car is pretty compact."

He glanced over at her tiny Toyota and back to her long legs. She must have the driver's seat pretty far back to fit comfortably, but he didn't say anything because he shouldn't be noticing her long legs even if she did wear short shorts.

As usual, Viv fell asleep five minutes into the drive. He was refreshed and awake from his nap.

"Do you mind if I get her a bag of M&Ms?" Lauren asked. "I'd just give her one as a reward for taking the medicine. Also for the potty if she likes them a lot."

He usually kept Viv away from candy except for three pieces at Halloween, but these were desperate times and so far Lauren's instincts for Viv had been right. "Sure."

"Okay, great."

He studied her profile for a while as she drove. High cheekbones, a narrow upturned nose like a ski slope, her chin came to a point. His fingers itched for his sketchpad.

She glanced over at him. "You okay?"

A heart-shaped face. That was what made him want to

sketch after not sketching for weeks. He needed to capture it —the angles, the curves, the shading for the hollow under her cheekbones.

"Alex?"

"Yeah. I'm good. Sorry, must've spaced out for a minute there." He belatedly remembered his manners. "How're you? Busy weekend?"

She rolled her eyes. "Not so busy. My dinner date didn't even make it to dinner."

He chuckled, suddenly remembering Hailey was performing a love service for Lauren. Cracked him up. "So love didn't bloom?" He bit back a smile. "TM," he added.

"It's Make Love Bloom TM," she said tightly. "And no, it didn't."

He suddenly felt bad for teasing. "Sorry."

"It's okay," she said. "He was very cute, as Hailey promised, but she didn't screen for oddities well enough. He had a python he considered family. Jeffrey. And rats to feed the python."

"Creepy."

"Even creepier, he wore a stuffed animal snake around his neck at the restaurant to test how I might feel about Jeffrey." She frowned. "Obviously I failed the Jeffrey test. It was very, very odd."

"Oh shit, and then Viv brought you a snake." He laughed. "You're a saint acting like it was awesome."

She smiled. "Well, she didn't know."

He shook his head. "Did he have to actually wear a snake to dinner? Couldn't he just have mentioned it?"

She slapped the steering wheel. "Thank you!"

He smiled. "So does Hailey guarantee the next one will be better?"

"It should be. It's a group thing over at Marcus's bar in the city."

His smiled dropped. "Marcus Shepard?"

"Yeah. And Ethan and Ben. That's all that could make it."

That stung. Everyone knew he was busy with Viv, but he didn't realize his friends weren't even bothering to invite him to stuff. Not that he could've gone, but it would've been nice to have been invited. Just because he had a kid didn't mean he fell off the face of the earth.

"Which guy is for you?" he asked.

She waved a hand airily. "It's a speed round to check for sparks."

"Sparks?"

"Oh, yeah. Very important. Without a spark, there's no chance for…" She stopped herself. "Never mind. You're going to laugh."

"I'd never laugh at you."

"You would. I've seen you kind of smirk and your eyes smile, so…never mind."

"How do my eyes smile?"

"I don't know. They just do."

He pondered that. Truth was, the whole thing did strike him as funny, but he definitely wanted to hear more about it. For some reason, it mattered to him who might be with Lauren. Even after the short time he'd known her, he knew she was naturally sweet and should have someone that treated her special. Marcus would be terrible for her. He had three girlfriends right now. An open relationship with all of them, everything aboveboard, but Lauren deserved better than that. He debated if he should warn her off Marcus. On the other hand, Marcus was a great guy, smart, funny, owned his own business, and maybe if he hit it off with Lauren, he'd be willing to be a one-woman guy. He debated between butting in and letting things proceed as Hailey planned. Then he considered every guy he knew that Hailey also knew and if they'd be right for Lauren. If they'd treat her the way she deserved.

Next thing he knew, Lauren was parking the car in the lot between the drugstore and the park. He suddenly realized he'd just spent ten minutes figuring out Lauren's love life and had rudely ignored her. She'd been quiet too, not interrupting his thoughts. Tammy had talked nonstop.

"You're quiet," he said.

She smiled. "I figured you could use some quiet time. I

don't imagine you get much." She turned off the car and, right on cue, Viv woke with an angry wail.

"Bingo," he said.

Lauren spoke loudly over the wailing. "Let's bring Viv into the store so she can see the candy—" her voice rose to a near shout on candy "—we're going to buy her."

Viv quieted. "Candy?"

Lauren turned to Viv with a sweet smile. All of her smiles were sweet. "We're going to get you some grape medicine to help with your teething. After you have some, you can have one M&M candy."

"Daddy," Viv said urgently, "up." She couldn't manage the seat belt herself with her little fingers. Thankfully.

Once in the store, Lauren made a big show out of buying the medicine. "Oh, Alex!" she exclaimed. "This grape medicine works perfect on two-year-olds!"

"Great!" he said, matching her enthusiasm.

Viv listened in rapt attention.

By the time they made it out of the store, after Lauren doing much exclaiming over the medicine and how the M&Ms were special for after the medicine, Viv was eager to get started.

And damn if Viv didn't listen to all of Lauren's instructions, taking the medicine with no problem and then letting the M&M melt on her tongue to avoid chewing. In fact, Viv looked very pleased with herself. Now why did she throw up the other stuff? Or maybe it was more like gagging. Either way, it hadn't stayed down.

"You taste all that wonderful chocolate?" Lauren asked.

Viv stuck her tongue out, melted green and brown with some purple from the medicine. Gross.

"Yummy!" Lauren exclaimed. "Ready to go on the swings?"

Viv nodded, took Lauren's hand, and walked toward the playground without a backward glance. He swallowed hard, watching them go. Their similarities in coloring, both of them with light brown hair, the happiness that radiated off the pair, hell, it looked like Viv had a mom.

Viv stopped suddenly and turned around. "Daddy!"

He got moving, catching up to them. "Right here."

Viv grabbed his hand with her other hand and they were off. His chest ached, looking down at his happy girl because for the first time it felt like Viv had a real family.

6

Lauren had a great first day with Viv and Alex. Viv was just as sweet and adorable as she remembered and Alex was easy to be around. The pair didn't have a schedule, more of a very loose routine. The only definite she discovered was a workout time in the afternoon. When it got close to the time, Viv seemed to know it because she looked to her dad, lifted her arms, and said, "Dance party."

Alex looked to Lauren, pink creeping up his neck. Adorable! A man who blushed. "We'll do that after dinner," Alex told Viv.

"Oh, it's okay," Lauren assured him. "Just do whatever you usually do." She turned to Viv, who was already jumping up and down in anticipation. Double dose of adorable. "Can I join in? I love dance parties."

"Kei-Kei!" Viv shouted.

"Kei-Kei?" Lauren echoed. "I don't know that one. Is it a new cartoon?"

"It's a movie," Alex explained.

"Ah. I missed that one."

Alex rubbed the back of his neck, mumbling, "It came out last summer. We have the DVD."

"Who is Kei-Kei?" Lauren asked Viv. "Is she a strong superheroine?" She lifted her arms and made some muscles.

"No!" Viv said through her laughter.

"Is she a powerful wizard doing her magic spells?" Lauren asked, waving an imaginary wand.

"No!" Viv shouted, seeming delighted to know something Lauren didn't.

Lauren lifted both her palms in surrender. "Then who is it?"

"A princess!" Viv shouted.

"Oh, a princess. Fancy."

Viv nodded. "Daddy?" She lifted her arms.

Alex glanced at Lauren, the pink creeping from his neck to his cheeks. "You want to take a break?" he asked Lauren. "Get some fresh air?"

She bit back a smile, knowing he found it hard to deny his daughter her Princess Kei-Kei fix. "I'm good."

He gave her a hard look before mouthing, "No laughing."

She shook her head, pursing her lips to stop her smile.

He jabbed a finger of warning at her. A small laugh escaped. She loved that he was willing to look uncool for his daughter's sake.

"Kei-Kei," Viv urged.

Alex sighed. "You got it." He pushed the coffee table out of the way, snagged a blue mat from the hall closet, setting it on the hardwood floor, and cued up the music on his phone. The music came out of some small speakers she hadn't noticed mounted high in the corners of the room.

A cute tinkling melody began. Lauren tilted her head, listening. Movement caught her eye. She turned to see Alex standing on the mat, doing curls with Viv lying across his forearms. Nothing embarrassing that she could see. He actually looked kind of studly.

"This is how you dance?" Lauren asked.

"That comes later," Alex said, doing another Viv curl. His biceps popped with a few veins showing prominently. It was primal, visceral, *hot* yet, holding his own daughter, tender too. Her eyes stung, touched, and she looked away, listening again to the music. The chorus played a happy refrain,

"Fruity toot, we are elves." The elves part was long and drawn out.

She smiled, crinkling her nose at the cuteness. "Elves?"

Alex did another Viv curl. "Yup. *Princess Kei-Kei and the Elves.*"

"Up!" Viv exclaimed.

Alex shifted Viv, lifting her over his head like a toddler barbell.

"Wee!" Viv exclaimed.

Lauren laughed.

Alex glared.

"Oh, I'm not laughing *at* you," Lauren assured him. "I'm laughing *with* you."

"Nobody else is laughing," he said, doing another lift.

She pressed her lips in a flat line, trying to hold it in.

"It gets worse," Alex said grimly, bringing Viv down to chest level.

"Yay!" Viv exclaimed as her dad brought her swiftly up over his head.

"That looks like fun," Lauren said. "I wish someone could exercise with me like that."

"Dancing!" Viv exclaimed.

Viv thought her daddy's workout was a dance. Looked like it was working for both of them.

Next Alex dropped to the mat, doing push-ups with Viv on his back, her little arms wrapped around his neck. She hoped he could breathe okay. Every time he lifted up, Viv exclaimed in delight. If that wasn't motivation to do more push-ups, she didn't know what was.

She did some push-ups next to them, mostly so she'd stop noticing all the fine muscular lines of her employer's body.

Alex spared her a quick glance before continuing his push-ups. Viv must be used to it too because Alex got a lot of reps in. Lauren only made it to ten.

Next was stomach crunches. Alex put Viv on his feet and got to work. Lauren did too, but she had to stop because the hardwood floor was a little rough on her back. She quickly shifted to sit on the sofa for the best view of the pair.

After Viv counted to ten, not entirely correctly, Alex told her to do it again. Then he told Viv to hang onto his bent legs. She did, wrapping her arms around his calves. He lifted her that way. Wow, now that was a good workout.

Viv squealed with every lift. "Horsee!"

Alex finished, lying on the floor, breathing hard. Viv leapt off him and started dancing crazy, her little arms flailing in the air, her feet stomping.

Lauren leapt off the couch. "Is this the part where we dance party?"

"Yes!" Viv hollered.

Alex slowly got up from the floor, sweating from his workout.

Lauren started dancing with Viv, copying her, which got Viv really excited and laughing. Alex laughed too. She hoped he was less embarrassed now that she was making a fool of herself right alongside his daughter.

"Daddy, dance! Sing!"

"Oh, there's trouble in these woods," Alex sang in his deep baritone.

"Trouble on the double!" Viv sang at the top of her lungs.

They sang together on the next line, Alex moving his hands like karate chops while Viv jumped from side to side, looking fierce. "So we'll fight with our might and all our powers!"

Lauren grinned and did some of her own karate chops. She didn't know the words and she didn't care. She was just happy to witness their beautiful daddy-daughter moment.

Viv slept that night until four a.m.—the longest stretch since she'd started teething. She woke Alex, standing next to his bed and pulling his hand. "Grape medicine," she said.

"I'll get it." He snagged the medicine from the bathroom cabinet and quietly gave it to her with no M&M, hoping if he kept it low-key, she'd go back to sleep.

"Night-night." She lay down on the floor next to his bed and went back to sleep.

He debated if moving her would wake her. Finally he couldn't bear to have her little face on the same rug his feet were regularly on. He scooped her up, transferring her back to her bed as gently as he could.

The moment her head hit the pillow, she said, "Yummy."

He smiled to himself. Probably dreaming of M&Ms.

He went back to bed and fell into a deep sleep.

"Wake up!" a tiny voice ordered. Now that Viv had a big-girl bed, she could move about freely. He'd moved her from the crib months ago because she was scaling the side of it and flinging herself to the ground. That was also why the entire house was toddler-proofed right down to baby locks, latches, and doorknob covers that required an adult-size hand to squeeze and turn. He always left his bedroom door open for her.

He stretched and opened his eyes. Nearly seven and he didn't feel like the walking dead. "Hey, pumpkin."

"Hungry."

"How about, can you make breakfast, please?"

"Please!"

"Can you make breakfast, please?"

Her face scrunched up in confusion. "Daddy do."

He let it go. "Yeah, okay. Let's change your diaper; then we'll have breakfast."

By the time he had Viv ready for her day and guzzled down his first cup of coffee, he actually felt good. It was a miracle. And he knew exactly who to thank for it.

He was beyond grateful for Lauren's part in helping them navigate the two-year-molar hell. Hope spread within for the first time in what felt like forever. He'd get so much done today. He'd get a chance to create, work on those fantasy covers, which he loved when he actually had energy. He could shut the door to his art studio since Viv seemed comfortable with Lauren.

Maybe too comfortable.

Because Viv felt good enough to be her usual hell-on-wheels self.

Lauren rang the bell to Alex's house, a large zipped tote bag at her feet full of outdoor toddler activities. She was determined that Alex would get some quiet time to work today. The door sprang open to a smiling Alex. She stared, momentarily dazzled by the change that beaming smile had. He looked vibrant, energetic, happy. His brown eyes were warm and pain-free. He was clean-shaven, the masculine angles of his jaw strikingly handsome. Wow. Had she done that?

"Morning," he said cheerfully.

"Morning," she said. "You look…great."

"Thanks. I feel great. Viv and I both slept well. Thanks so much for your help with her medicine."

"No problem."

"I'll get that." He snagged the bag. "It's heavy."

She stepped inside. "It's my goody bag for Viv. Where is your little cutie?"

He turned around. "She was right here a minute ago." And then louder. "Viv!"

Viv appeared, her hair down, barefoot in a red and white striped short-sleeved shirt with pink and orange polka dot leggings. *Somebody dressed herself today.* She ran and hugged Lauren's legs quickly before inspecting the bag.

Lauren lifted the bag, tucking it over her shoulder. "Let me get your hair back first. You can have a braid like mine." She turned to show her the braid. "We're going to be very busy playing with the stuff in this bag."

Viv stared at the bag in fascination.

Alex spoke up. "I was thinking I'd try to get some work done since she's so comfortable with you."

Lauren smiled. "Absolutely. That's what I'm here for."

Alex stared at her for a long moment before turning to Viv. "Listen to Miss Lauren today."

"Bye, Daddy." Viv waved him away.

"You heard her," Lauren said with a laugh.

Alex shifted from foot to foot like he couldn't decide if he should really go. "I'll be just down the hall in my art studio. I'm closing the door and putting my music on. You need me, you just walk right in."

"Got it," Lauren said.

"Got it," Viv mimicked.

Alex stared at Viv and then turned to Lauren. "It's one of those childproof knob covers. You know how to do those?"

She nodded. "I do. I noticed those yesterday."

Alex put his hands together like a prayer and pointed them at her. "Thank you, thank you, thank you."

She shook her head. "It's really no problem. Me and Viv are going to have a blast."

He turned to Viv. "See you at lunch, my superstrong girl." He put out his fist for a fist bump.

Viv left him hanging on the fist bump, instead lifting her hair and twisting it together, trying to make a braid. "Hair."

Alex stared for another long moment, looking from Viv to Lauren and back, almost like he didn't want to leave. Lauren shooed him out.

"Thank you," he mouthed and left. So sweet.

She turned to Viv. Another sweetie. She was so happy she got this opportunity to help Alex and Viv. What a wonderful day they were going to have.

That lasted approximately five minutes.

It wasn't that Viv was *bad*. She was more like...curious and energetic and...reckless. Lauren couldn't take her eyes off her for one minute. By the time lunch rolled around, Lauren was embarrassingly exhausted. She hated to push the issue, but she really thought she needed to take Viv to a playground or a kiddie pool. Something that would get her energy out. She'd have to broach the topic with Alex carefully.

7

─────

Alex was in that beautiful place where creativity flowed, guiding his fingers as he sketched an intricately interlocked picture with a dragon, castle, shield, and the shadow of two kids on the move. He felt like only minutes had passed when he heard his name.

"Daddy!"

He set his pencil down, turned down the music, and stood, arms open wide. Viv ran and body slammed him with a hug around the legs. He lifted her and kissed her temple.

Lauren stepped inside his studio. "Sorry to bother you. She wanted lunch and I thought you might want to join us. If you're too busy—"

"Not at all." His eye caught on Viv's hair. "Nice braid." He didn't know how to braid, so she was probably pretty happy to have one.

Viv wiggled to get down. He set her on her feet and she did a few model poses, hand on her hip, flipping her braid back and forth over her shoulder. He laughed, turning to Lauren. "Where'd she get that modeling thing?"

"Got me," she said.

He gestured to go. "Okay, Miss Vivian, let's eat."

Viv raced to the kitchen. Lauren looked around his studio. "So this is where the magic happens."

He glanced around. It was a mess. "Nothing fancy." He had a drafting table for drawing in front of the window. The blinds lowered from the top to let in some natural light. Adjacent to that was a black futon from his apartment days and a small bookcase with some art school books. Opposite the window on the far side of the room was a desk with the computer and a large monitor, where he did most of his work, using Photoshop and a digital painting tablet. Two rows of long wire hanger mounted high on the walls had works-in-progress clipped to them—drawings for cover concepts or the occasional picture book illustration.

She stopped by his drafting table, inspecting his work. She turned back to him with a look of wonder. "You're quite a gifted artist."

He flushed at the compliment. "Thanks. I missed it."

"Is this what you do for a living? Fantasy illustrations?"

"Not always. This is for a trilogy. Book covers. Sometimes I illustrate picture books too. But that work is only part time. The rest of the time I'm doing graphic design and programming for websites. That's more of a pay-the-bills steady job."

She turned back to the cover he'd been working on and then over to the other two. He'd actually done all three in record time, flying high with the rush of creativity he'd missed so much. Of course, that was just the sketch work. He needed to do tighter line drawings and then scan and upload them to Photoshop, where he'd do the color work. Still, he was proud of what he'd accomplished after being stuck for weeks.

The sudden silence alerted him to possible toddler mischief. "Gotta go check on Viv."

"Of course," Lauren said with a sweet smile. "I'd love to see more of your work when you have a free moment."

"Don't get many of those."

"Viv," they said at the same time.

They bumped into each other trying to get out the door. "Sorry," he said. "After you."

She laughed and looked up at him, her green eyes bright and smiling. "Oops."

He was suddenly hyperaware of her—the flush of pink along her cheeks, the heart shape of her face, the heat of her body, her sweet flowery scent with a hint of something sharper, some kind of spice. She slipped past him, her bare arm brushing against his, and he actually got goose bumps on the spot. He stayed rooted in place, surprised at his own reaction. He hadn't been with a woman since Viv was born. Maybe it was catching up to him.

When he got to the kitchen, Viv was on a chair next to the counter, one leg hitched up, and Lauren was pulling her down.

"Nope," Alex said, taking Viv from Lauren's arms. "No climbing on counters. That's dangerous. What do you want?"

Viv put her hands on his cheeks and stared into his eyes. "M&M. Grape medicine."

Alex did a quick calculation and determined it was too soon for the next dose. "Not time for that yet. What do you want for lunch, chicken nuggets or grilled cheese?"

"Grilled cheese," Viv said.

"Grilled cheese, please," he prompted.

"Please," she said, hugging his neck tight. "Please, Daddy."

He kissed her temple and set her down. "Coming right up."

"You want to help me set the table?" Lauren asked Viv.

Next thing he knew, they were having one of those "family" moments. Lauren directing Viv; him at the stove cooking. He glanced over at Viv, looking proud and full of purpose as she set three paper napkins out. He swallowed down a lump of emotion. Her happiness was everything. His gaze trailed to Lauren as she flopped down in a kitchen chair, her cheerful expression dropping for a moment as Viv carefully folded a paper napkin in half at Lauren's direction. Lauren looked tired, and he hated to say it, a little worse for the wear. Her hair was coming out of its braid, her knees looked a little dirty, and she was kind of slumped in her seat.

"She wearing you out already?" he asked.

She straightened immediately and smoothed loose

tendrils of hair back over her ears. "I'm fine. I just need to eat."

"What'd she do?"

"Nothing beyond any other two-year-old."

"Uh-huh. I don't know many other two-year-olds with her athletic abilities and *spirited* curiosity." He said spirited loud enough to get Viv's attention.

Viv looked up and smiled, her chest puffing out with pride. "Spirited."

He nodded and turned back to the grilled cheese, flipping it over. It was what the last nanny had called her right before he fired her. "Such a spirited girl," the older woman had said. "You need to get that out of her, make her conform to the rules." He'd be damned if he'd ever break his little girl's spirit.

"I like her spirit," he'd returned. "You're fired."

He'd reclaimed the word *spirited* to be a good thing in case the old witch had been telling Viv she was spirited in a bad way.

Viv helped Lauren set out plates and cups. He finished up the grilled cheese sandwiches and served them up. He suddenly realized he didn't have to do anything else. Lauren had taken care of the strawberries, milk, and getting Viv into her high chair. He took a seat, surprised to actually be able to eat while his lunch was still warm.

Viv ate two triangles of grilled cheese, leaving the crust, but at least she was eating. Lauren asked him about his process for book covers and illustrations and he explained it as best he could, though he told her it was easier to show her. Maybe one day he would, if he ever got a spare moment and Viv was occupied.

Lauren passed Viv a strawberry, who took a big bite, chewed, and then started crying, holding her cheek.

"Let me see your teeth," he said. "Say ahh."

She opened her mouth wide. Maybe he should've waited for her to finish chewing. In between the gross bits of chewed-up berry, he could see just the corner of both molars were poking through. The swelling was down a bit so the medicine was doing its job. He checked the time. Close enough to the time for the next dose. "I'll get your medicine. Drink your milk."

"M&M," Viv said.

He stopped. "Do you need medicine or do you just want an M&M?"

"Medicine," she said. "M&M."

He exchanged a questioning look with Lauren. Had they taught her to ask for medicine just to get candy?

"M&Ms are all gone," Lauren said. "Just medicine today."

"You still want medicine?" Alex asked.

Viv nodded.

He left, but he heard Viv ask loudly, "Where M&M?"

"I'm not sure," Lauren said. "Maybe I left them at my apartment."

After medicine, Alex "found" the M&Ms and gave Viv one. Lauren helped him clean up the kitchen and left to change Viv. When she came back, she asked, "Would you mind if I took her to the playground this afternoon? I just think she needs to, you know, expand her horizons beyond home. She's so smart and curious. I think she gets bored and makes her own fun."

He tensed. He'd wanted to get back to his art studio. "Just stick around here."

Viv took off, running up and down the hallway from the living room to the bedrooms.

"She has so much energy," Lauren said. "I wouldn't take her far. I was thinking of the fenced-in playground at Baldwin Park."

He rubbed the back of his neck. "I wanted to do a little more work."

"You can. I'll take her."

"She's not ready to go out somewhere without me," he said tightly. "I told you she's only been alone with my dad before."

"Then we could visit your dad maybe?"

He let out a breath, not ready for that either. Not without him. Viv came racing down the hall with a weird hat. Fuck.

That was his underwear. He snagged it off her head and tossed it back in his room, shutting the door.

He caught Viv mid-run and lifted her to eye level. "We don't wear underwear on our head."

Lauren giggled, and he felt himself flush. The stuff that came out of his mouth now that he was a parent. He set Viv down and shook his head.

Viv ran to the open space in the living room and started spinning.

Lauren crossed to his side. "See how she entertains herself? But it's not always good to have the same experiences over and over."

He watched Viv spinning, spinning, spinning. Didn't take much to entertain her. "She's two. She's fine."

"I understand you have a close bond and that's fantastic, but…" She trailed off as Viv landed on her bottom and swayed, but didn't tip over. "I'm just saying I think she'll be happier if she can expand her horizons."

He tensed, irritated she was pushing him. It was only Lauren's second day. "She's happy enough," he snapped. "I do as much as I can," he added defensively. As always, he felt the pressure of being a single parent to Viv and feared he was coming up short.

Lauren put her hand on his arm and squeezed, the touch gentle and reassuring. "All I'm saying is a little more freedom would be good for her."

"If you're not up to the task—"

"No, I'm okay." She smiled tightly. "Sorry. I didn't mean to push something you're not comfortable with. We'll hang out here. Do you have some bigger outdoor toys like a tricycle?"

"Everything's in the garage. Door's just off the kitchen."

They both turned as Viv stood, swaying unsteadily. "Whoa. Bizzy."

"I bet you are," Lauren said. "Spinning can make you *really* dizzy. Let's go get a toy from the garage."

"I'll be in my studio," he muttered.

He left, feeling irritated and judged and still not ready to let Viv out without him. He was her protector and it was very hard to trust anyone else to look out for her the way he could. His dad was the exception, the only one he trusted. His dad had raised six kids on his own and mentored a lot of other troubled kids who'd needed a father figure. Even Lauren, as great as she was, couldn't take Alex's place. What if Viv hurt herself? What if she was crying and asking for Daddy and he wasn't there? He didn't want Viv to think for even one moment that he wasn't there for her. It was a vow he'd made the day she was born. He would make up for her loss of a mom by being her everything. He wouldn't break that vow for anyone.

He shut the door of his studio and put the music on. This time, things didn't flow. He started a more detailed line drawing, screwed it up a few times, and felt suddenly immensely fatigued. He found himself at the computer, clicking over to Tammy's artwork. He looked at it daily, an itch he had to scratch. Like him, she liked digital painting, though hers were superimposed on photographs. She'd taken pictures constantly, all around the city, none of them of people. All urban elements—graffitied buildings, vacant lots, broken sidewalks, garbage. Then she'd mess with them on the computer, painting them with different effects.

He studied the pieces she'd made during their time together the most. Her reluctance to marry him had made him doubt her love. Sure, she'd told him she'd marry him once the baby was born, after he'd asked several times, but when he gave her a ruby engagement ring (her favorite gemstone), she'd worn it on a chain around her neck. Some part of him wondered what would've happened if she'd lived. Would they have married and been a real family?

He clicked over to the last thing she'd created at nine months pregnant only two weeks before Viv was born, a picture of a vacant lot with one rose blooming in it. He hadn't seen this one when she was alive and wished he had. It haunted him. The rose always made him think of the baby growing inside her, but then she'd painted the petals black. A dead rose all alone. Had she known she was going to die? Did she want the baby to die? Or did she feel all alone in an empty space, darkness closing in on her?

He kept clicking through her work, looking for meaning and finding none. Sometimes she superimposed one image over another, making an otherwise innocent object look spooky. A knife superimposed on a grassy hill, broken glass next to a fluffy dog. It occurred to him that he never really knew her until after her death. She'd been full of energy, always on the go. By day she was a dog walker and part-time personal assistant to a wealthy eccentric woman. She saved her art for late night, her favorite time. He'd never realized the darkness in her until he'd studied her work as a whole. These images were the only material thing he'd kept of hers, transferring all of her work from her laptop to his computer. He'd been in shock with her sudden death and his own new role as a single dad, so he'd left going through their apartment to his dad and her parents. He'd told his dad he only wanted the laptop. She'd told him her password, Psychobitch101, when he'd first met her.

He'd liked her forwardness, her unapologetic defiant attitude. He'd thought she was edgy and badass. She dressed in black, tight, revealing clothes, her blond hair dyed black in striking contrast to her fair skin, piercings running up both earlobes, her bellybutton, and small silver hoops through her nipples. A dragon tattoo breathing flames ran up her right side. She lived life her way on her terms until the pregnancy forced her to think of someone else. She'd hated having to wear maternity clothes. Her indifference to Viv had worried him. She called the baby a parasite sucking her life's blood. He'd hoped her maternal instinct would kick in after Viv was born. Now he'd never know.

His eyes felt gritty. He scrunched them tight, closed the Tammy folder, lay down on the futon, and was out cold.

When he woke, he got himself some coffee and went to check on Lauren and Viv. His little girl never gave him a moment to wallow in the past. It was probably the only thing that had kept him going in those early days. He saw them through the large front window of the living room. Lauren was pushing Viv by the handle of her red plastic car down the sidewalk of their block. Viv looked happy, steering and occasionally slapping the horn. He smiled, as he always did at Viv doing her thing.

He stepped outside to a hot June day. Viv was in the shade provided by the roof of the car, but what about Lauren? Had she been trudging up and down the sidewalk in the heat for the past two hours? Guilt pricked at him because he knew she was just trying to keep Viv busy and out of his hair.

He caught up to them at the end of the block. Lauren stopped and wiped a sweaty tendril of hair back from her face. "Hi. We're just taking a drive."

"Go!" Viv hollered, slapping the horn in the middle of the steering wheel.

He bent down to Viv. Her doll, Dolly, with the chopped-off yellow hair was in the passenger seat. "You're stopping for gas while I talk to Miss Lauren."

Viv nodded and got quiet. He pretended to put a gas pump to the side of the car. He turned to Lauren flushed from the heat, her hair coming out of its braid in soft tendrils. He suddenly wished he could bring her back to the studio and sketch the soft curves and lines of her beautiful face. His gaze caught on a trickle of sweat running down the side of her neck. He had the urge to lick it.

He blinked, surprised at the unusual sharp edge of lust. He focused on her green eyes, noticing, in this light, tiny flecks of blue and gray in them. He had to do more than sketch her, he needed color, maybe soft pastels.

"Did you get a lot of work done?" Lauren asked.

"Yes," he said just so she wouldn't feel like she'd made all this effort for nothing.

She beamed and his whole world lit up with sunshine. "Good."

He looked away, wondering what the hell was wrong with him. Of course his world was lit with sunshine. It was a sunny day. "Have you been pushing her in the car for the last couple of hours?"

"Has it been that long?" she asked, brushing the bead of sweat from her neck.

"Yeah. Unless you did something before this."

She rocked back on her heels. "No wonder my feet are sore."

"Lauren—"

"It's okay. I needed the exercise." She put a hand to her lower back and arched. She was tall, slender, graceful. Her breasts full, her hips narrow, long, long legs. He wanted to do more than sketch her. He wanted to touch.

"I'm not sure you really did need the exercise," he murmured. His gaze trailed back up to her face. "You could've come inside."

She straightened, hands on her hips. "I wanted to let you get some work done."

"I did. And then I took a nap. You should've come back in. Don't wear yourself out."

"I wouldn't want to disturb your nap either."

Viv honked the horn three times. He bent down to Viv and held out his palm. "Fifty bucks for gas." She slapped his hand with invisible money.

Lauren went on. "Besides, for a while there, Viv was pushing the car with Dolly, so she was the one getting the exercise."

He was sure Lauren walked right alongside her. He straightened and pulled out his cell. "Hold on. I'm going to see if my dad's home." He called his dad, got the go-ahead, and hung up. "My dad lives across town. We'll go visit and then, if you're comfortable hanging out there, you can take her to visit whenever you want without me."

"I'm sure I'll be comfortable," Lauren said. "I know your dad from when Mad lived at home. We hung out there sometimes."

Twenty minutes later, he pulled into his dad's driveway. Lauren got Viv and walked hand in hand with her to the front door.

His dad, tall and still fit at fifty-four with dark brown hair and some gray interspersed on the sides, answered with a smile that made his brown eyes crinkle at the corners. "There's my favorite girl!" he exclaimed to Viv.

Lauren picked up Viv and handed her over to his dad just like Alex would've done so his dad didn't have to bend down.

His dad smiled at Lauren as they stepped inside. "Nice to see you again, Lauren. I heard you were helping out this summer."

"Nice to see you too, Mr. Campbell." Lauren smiled sweetly. "I'm happy to help out. Viv is awesomesauce." She sang the last word and gave Viv a high five.

His dad studied Lauren for a moment. Alex was sure his dad was seeing that same angelic quality he did. "Call me Joe, please."

"Okay," Lauren said. "If you don't mind."

"I insist," his dad said. He turned and studied Alex with his sharp cop gaze. "You're looking a lot better than the last time I saw you. Did the two-year molars come in?"

"Almost," Alex said. "I got my first good night's sleep last night thanks to Lauren's help."

Lauren blushed, and he suddenly realized that sounded dirty. He hadn't meant Lauren helped him with anything to do with bed. Before he could explain, Lauren jumped in.

"It was nothing," she said. "I just helped with the baby medicine."

"M&M," Viv told his dad.

"Oh, is that what they call medicine these days?" his dad asked.

"Grape medicine, then M&M," Lauren explained.

"That'll do the trick," his dad said.

They ended up staying for dinner. His dad ordered a pizza. Viv just ate the cheese, but she was plenty happy to have so many adults doting on her. His dad kept watching Lauren and how good she was with Viv. It was hard to miss the bond that had formed so quickly.

The moment Lauren excused herself for the bathroom, his dad turned to him. "She's a keeper. Don't let her slip away."

Alex shook his head. "It's just for the summer. She teaches

second grade." He glanced at Viv playing with a small rainbow slinky toy Lauren had in her purse. Lauren had given it to her just as Viv finished eating, buying the adults the time they needed to finish dinner.

"Shame she can't be with Viv year-round," his dad said. "She's fantastic with her."

He inclined his head. "I got lucky. She's completely overqualified for a nanny job." He rattled off her impressive credentials.

"She still single?"

He flushed. Seriously? His dad was going there? Then he remembered Lauren had signed up for Hailey's silly love service. He didn't like to think of sweet Lauren out with some loser like that guy who kept a snake and rats.

"I don't know," Alex bit out. "It's none of my business."

"Uh-huh."

He stood, busying himself wetting a paper towel and then cleaning up Viv's messy face and hands as she sat in her high chair. He had to clean the slinky too.

Lauren returned.

"So Alex tells me you're single," his dad said.

Alex stiffened.

Lauren blushed furiously and shot Alex a questioning look. Alex just shook his head. Finally she took her seat and replied, "I guess he told you about Make Love Bloom (TM)?"

Alex made a slashing motion across his throat that Lauren didn't notice. She was looking to his sneaky dad.

His dad smiled widely. "Tell me more. Is this one of those Hailey matchmaking schemes?"

Lauren started to fill him in, beginning with the fact that it was a legitimate service with a trademark and everything when Alex cleared his throat. She stopped and turned to him. "What?"

"We should get going. I don't want it to get too late before I do the whole bed-bath routine. Trying to keep Viv to an earlier bedtime now."

Lauren stood. "Oh, of course." She turned to his dad. "Thanks so much for dinner, Joe."

"No problem," his dad said, smiling like he'd won the lottery. "Stop by tomorrow same time. I'll show you some of Viv's favorite games."

"Football!" Viv shouted from her high chair. She threw the slinky like a football. It wobbled in the air and crashed halfway across the room. She had a good arm.

His dad fist-bumped Viv and ruffled her hair. "That's my girl. We'll teach Lauren all the best stuff."

"Okay, we'll see you then," Lauren said cheerfully as she got Viv out of her high chair. She held Viv on her hip.

"Bye-bye!" Viv said.

His dad leaned in and Viv gave his cheek a noisy kiss.

"Thanks for dinner, Dad," Alex said, his voice trailing off as he watched Viv pop a thumb in her mouth and lean her head on Lauren's shoulder. No reaching for Daddy? No calling for him? Lauren headed for the door.

His dad clapped a hand on his shoulder, startling him. "Real good to see you all. Real good."

"Yeah, bye." He followed them out the door, still not used to the way Viv seemed so content with Lauren so quickly. Probably all kids were like that with Lauren. She was like a supernanny or something.

At the car, he waited behind Lauren while she put Viv into her booster seat, wanting to check that she did the seat belt right. She turned and walked right into him with a startled cry. He caught her around the waist to steady her, suddenly aware of her breasts pressed into his chest. Her head lifted, her green eyes soft on his.

"Sorry," he whispered because she was so close. "Didn't mean to startle you."

"It's okay," she whispered back.

His fingers tightened around her waist even as he told himself to let go. "I was just going to check the seat belt."

She nodded so close that her lips nearly touched his. He felt her soft breath and gazed at her parted lips. He found himself slowly lowering his head, irresistibly drawn in. Her breath hitched and the blood rushed through his veins, waking him to long-neglected need.

"Go!" a little voice ordered, snapping him back to reality.

He jerked back, dropping his hold on Lauren, who quickly skirted around him and got in the car. What the hell was he doing? He'd almost kissed Lauren. He checked Viv's seat belt and it was fine. Viv was sucking her thumb and twirling her hair, nearly asleep. He quietly shut the door.

He took a deep calming breath. He couldn't screw things up by lusting for the nanny. She was fantastic with Viv. He was just starting to get himself back together—all thanks to Lauren.

He got in the car and turned to Lauren, who was staring straight ahead, not even blinking. He opened his mouth, had no idea what to say, and started the car instead, backing out of the driveway.

Viv fell asleep before he'd even left his dad's block. Lauren was so quiet he feared he'd crossed the line.

He glanced over at Lauren. "You okay?"

She nodded, her smile tight.

He let it go. It wouldn't happen again, he told himself. "You must've done a good job wearing Viv out."

"I try. Truthfully, I'm a little worn out too."

He felt guilty over the huge effort she'd made just for him to get a little work done and nap. "It's late," he said. "You're two hours into overtime. You can come late one day or leave early to make up for it."

"Don't be silly. I got a free dinner out of it. I'm fine."

"I'm starting to believe you have supernanny powers," he said, only half joking.

She laughed. "I love kids. And I guess they love me too."

He stopped at a stop sign and turned to her. "Viv sure does."

She met his gaze steadily. "That's partly why I decided to get serious about finding Mr. Right this summer. I'd like to have the husband before the kids."

No. The voice in his head spoke up loud and clear. He kept his mouth shut. He had no right to tell her no to finding her Mr. Right.

She stared at him for a moment, searching his features,

seeming to be waiting for him to say something before giving up and facing front. "You probably think it's stupid to have a plan, but—"

"Not if it's what you want," he said gruffly. He hit the accelerator. It wasn't that he didn't want her to have a husband and kids. She absolutely deserved that. Mostly he felt dread because he knew she'd find that. Anyone could see what a catch she was as a future mother of their children— sweet, smart, patient, and, though he wished he didn't notice, beautiful in a wholesome angelic way. That had never been his type and he wasn't sure why it drew him in so much now. Was it just because she seemed to adore Viv as much as he did?

He was already dreading when the summer ended and his little girl didn't have Lauren in her life. He knew it wasn't fair to ask Lauren to stick around. He had nothing to offer her. When it came to loving anyone but his daughter, that was a hard stop.

8

———

The next afternoon, Lauren had to talk Alex down as she prepared to take Viv to Joe's house. He was hovering instead of working or napping like he should've been. "Alex," she said gently, "I've got this."

She took the diaper bag from him and set the strap over her shoulder.

"Call me for any reason," Alex said anxiously. "You have my number, right?"

"You gave it to me the day you interviewed me." She put a hand on his arm in a reassuring gesture and met hard muscle that went taut before he pulled away.

She ignored the sting that provoked. He'd almost kissed her yesterday, she was sure of it. She was also sure he understood she was looking for a relationship. Clearly, he wasn't. Therefore, they would remain friends. Coworkers for the summer. Obviously he agreed that was the best course of action because he'd been careful to keep his distance from the moment she'd arrived this morning.

She swallowed and pasted on a smile. "It'll just be for a couple of hours. Don't forget I'm certified for pediatric first aid and CPR."

His mouth crooked to the side. "I remember."

"Come on, Viv," she said, "let's roll."

"Roll!" Viv hollered. "Bye, Daddy!" She didn't look back.

Lauren glanced back to see Alex looked a little stunned and then hurt flashed in his eyes. This little outing had been a big deal to him. Viv venturing out without him.

She bent down to Viv. "Give Daddy a hug goodbye."

Viv ran back and hugged Alex's legs.

He ruffled her hair. "Have fun, pumpkin."

"Bye-bye!" Viv ran back to Lauren.

Alex slowly backed away.

Lauren took Viv by the hand and gave Alex a wink. "We'll see you after your boring nap." She figured it'd be easier on Viv if she thought nothing fun was happening at home.

"Bye," he said, sounding very forlorn.

She almost felt guilty, but it was just a short trip to visit Viv's grandfather. Alex would be okay. She wanted to give him the space he needed to get his life back on track, whether that meant catching up on work or sleep or whatever he needed.

She was just buckling Viv into her booster seat when a masculine voice behind her made her jump and hit her head on the top of the car.

"Just checking if you have her blanket," Alex said.

Lauren rubbed the back of her head and turned to him. "It's in the diaper bag, right?" She patted the bag over her shoulder.

He peered inside the bag. "Yeah."

She left the car door open until she could turn on the air-conditioning. "She'll be fine. I promise." She made a small crisscross over her heart.

He stared at her heart. "She's my everything," he said quietly.

"And you're hers, but that doesn't mean there isn't room for more people in there, right?" He met her eyes and she saw that old pain and sorrow there. "I say this as a friend, Alex, you need to give her a little freedom. Just a little."

He pinched the bridge of his nose. "Yeah, okay." He dropped his hand and leaned toward Viv. "Have fun with Miss Lauren."

"Mommy," Viv said loud and clear.

Lauren froze and exchanged a shocked look with Alex.

"No," Alex said tightly, "she's not your mommy. Your mommy is sleeping with the angels in heaven."

"Mommy," Viv said stubbornly.

Alex paled.

Lauren shook her head and smiled at Viv. "You can call me Super L and I'll call you Princess Kei-Kei." She tapped her on the nose.

Viv beamed. "Kei-Kei!"

Lauren shot Alex a sympathetic look, knowing how he mourned the loss of Tammy. His return look wasn't sad like she thought it would be. He looked somewhere between shock and wonder. He took a step back.

She carefully shut the car door, making sure Viv didn't stick out an arm or leg at the last minute. She turned to Alex. "Sometimes my students slip and call me mommy too. Like when they're tired or upset. It's no big deal."

His voice came out hoarse. "She's never called anyone mommy before."

She bit her lip. Maybe Viv really wanted a mom now that she was old enough to realize she didn't have one. "I'm sorry. I know it's hard for you to hear after—"

"No, it's okay. You handled it great. Thanks, Super L."

She smiled, glad he wasn't dwelling on the awkward mommy moment. "No problem."

She got in the car and blasted the air conditioner, still flushed from all the awkwardness. She pulled into the street and glanced in the rearview mirror to make sure Alex had gone back inside. He was just standing there, watching them drive away.

In the backseat, Viv started singing the *Princess Kei-Kei and the Elves* theme song at the top of her lungs. Lauren smiled to herself and joined in.

Joe greeted them like long-lost family when they arrived, bowling her over with his enthusiasm. "Welcome! Come in, come in. So glad you could make it."

Lauren stepped inside and lifted Viv to give him a kiss. Joe surprised her by kissing her cheek too. Then he rubbed his hands together. "So what should we do first, Miss Vivian? Tee-ball or football?"

"Football!" Viv exclaimed.

"Let's go," Joe said, gesturing them toward the back door. Once outside, Joe opened a shed and handed Viv a little kid football helmet.

She put it on and grinned. "Football," she told Lauren.

"You look so professional," Lauren said, pulling out her cell phone and snapping a picture. "Like a real football player."

Joe handed Viv a toddler-sized football. He quickly backed up a few steps and Viv fired a perfect spiral pass at him. He caught it and pretended his hand burned. "Woo, Viv! Bringing the heat!"

He lobbed the ball back in an easy underhand pass and Viv fired it back. Lauren texted the picture to Alex with the caption, *Future Hall of Famer.*

He texted back immediately. *Adorable.*

She watched Viv and Joe toss the ball a few more times before Joe called to her, "Go long."

She stood there, unsure what to do.

"Run!" Viv shouted.

She ran half the length of the yard. Joe tossed her the football and she bobbled it. Viv charged forward and grabbed it, passing it back to Joe. They played pass the football for a while until Viv took off her helmet and headed for the shed. Apparently that was the cue for the next game. Viv emerged with a plastic bat.

"Time for tee-ball," Joe announced, putting back the football stuff and bringing out the plastic tee and two large plastic softballs.

He set it up and Lauren watched Viv whack both the ball and the stand, drop her bat, and race from tree to tree in the pattern of a crooked baseball diamond. Lauren snapped a picture of the tee on the ground and texted Alex. *Power swing took out ball & tee.*

That's my girl, Alex texted back. Lauren smiled, loving his pride in Viv.

"Home run!" Joe hollered.

Viv threw her arms in the air in a little V of victory. She snagged the bat and handed it to Lauren. "Mommy turn."

Joe sucked in an audible breath.

"Thanks, Princess Kei-Kei," Lauren said, taking the bat. "Looks like it's *Super L's* turn."

Viv nodded.

Lauren hit the ball and it took off in a nice arc. She jogged around the tree bases and Viv ran with her. They double high-fived back at home plate.

Joe joined them and said, "My turn. Viv, go long. This is going to be a homer." As soon as Viv was out of earshot, he said quietly to Lauren, "Did Alex hear her call you mommy?"

"Yes. I corrected her. Sometimes my students call me that if they're tired. I guess I just have that maternal quality."

"Yeah." He studied her for so long she felt like squirming. "I guess you do."

After an hour of sports, including basketball with a mini-net on a stand, they headed back inside for a drink and snack. Lauren put Viv in her high chair and filled her sippy cup with fresh water from the sink while Joe got out some Goldfish crackers for her and put them in a bowl. Viv fell asleep right in the middle of eating crackers. Her mouth hung open with bits of chewed-up crackers, her head resting on the side of the high chair. Joe swept a finger in, clearing out the remaining crackers from Viv's mouth, and leaned back the high chair seat to let her sleep.

"Does she fall asleep in the middle of eating like that a lot?" Lauren asked. She'd never seen a kid fall asleep mid-snack before. She snapped a picture. "For Alex," she explained, sending the picture with the caption: *Power nap!*

"She naps after sports," Joe said. "I think eating is one of those rare times where she's still. Catches up to her. Plus she feels comfortable here with me."

She took a sip of ice water. "So, how are things with you?

Still working part-time?" She knew he was a security guard since retiring as a cop.

"I am. It's just for pocket money. I've got a full pension from my old job."

"Do you miss being a cop?"

He dipped his head. "It's a younger man's game, but I liked it when I was. You always want to be a teacher?"

"Oh, yes. I was a nanny every summer through high school and college, but I couldn't wait to have a whole classroom of my own full of kids."

"You grow up in a big family?"

"No, just me, my mom, and my sister. But my sister is ten years younger, so I felt more like a mom to her." He nodded and he was such an attentive listener, she went on. "My parents divorced and my dad moved to Vermont to be with his new family. I saw him on school breaks."

"I didn't have a large family until I had my own," Joe confided. "I love it, though. Love kids. We have that in common."

She nodded. "That must be why Alex is so good with Viv. He took after your example."

Joe sipped his water and glanced at Viv still sound asleep. He turned back to her. "He's doing great." He lowered his voice. "I think he'd do better if he let go of the guilt."

"You mean survivor's guilt?" she whispered.

He stood and gestured for her to follow to the adjoining living room. He stopped at a spot where he could keep an eye on Viv before saying, "Tammy didn't want the baby. It was an accident. Honestly, I'm surprised it didn't happen before it did. Both Alex and Tammy were wild, living the bohemian artist life in the city. Anyway, Alex wanted his child. Very much. He offered to marry her and promised he'd do most of the child care if she'd keep the baby."

She stared at him, unsure why he was telling her all this. "Of course he'd want his child. Anyone could see you've raised him to have a strong sense of family."

Joe pinned her with his eyes. "When Tammy died, Alex blamed himself since he was the one that convinced her to go through with the pregnancy. He has tremendous guilt over her death. I've tried talking to him about it, but he won't hear it. He's like superdad trying to make up for her loss. I'm afraid he's going to crash and burn." He turned back to Viv. "No one can be superdad forever."

Her heart squeezed painfully hard. All this time she'd thought Alex's pain was sorrow over losing his fiancée, but it was so much worse than that. Blaming himself for her death, something completely out of his control, just because he wanted the baby more than Tammy did. Tammy must've wanted Viv at least a little to go through with it. No man was that persuasive.

"How can I help?" she asked.

Joe spared her a glance before turning back to Viv. "Just be a friend. When he's ready, he'll move on from it. It helps that you're so good with Viv, takes some of the pressure off him."

She let out a breath. "Good. I'm glad I could do that at least."

"It's good you're friends of the family now. It'll give Viv some continuity." He pinned her with his eyes again. "She won't have to lose you after the summer."

So that was what this was all about. He wanted to make sure Viv wouldn't be abandoned. "Absolutely. I'd love to visit on the weekends and breaks."

Joe grinned. "You're on the list. Birthdays, holidays, barbecues, you're in."

"Thank you, that's sweet. Alex and Viv are lucky to have you."

He smiled warmly, still a handsome man. Alex looked a lot like him. "I could say the same to you too."

She felt herself blushing.

"You want something to eat? I've got fresh blueberries."

"I'd love some."

She followed him back to the kitchen. He retrieved the bowl of washed blueberries from the refrigerator and set them on the table. "Help yourself."

She took a handful and he did the same. She looked over at Viv and smiled. She looked like an angel when she slept.

"You're much sweeter than he's used to," Joe said. "Don't let him steamroll you."

Her head snapped back to Joe. "Oh, no. Alex has been very respectful. He even wrote up a contract for both of our benefit."

"He did, huh?"

"Yes. He's had some trouble with nannies in the past, so he made sure everything was nice and clear, hours, pay, all that stuff." She left out when she'd reassured him he didn't have to worry about any untoward advances from her. Not that she'd ever made an advance in her life. Men generally made the moves on her, not the other way around. And she was definitely not going to make any advances on Alex after he'd so clearly drawn the line between them. Though part of her wondered what that would feel like, would he pull away or would passion take over, his ravenous need—

Joe interrupted her spiral of out-of-control longing. "Yeah, Viv can be a handful. You just have to keep her energy focused or she'll find her own fun."

"Found that out after one day," she said with a laugh.

He ate some blueberries. "She'll try your patience, but once you get to know her, you can't help but love her."

"Agreed."

"Can I give you a little advice?"

"Sure," she said, figuring he'd have some good tips on Viv.

"Alex will resist you, dig his heels in. He won't want to change the way he does things, but you push through that because he needs it. He *needs* to change things up. He can't keep going the way he has."

Her brows scrunched in confusion. "I'm not sure what you mean."

Joe leaned forward. "I mean when he puts up a wall, you push through it."

"What kind of wall?" She had an uneasy feeling he meant more than her responsibilities toward Viv.

He leaned back. "You'll know it when you see it."

She nodded, though she was still a little uncertain. "I'll do my best." She popped a blueberry in her mouth and chewed, telling herself she was imagining things. Joe wasn't picturing anything between her and Alex. For sure, Alex wasn't. Besides, she should be focusing on this weekend's singles mixer at Marcus's bar. "So you got any dirt on Ethan, Ben, and Marcus?"

He grinned. "I got dirt on all three of them. Why?"

"Hailey invited them to meet us at Marcus's bar. Part of her Make Love Bloom (TM) service. I do online dating too, but this is more like a speed round to check for sparks."

Joe cleared his throat. "Uh-huh. What about the rest of the guys?"

"They couldn't make it."

"Well, which one are you interested in?"

She lifted one shoulder up and down. "I don't know. I'm supposed to talk to all of them one-on-one and then report back if there's a spark."

Joe chuckled. "Sure is different than dating in my day. Your friends going with you?"

She nodded and took a sip of water. "Everyone except Mad and Charlotte, they're not single anymore." She'd invited them anyway, but they wanted to hang with their guys. She kinda missed them, even though she still saw them at book club and post-book club drinks. She hoped once they all moved on with the next phase in their lives—marriage and kids—they'd still be as close as they were now. She'd make every effort to keep them close. Their kids should all grow up together. And wouldn't it be nice to live within walking distance? Maybe even the same street. Now she was just being silly. Not everything worked out like her favorite sweet TV show *Cherry Blossom Lane*. Joe interrupted her fairy-tale thoughts.

"What if one of your friends has a, um, spark before you do?" he asked.

She waved that away. "If it's meant to be, it will be. Anyway, if there's any dirt you'd like to share ahead of time, it would really help me out. I'd like to move forward with a suitable candidate sooner rather than later." She laughed. "Or as Hailey says, for my happy ending. You know how she likes to help out."

He chuckled. "That she does." And then he proceeded to dish the dirt on all three guys.

Lauren frowned, her hopes taking a spectacular dive. She thought about cancelling altogether, but feared it was rude after all the effort Hailey put into organizing the event. Apparently, Ethan was a sex addict, which was definitely not relationship material! Ben refused to ever get married because he thought the whole institution was "the man" keeping him down. And Marcus, my goodness, Marcus already had a harem of girlfriends. He didn't believe in monogamy.

She shook her head. "I had no idea."

Joe smiled gently. "Hang in there. I'm sure you'll meet someone decent. Just not those guys."

She realized Joe had done her a huge favor with his honesty. "Thank you. You've saved me a lot of heartache and terribly dashed hopes."

He chuckled and took a long drink of water. Was it her terribly dashed hopes that made him chuckle? She'd read that once in a book and thought it fit the occasion. Though it was rude of him to laugh. Maybe he was pulling her leg with all that dirt.

"Is something funny?" she asked.

"Nothing," he muttered, his glass up to his mouth. He set it down and quickly stood. "Keep an eye on Viv for me for a few minutes." He strode out of the room.

She sighed. Well, she supposed it was better to be in the know. She had asked for the dirt. It was just a shame not to have any hopeful anticipation for her big night out. She'd have to warn her friends off those three men too. Ugh. Dating sucked.

She thought of Alex taking himself off the market and it sure sounded like he had the right idea. Except Alex already had a beautiful child. She'd have to continue wading through the murky dating waters if she was ever going to get the same.

She gazed at a napping angelic Viv and smiled. She pulled

out her cell and took a smiling selfie next to Viv, texting it to Alex with the caption, *Nanny 2 Viv = best job ever.*

Alex texted back. *Thanks for all the pics. You want to bring her home now?*

Sure. Let me just say bye to your dad. We had a nice talk.

Was he talking about me?

She hesitated. Shit. She shouldn't have mentioned the talk. Joe had shared intimate details that Alex might not be happy about.

She quickly texted. *Nothing bad.*

Don't listen to a word he says. He's like Josh, calculating, always with a plan.

Her fingers flew over the keys. *Your dad is a sweetheart. So's Josh.* (Mostly anyway, she added silently. Josh was less than sweet with Hailey.)

You got the hots for my dad?

She rolled her eyes and then texted: *Yes, Alex, I'm going to be your new mom.* She slapped a hand over her mouth. His mom had left when he was little. She knew the family history from his sister, Mad. And then with Viv being motherless and calling her mommy, there was just nothing funny about a mom joke.

No response from Alex.

She texted again. *Sorry. That was in poor taste. I probably shouldn't text.*

Silence.

Her stomach dropped. She'd upset him. She felt sick. She was supposed to be helping him. Another text popped up from Alex.

Text me anytime.

He forgave her. Oh, thank God. She texted back, *I will.* She smiled at the phone, even though he couldn't see her, and texted again. *How come you didn't ask if I had the hots for Josh?*

Josh would chew you up and spit you out.

Nice.

Fact. You're too sweet for him.

Geez, first Joe and then Alex said she was sweet like it was a bad thing. Just because she was kind didn't mean she let men walk all over her. She had her dignity. She had bound-aries and pride and self-respect. All that good stuff. She tried to formulate a firm, but nonconfrontational response, but Joe returned, so she tucked her phone away.

She stood. "I'm going to get Viv back home."

"Sure thing," Joe said easily. "Thanks for stopping by."

She carefully lifted Viv out of the high chair, still sound asleep.

Joe kissed the top of Viv's head. "You should check out the new Spray Bay they have over in Fieldridge at the rec center. It's just sprinklers and sprayers, perfect for her age."

"I heard about that. I'll check with Alex, thanks."

She returned to Alex's house with a number of rehearsed lines that spoke to the fact that just because she was sweet, she wasn't a pushover. Viv woke up when she pulled in the driveway. She carried her anyway because Viv was still a little groggy.

She rang the doorbell and the door swung open to a smiling Alex. "I'm so sorry about my stupid mom joke," she blurted.

"You're forgiven," he said, taking Viv from her arms and tucking her against his chest. He gazed down at Viv with so much love in his eyes, Lauren's eyes stung and her throat clogged with emotion.

All of her carefully rehearsed lines about herself flew from her mind. She melted on the spot. She had to fight the impulse to hug them both, to join in their lovefest. Viv rested her head on her dad's chest and popped her thumb in her mouth.

He lifted his head and met Lauren's eyes. "I'm getting you a key to the house."

"Thank you," she said over the lump in her throat.

"Everything okay?" Alex asked.

She nodded and that was all she could manage because she'd just realized she was longing for what she could never have. Alex had Viv and that was all he needed.

9

———

By Thursday Alex was all caught up on sleep and making fantastic progress on the book covers. Lauren had taken Viv for a picnic lunch and a visit to the new Spray Bay in Field-ridge, the next town over. She'd texted a picture of Viv looking thrilled to hold a huge slice of watermelon. That had made him smile. Viv probably didn't remember eating watermelon last summer. And even though Lauren explained she was putting her cell in the waterproof tote so she could be with Viv in the water, the lack of communication made him feel like he was missing something important. He'd been there for all of Viv's new experiences. This was the first time she'd been to a water playground and, though he knew she was in good hands and knew he needed to work to pay the bills, it still made him depressed to miss out. He would've shown up there if Lauren hadn't taken his car. Lauren had texted when they were ready to head home. He'd been waiting impatiently ever since.

As soon as Lauren pulled into the driveway, he went outside to meet up with them. Lauren stepped out, giving him a sunny smile and a wave. She looked tan and happy.

"How was it?" he asked, already on his way to get Viv from her booster seat.

"We had a great time," Lauren said, joining him by the

passenger side. She smelled like the beach—sunscreen, fresh air, and a sunny day.

He gave himself a mental shake, opened the door for Viv, and poked his head in the backseat. "Hi, Viv!"

"Daddy!" She beamed her little baby-toothed smile and held out her arms to him.

His little sunshine was back.

Her hair was still wet in crooked pigtails, no sunburn that he could see. Lauren did a good job. A deep sense of contentment washed through him as he lifted Viv out and held her in his arms. "Did you have fun in the water?"

"Yes! And Kaitlin and sprinkler and flower and ice cream and *babble, babble.*" She was exuberantly excited and he couldn't keep up with what she was trying to tell him.

Lauren interpreted, smiling at Viv. "She made a new friend Kaitlin. She's three and they held hands and played in all the sprinklers. Some of them were flower sprinklers."

He headed back to the house, still holding Viv because he'd missed her, and Lauren kept up, filling him in on what he'd missed.

"There were also multiple pipes in all directions where water came out, buckets that tipped water out, and a couple of dolphins spouting water. We got them ice cream from the ice-cream truck afterwards. I made plans to meet up with Kaitlin's mom there again tomorrow if that's okay."

"Yeah," he muttered. "Of course." He turned to Viv. "Sounds like a great day. Wish I had been there."

Viv patted his cheek. "Daddy go."

He smiled. "I will. But don't you squirt me with water."

Viv giggled. "I get you."

"You sure you don't want to get caught up on work?" Lauren asked. "You could always take her on the weekend."

He spoke to Viv. "Then how would I meet Kaitlin?"

The next day he helped pack what they'd need for the water playground while Lauren got Viv ready. Lauren put one of her own T-shirts on top of Viv's bathing suit as a cover-up. It looked like a little dress on Viv. He wore his swim trunks and a T-shirt.

He hadn't given much thought to seeing Lauren in a swimsuit until after lunch when she directed them to a set of outdoor lockers to tuck their stuff away and quickly stripped out of her tank top. The black bikini top was strapless, just a black band that held up beautiful tempting breasts. Her hands went to the waistband of her shorts and he held his breath.

"Kaitlin!" Viv shouted, jumping up and down. "Kaitlin!" She took off toward a little girl with shiny black hair that curled under by her jaw, walking with her mom on the path to the spray bay.

"Wait!" Lauren shouted, taking off after her in bikini top and shorts.

He should've moved to grab Viv, but he was mesmerized by Lauren. She swooped in on Viv, scooped her up, and put her on her hip while she smiled and chatted with Kaitlin's mom. Viv was leaning down, chattering to Kaitlin, her little hand on Lauren's bare shoulder. In fact, most of Lauren was bare. Her hair was up in a ponytail, tucked into the band, leaving her neck and back bare. His fingers tingled with the urge to move over all that smooth skin.

This had been a mistake.

He should've stayed home, where he wouldn't be tempted by soft curves. He hadn't pictured her in a bikini top. Soon she'd strip out of those shorts, exposing more skin, ratcheting up the temptation level. He'd pictured something modest like a one-piece. He shouldn't have been picturing her at all. She woke the sleeping beast.

Lauren turned and pointed to him, smiling her sweet angelic smile, taking his breath away.

Just focus on the kids.

He met up with them. Lauren set Viv back on the ground and introduced him to Kaitlin and her mom, Michelle. Viv and Kaitlin held hands, smiling at each other. Kaitlin was adorable with big round cheeks and blue eyes, about Viv's size. "Nice to meet you," he said. "I heard you had a great time yesterday. Viv, maybe you and Kaitlin could show me how everything works."

Viv took him by the hand and pulled him toward the fenced-in spray bay. Lauren veered to the lockers probably to finish getting ready.

"Just a minute," he told Viv. "Let's go put my stuff in the locker and get some sunscreen for me."

"Hurry, Daddy!"

"If it's okay with you, I'll take her in with us," Michelle said. "You can meet us."

He glanced over at the fenced-in area. "Sure, thanks." Viv already wore her orange wristband that showed they'd paid for the day.

He headed to the lockers, where Lauren was sitting on a bench, pulling her shorts down the length of her long tanned legs. He swallowed. Her bikini bottom was a modest black and white polka-dot piece that stopped just below her belly button. He tore his gaze away.

He took off his shirt and hung it on the hook in the locker, risking a quick look over his shoulder where Lauren was now standing. His mouth went dry. She was trim, toned, curvy, and so damn sexy. Like a freaking bikini model. He was sure she had no idea how sexy she was because otherwise men would be swarming her, instead of her going through an online dating service. Before he could get his brain in gear for some kind of compliment that wouldn't give away the depth of his lust, she spoke.

"Someone hasn't been in the sun for a while."

He glanced down at his pale chest, figured his back was the same, and turned to face her. "Haven't been shirtless in the sun, but I get outside with Viv."

Her gaze took him in from shoulders to chest to stomach, bringing a soft flush of pink to her cheeks. "For some reason I pictured you with tattoos."

"Why? Because I'm an artist?" He'd almost gotten a dragon tattoo to match Tammy's dragon, but then when it looked like she was going to bail (before they knew she was pregnant), he didn't. Now he was glad. He didn't need that constant reminder on his body. He already had it every time he looked at Viv.

"Yeah." Her gaze drifted back to his chest before she met his eyes. "And you have a little bit of an edgy vibe."

He smiled. "You like edgy?"

She opened her mouth, closed it, and then smiled, shaking her head.

So, yeah, she did. He could be edgy.

He stepped closer and lowered his voice. "I took out the piercings before Viv could yank them out."

"Where?" she whispered.

He pointed to the various locations—brow, ear, nose, nipple.

She cringed, staring at his nipple. "Ouch."

"There's more painful areas to get pierced."

She shuddered. "I can imagine."

"Where's your edgy?" he teased, knowing she had none.

"You need sunscreen," she announced. "It's in the bag."

He turned to get it from the locker at the same time as she reached for it, colliding breasts to chest. He grabbed her waist automatically.

She looked up at him under her lashes, her lips curling into a small smile. "We have to stop running into each other like this."

Everything in him said this was a bad idea, but he liked it too damn much. "Lauren."

She gave him a small almost regretful smile and stepped back. "Meet you over there."

He watched her go, taking her in—the line of her spine, the flare of her hips, sweet ass, long legs. He didn't think he could ever look at her again without seeing her just like this. Like a sexy work of art.

He turned to finish getting ready. It was the spray kind of sunscreen, so it didn't take long. He bought the organic hypoallergenic kind for Viv that you had to rub on, which took a lot longer. He never took shortcuts with Viv. She got the best that he could give her in every way.

He quickly found Lauren and Viv, cold water splashing him from other kids as he made his way over. He felt like a total perv watching Lauren playing with Viv—bending, squatting, standing, her smooth skin slick and wet. He was stupid with lust, dizzy and hot and hungry.

It was completely inappropriate with his nanny, especially with someone looking for love. How was this possible? Standing in a playground full of kids and moms suddenly alert and aware of a woman, really aware, not just a quick acknowledgment of beauty, but an aching need for her. It was the first time he'd felt a strong attraction for anyone since Tammy had died.

Lauren was life—laughing, smiling, squealing as she matched Viv's delight, making it fun for his little girl.

"Hey!" Lauren waved at him. "Kaitlin and her mom went for a potty break."

Just like that he was back in parentland. Potty breaks, diapers, sippy cups and all.

She whispered something to Viv and a moment later twin streams of water were aimed his way. He joined Viv, teaming up to squirt Lauren with water, who put on a great show with lots of "yikes!" and "you got me!" that had Viv in stitches.

Time flew by. And even though everything he did was to entertain Viv and her little friend, he probably enjoyed it more than they did. He loved seeing Viv happy, loved seeing her make a new friend. And Lauren was right there with him, playing with the girls and occasionally giving him a playful splash too. She made things more comfortable with Kaitlin's mom too. Usually moms either ignored him or flirted with him, both of which made him feel like the odd man out. He couldn't remember having such a fun day. His old kind of fun, partying, hadn't appealed since Viv was born. Maybe it was time for him to live a different kind of life.

He drove them home, turning the idea over in his mind of him and Lauren and what could happen if it went bad (he'd lose a fantastic nanny) or if it went well (maybe she'd stick around). It was risky either way because he was definitely not Lauren's ideal candidate for love. He didn't deserve it, not after what he'd done—his own carelessness had terrible consequences.

But he wanted her.

The first woman he'd wanted at all after not wanting anyone in two long years. And she was good for Viv. That was enough for him.

He turned to Lauren once he parked in his driveway. She'd left him to his thoughts in her quiet considerate way. "I had a great day," he said.

She smiled. "Me too. Bonus, all the sun and fun wore out Viv." She hitched a thumb toward the backseat.

He glanced in the rearview mirror. Viv was out cold, her mouth hanging open. He smiled. He had that good tired feeling after a day in the sun.

"You should put some aloe on your back before you go to bed tonight," Lauren said.

He'd gotten a little burned because the water had washed off some of the sunscreen. "You're good at taking care of people."

"Thanks," she said. "I'm just one of those nurturers. My mom says even when I was Viv's age I was fussing over my dollies, tucking them into bed, talking to them, hugging and kissing them."

"That's sweet."

She crinkled her nose. "Good or bad kind of sweet?"

"Is there a bad kind?"

"Some people say I'm sweet like maybe I'm a pushover or something."

"The good kind of sweet." He winked and she blushed prettily. Her cheeks would be flaming red if she knew what he was really thinking. She was the kind of sweet that would be soft and pliant in bed. He knew it on a primal level and liked it.

She interrupted his dirty line of thinking. "Speaking of dollies, do you mind if I get Viv another one with hair?"

He laughed. "It is kind of sad looking, isn't it? I left it like that so she wouldn't get the idea to cut her own hair."

"She already did a little."

He stared at her, shocked. "What? How did I not notice that?"

"It was just the tiniest lock of hair. She got my safety scissors and did it before I could get them back. Then she tried to make it stick to Dolly's head by pressing really hard."

He shook his head. "That's just sad."

"I know! That's why I wanted to get her a new doll."

"You don't have to do that. I'll get her one."

"Maybe we could take her shopping. Get her a doll and some big-girl panties. Something pretty to encourage potty training."

"Absolutely." It occurred to him that when he was with Lauren, he didn't feel like a struggling single parent. He felt like he had a partner. That was it. He was going for it. Then he remembered she was dating random guys on the weekend.

"What's next for your dating adventures with Hailey?" he asked.

She laughed. "Not with Hailey. My adventures are with a guy."

He grinned. "So what's next on the agenda?"

"Singles mixer at Marcus's bar."

He remembered she'd mentioned that. Marcus, Ethan, and Ben. Of the three, Ethan was the one to watch. Very smooth with the ladies. He tried to think of something to put her off Ethan, but there was nothing. He was a cop, upstanding citizen or whatever.

"Marcus is already busy with a few girlfriends," he told her.

"So not him," she said.

He turned off the car, his plan slowly forming in his mind.

"You want to get her, or should I?" Lauren asked.

"Hold on a minute." He glanced back at Viv still out cold. "Yeah?"

He turned back to Lauren. "Do you mind if I sketch you?"

She gave him an impish smile. "You'll have to buy me dinner first."

They laughed.

He shook his head. "I didn't mean that like a line."

She let out a short *ha-ha* that sounded forced. "I know."

He gestured around her face, tracing a curved line in the air. "You have a heart-shaped face. Most people have oval."

"Oh," she said softly. "Well, I guess if you want to. I never thought it was anything special."

"Speaking as an artist, it is special."

She tilted her head, studying him.

He laughed. "I swear I'm not trying to be cheesy." He was damn rusty at this was the problem. "I've sketched Viv too. You want to see?"

Her green eyes lit up. "I'd love to."

He took off his seat belt. "Alright. I'll get her. If she stays asleep, I'll show you."

He got out and carefully scooped up Viv. Lauren had the key now and let them in. He settled Viv in her room. He figured he'd wake her in a half hour so she'd still go to sleep on time tonight.

He stepped back in the hallway and gestured for Lauren to follow. She did, coming up behind him and whispering, "Shouldn't we hang up our wet stuff?"

"Later," he said, stepping into his studio. "We're on the Viv clock." He pulled the Viv sketches from the top shelf of the closet. There was a series, one for each month of her life with the date and her age marked on the back. "Have a seat."

She sat on the futon. He sat next to her with the stack of loose pages and set them in her lap. She carefully lifted the first one, studied it, and placed it in the back of the pile before looking at the next one. He tensed because she wasn't saying anything. These sketches were probably his best work, done out of love.

Finally she looked up and met his eyes. "Oh, Alex, these are so precious! I love them. So these are, like, every few weeks?"

He relaxed. "Every month."

She kept looking through them. "Oh, wow, look at the difference here between three and four months."

He smiled. "Yeah. It was like she suddenly noticed the world."

Lauren gestured to the sketch. "And she's holding up her head, eyes big and wide and so aware." She got it. She saw the Viv he saw.

"Yes," he said quietly.

She went through the whole set and then handed them back. "What a gift you've given her with this collection. You should sign them. They'll probably be worth something one day."

He warmed at the compliment. "Nah. It's just something I do for me."

She gazed at him. "Thanks so much for showing me these."

He stood and crossed to the closet, carefully storing them where little hands couldn't reach. He turned back to her. "Can I sketch you now?"

She flushed and smoothed her hair. "I'm a mess. My hair is still wet and scraggly. I didn't even get a chance to comb it out."

"It looks natural." He just wanted an excuse to touch her, to angle her head, trace the shape of her face.

She put her hands to her cheeks. "I can feel the sunscreen. No makeup. I'm not sketch-ready."

"You look fine." *You look amazing—sunkissed and sexy.*

He sat next to her, tracing his finger near the line of her cheek, close but not touching. "It's the shape, the lines, the shadows I want to capture." His gaze trailed to her mouth and then her neck where a pulse was beating rapidly. A surge of lust heated his blood. He met her eyes and she gazed back, her lips parting, the air practically crackling with tension.

He slowly brought his hand up, brushing a loose tendril of hair back from her face and then letting his fingers graze over the pulse point of her neck. "You ready?"

She stood abruptly. "I'd better...I have a thing! And my wet towel and this hair!" She rushed out of the room. A moment later he heard the door to the bathroom close.

He blew out a breath. He'd scared her away. In his old life, he'd met experienced women at parties, who were ready to hook up right out of the gate. Hell, the places he used to hang in the city were made for that. Meet, greet, drink, and fuck. Lauren obviously required more finesse.

The moment he heard the bathroom door open, he

stepped out into the hallway. "Hey," he said in a low soothing tone.

She jumped. "Hi."

"I hope I didn't make you uncomfortable there."

She smoothed her sleek combed-out hair and tucked it behind her ears. "Don't be silly." She laughed her forced *ha-ha* laugh. "I'm perfectly comfortable. I'm just not used to artists wanting to sketch me."

He took a step closer. She'd washed off the sunscreen, added some lip gloss, and the dusting of freckles across her nose were less pronounced. She wore a tank top and shorts, but all he saw was bare skin in a black bikini. He gestured back to his studio. "Do you want to try again?"

"Wh-what do I have to do?"

"Nothing. Just sit still long enough for me to get some of the lines down." He gestured for her to go ahead of him into the studio. She didn't move.

Instead she eyed him suspiciously. "You know, I checked in the mirror, and I'm not seeing this heart shape you're talking about."

He was going to have to dial it way the hell back for her. Suspicious distrust did *not* lead to where he wanted.

"It's there," he said. "I'll show you on the sketch pad. Come on." He gestured for her to follow and headed back to the studio.

She sat on the futon while he grabbed a pencil and his sketch pad from the drafting table. He stayed at the table, turning his head slightly to watch as she fidgeted every which way. First she crossed her legs and rested an elbow on her leg. Then she uncrossed her legs and put one hand on each knee. She caught him looking and crossed her arms; then she uncrossed them and crossed them the other way.

He smiled and stood next to her. "All done?"

She held up her palms. "My arms don't know where to go."

"Just put them at your sides." He took a seat close enough to touch if he reached out, far enough to keep her from getting too nervous.

"And what about the rest of me?"

He kept his eyes on his sketch pad, giving her some time to calm down. "Just sit like you normally would."

"But it doesn't feel normal because you're judging me."

He looked up, surprised. She had no idea how beautiful she was. If he told her now, though, he'd show his hand. "I'm not judging. I'm observing like any artist would. I never stop observing, so it's nothing new. That's how I noticed the first day you were here that your face is a heart shape—" he let his gaze follow his words "—and your eyes are green with blue and gray flecks, and you have a light dusting of freckles across your ski-slope-shaped nose." *And a plump lower lip I want to sink my teeth into.*

She covered her nose, her cheeks pink.

He leaned close, pulling her hand off her nose and holding it. Her eyes widened. He stayed close, his gaze drifting to her mouth, on edge with a sharp need for a taste of her sweetness. She moved so quickly she nearly knocked into him as she assumed a pose, propping her chin on her hand and smiling. "How's this?"

He leaned back. "Perfect."

All the lines of her jaw and chin were obscured by her hand, so he focused on her eyes. He captured the shape of them, the expressive openness, the lashes, the arch of her brows, but the guileless innocence, the sweet vulnerability was harder to capture. It was a tangible thing that drew him in, even knowing he didn't deserve sweet, knowing he was a man who took. And she was a woman who gave. But Lauren deserved better. She deserved someone who gave back with the same open generosity that she did. What the hell was he doing?

He set his pencil down, his gut churning. Why was he attracted to her when he was all wrong for her? Was it just because she was so good to Viv? That was messed up. He suddenly felt like he was using her. Fuck. He was. He wanted her for what she could do for him.

She dropped her hand and straightened. "You're done already? Can I see?"

He closed the sketchbook and stood. "Not yet. Might take a few more sessions." He put everything on the high shelf of the closet next to Viv's stuff.

"You didn't draw my freckles, did you? Because I think you can leave those out."

He turned, smiling. "No freckles."

"Good. Can I have it when you're done? I've never had an original work of art."

He shook his head. "It's just a sketch."

She stood. "I still want it with your signature."

"Okay, but it's not worth anything."

She moved to look at his concept art hanging on the two long wire hangers above the bookcase and the adjacent desk. They were pieces from a picture book he'd illustrated about a robot who wanted to be a boy. Normally he didn't take the old stuff down until he needed the hangers for new stuff.

She spoke while looking at the drawings. "That's where you're wrong. You're going to be famous one day."

"Aw, shucks," he said, not believing that for a minute.

She whirled, green eyes flashing, jolting him. "I mean it! You're not just technically proficient, you're capturing emotions on the page. Conveying concepts in a visual way is not easy."

He was shocked she noticed all that. Most people thought it was the text of a picture book that brought the concept and emotion to the page. And just like that, he was drawn back in. He closed the distance between them. "Thank you."

"You're welcome," she said softly, her cheeks pink.

He turned back to the drawings, trying to keep himself in check. "What do you see on the pages?"

"Longing, sadness, loneliness…" She gave him a long look that he felt in his gut, like she saw all of that in him, before turning back to the pictures. "Ultimately joy."

She nailed it. He felt understood, even though it wasn't his story. He'd just helped bring it to life. Of course he hadn't given the robot or the boy any of his darker issues, those stayed buried deep.

She turned to him. "Have you ever thought of writing a picture book of your own?"

"I've thought about it. Just haven't had time."

"You should make time," she said firmly. "Maybe this summer while I'm here with Viv."

He met her gaze and held it, tension crackling between them. It couldn't just be him that felt that. She blushed like a virgin whenever he got close. "What's your schedule look like after the summer?" Idiot. He should be asking her about this weekend not looking to the future and her availability. Somehow he'd gotten Viv and her care tangled up in his attempt to get closer to Lauren. Did he want Lauren for himself or Viv? Both, he quickly decided.

She stepped sideways and brought her hands together in front of her and then switched them to the back. "Typically eight thirty to four. Then I have to do some prep work at home for the next day." She rocked on her heels, looking everywhere but at him. "I wouldn't be much help to you as a nanny."

She was ideal in every way. He didn't care about love. All he needed was a partner, a mom for his little girl and someone to warm his bed. Not just anyone in his bed, though, he wanted her, the woman who'd woken him from his coma of celibacy. If he was clear right from the beginning, spelled out what she could expect from him—an arrangement of sorts based on mutual compatibility—maybe it would work. He didn't want to hurt her. If they were both agreeable...fuck it, he was going for it.

"Lauren." His tone was harsher than he intended, and maybe that made her nervous because her brows shot up over wide eyes. He needed to get the words out there, so he tried to gentle his tone. "Maybe we could—" He stopped himself. This was one of those lines of no return. Lauren was special. She deserved the best. He couldn't give her what she longed for. He was nobody's Mr. Right.

"Maybe we could what?" she asked softly.

His heart thudded hard against his rib cage. Her voice was

soft, her eyes were soft, her skin looked soft. So much softness he longed to sink into.

"Would you like a hug?" she asked gently.

"Yes," he croaked because he desperately wanted to touch her.

She wrapped her arms around his torso and hugged him. His arms closed around her with almost painful relief. She tightened her hold, but he felt anything but comfort. The need intensified, sharper than he could ever remember feeling.

He stroked a hand down her back and spoke near her ear, the words dragged from somewhere deep inside. "I haven't wanted—"

"Hi, Daddy!" a little voice said from behind him.

He whirled and took a step away from Lauren, flushed with guilt over his unfinished sentence, *I haven't wanted anyone the way I want you.* He didn't get to have that. Not for a long time. He had a little girl depending on him.

Viv hugged his legs and he cupped her head, her hair was mostly dry. He cleared his throat. "How was your nap?"

"Okay," Viv said, looking up at him. "Hungry."

Lauren rushed past him. "I'll take care of her. You go back to what you need to do."

Viv followed Lauren like a duckling to her mama. He followed close behind because *that* was what he needed to do.

10

Lauren was in the front passenger seat of Hailey's orange Mini Cooper convertible on the drive over to Marcus's bar in lower Manhattan. It was the only seat where she didn't have to squish to fit her long legs. Carrie and Ally were in the backseat, both of them shorter than her.

"So-o-o, are you excited, Laur?" Hailey asked in a super-perky voice.

Lauren hesitated. She didn't want to be rude. On the other hand, Joe had told her the dirt and it wasn't pretty. Best to be honest, she decided. "Hailey, I'm really sorry because I know you went to a lot of trouble to plan tonight, but I already know these guys aren't for me."

"What?" Hailey barked. "Hold on now. You can't say that before we even get there. What are you even talking about? Did you meet someone?"

She fought back a blush. She'd met someone all right, but he was off the market and rightly so. She liked Alex way too much—her longing/lusting/craving was off the charts—but he just wasn't all there. She could see it in his eyes, in unguarded moments, a dark pain. A wall, like Joe had said. And she knew she wasn't the one to push down those walls. He had them for a reason and would keep them until he was ready, not because she pushed him to be ready.

"Lauren, did you?" Ally piped up from the backseat. She was easily excitable.

"Omigod!" Carrie exclaimed. "She's falling for her boss. The forbidden romance!" Carrie was obsessed with forbidden romances lately, reading tons of them. Not to be unkind, but by no stretch of the imagination was Carrie *ever* going to have a forbidden romance. She was textbook girl next door, even more so than Lauren.

Lauren turned to look at Carrie's no-doubt eager expression. In the dim streetlight, all she could see was Carrie's bright blond hair and big round black-rimmed glasses that were supposedly geek chic (but were more geek than chic). "Carrie, *please* stop with the forbidden stuff."

"It's exciting!" Carrie exclaimed. "Boss and assistant, teacher and student—"

"Bad boy and good girl," Ally put in.

"Yes!" Carrie exclaimed. Then in a forlorn tone, "Good girl, good boy is so boring."

"Good doesn't mean boring," Lauren said. "You definitely don't want someone bad. What do you want a criminal or something?"

"I'm just saying—" Carrie started.

"Ladies, please!" Hailey interrupted. "We're almost there and I need to know what's up with Lauren. She's the one putting herself out there and I want tonight to be a success."

Lauren faced front and sighed. How could tonight be a success when the men were completely unsuitable as Mr. Right?

"Then what are we here for?" Ally asked.

"Backup," Hailey said.

Lauren turned in her seat. "If either of you feels a spark with any guy here, I'll back off immediately. But I should warn you off Ethan, Ben, and Marcus." She winced and faced front. She hated saying anything bad about anyone, but it was true. Joe had told her everything about them. Now that she thought about it, she'd have to be careful what she shared with Joe. He was quite the blabbermouth.

"What's wrong with Ethan?" Hailey asked. "He's

gorgeous and a cop. That's an honorable profession."

"Sex addict," Lauren mumbled.

"What?" Hailey asked.

"Yeah, we can't hear you back here," Carrie piped up.

Lauren spoke up loud and clear. "I said sex addict."

Dead silence. They were probably trying to match up Ethan with sex addict. It was odd. He didn't seem overly sexed. Sure, he was sexy, very sexy, especially in his uniform, and he smirked a lot in a sexy way. Maybe he smirked because he was imagining having sex with them!

She glanced over to find Hailey staring at her, jaw dropped.

"Look at the road!" Lauren ordered.

"Are you serious?" Hailey exclaimed.

Lauren nodded. "It's true. Joe told me."

"Who's Joe?" Hailey asked.

"Mr. Campbell."

Hailey glanced over at her. "You're hanging out with Mr. Campbell now?"

"Ooh, is that who you met?" Carrie asked. "The forbidden older man? Daddy figure?"

Lauren swiveled her head around to glare at Carrie.

She shrugged. "Sorry."

Lauren turned back in her seat. "I brought Viv over to visit and Joe told me all about it."

"Huh," Hailey said. "Well, maybe a sex addict could be fun. He'd certainly be skilled."

"Yeah," Ally piped up.

"I'd do him," Carrie said.

"Please, Carrie, you've slept with one guy," Ally said. "You can *not* handle a sex-crazed man."

"Really?" Hailey asked. "Just one guy? But you're twenty-six, right?"

Carrie huffed. "We dated six years, okay? And we did everything."

The women got quiet. Lauren thought that breakup must've been tough. Almost like a divorce after six long years.

"At least I thought we did everything," Carrie added. "Now that I'm reading all these sexy books…damn, ladies, I missed out."

"Oh, Carrie," Hailey murmured. "I'll help you as soon as I've gotten Lauren on the right path."

"It's not happening tonight," Lauren said.

"So what's wrong with Ben and Marcus that makes them not for you?" Hailey asked.

"Ben doesn't believe in marriage. Marcus doesn't believe in monogamy." Now those two she really felt sorry for. They'd never get to experience the deep and lasting love of a committed relationship. Neither had she, but she knew for sure she wanted that and was at a point in her life where she wouldn't settle for less.

"*Pfft.* Totally fixable," Hailey said confidently.

"I don't think so," Lauren said.

Hailey let out an exaggerated sigh. "The problem is you want a unicorn."

"What's a man have to do with a unicorn?" Ally asked.

"Obviously she wants a big *horn*," Carrie said. "Right, Laur?"

Lauren remained silent, not wanting to encourage them to explore what her unicorn was. It was one of the things Hailey had intuitively picked up during her intensive questionnaire and interview process for Make Love Bloom (TM).

Ally ran with the horn idea. "You never know what you're going to get until the big moment arrives; then it's either tiny banana, big horn, or something ho-hum in between."

"Please," Hailey said, "like size matters. No, Lauren is looking for a sweet alpha, which I've already informed her *doesn't exist*. That's her unicorn. A fantasy."

"Charlotte says Ty is sweet," Ally said. Charlotte and Ty had recently married.

"He's definitely alpha," Carrie said enthusiastically.

"Okay, well, maybe Ty is the unicorn," Hailey said. "Lauren, you're simply going to have to be more open to either sweet and gentle or alpha and rough. You can't have both. It's just *not* realistic."

Lauren looked out the window. Alex was sweet. She saw it every day with him and Viv. He also had alpha potential with his edgy vibe and delicious muscles. But he ranked zero on relationship potential. She sighed. Maybe Hailey was right and she just needed to move on and accept that what she longed for wasn't realistic.

"How's your nanny job working out?" Carrie asked.

Lauren jolted, almost like Carrie knew she was lusting over Alex, though she hadn't confided her secret lust to her friends. "Viv is great," she said a little too loud. She filled them in on Viv's adorable antics. The women listened, but no one was all that enthusiastic. "I guess you had to be there," she finished lamely.

"How's Alex treating you?" Hailey asked.

Lauren fidgeted, unsure why they were back to her employer. "Fine."

"Just fine?" Hailey chirped. "I'm hearing five more layers of *not* fine in that fine." Hailey was surprisingly intuitive. And a good listener too. Still Lauren kept quiet.

"Spill," Carrie said.

"You know how he's an artist?" Lauren said hesitantly.

"Yeah?" the women chorused like *go on*.

"He asked to sketch me," Lauren said in a carefully neutral tone. She wanted to hear what they thought of it because she was confused. He'd backed off after their near kiss and then almost, sort of flirted.

"Were you naked?" Hailey asked.

"No!" Lauren exclaimed. She couldn't imagine posing naked for a sketch. Alex staring, studying her every flaw. She wasn't exactly full of curves like men seemed to like. She'd always been tall and lean, medium-size breasts and narrow hips. A swimmer's body, not a sexpot.

"Were you in a sexy pose?" Ally wanted to know.

"Or did he put you in a sexy pose?" Carrie asked gleefully.

"What were you wearing?" Hailey asked.

"Tank top and shorts. I posed like this." Lauren put her chin in her hand in the classic portrait pose.

"Oh," Hailey said. "You look like you're thinking."

"I thought it was a good sketching pose," Lauren replied.

"Then what happened?" Hailey asked.

Lauren sighed. "That's it. For a brief moment, it seemed like maybe a small flirt? Like how an artist might flirt, but then I thought maybe I was reading too much into it." She shook her head, sure she was reading too much into it.

"Did you want it to be a flirt?" Hailey asked.

"I don't know," Lauren said. This was why she was confused. And overwhelmed. And, terrified, actually, over her growing feelings for him. There were moments when she was sure the attraction went both ways and then they vanished. Like Alex shut them down because of his pain. That was probably a good thing. The *right* thing to do. After what Joe confided, she knew Alex had a lot to work through before he could be there for anyone besides Viv.

"What do you mean?" Ally asked. "He's hot."

The women all murmured agreement.

"You should see him shirtless," Lauren confided. "Totally ripped. He works out with Viv." She smiled remembering their adorable dance. Viv looked so ecstatic to dance with her daddy.

"Oh-kay," Hailey said. "So what's the problem?" She honked the horn and swerved around a double-parked car. "He's hot, he's maybe flirting with you, and you think he's ripped."

Lauren tried to explain without revealing the intimate details Joe had shared. "It's just that, well, his fiancée's death was hard on him." Alex felt like it was his fault. That was something he needed to forgive himself for, not something she or anyone could help him with just with words. It was difficult emotional territory and a decision he had to come to terms with on his own time.

"It's been two years," Hailey said gently.

"I don't think he ever had time to really deal with all the emotional fallout," Lauren said quietly. "Too busy being a single parent. He's not looking for a relationship, that's for sure. He sort of warned me away at our interview, telling me how he fired two nannies that hit on him. He flat out said he was unavailable and not looking for anyone."

"You don't have to be looking to find someone," Hailey sang.

Lauren's brows shot up. "I can't believe you just said that. You're the one running the Make Love Bloom (TM) service to help people find someone."

"What's that?" Carrie asked.

"Lauren!" Hailey exclaimed. "You're supposed to keep that under wraps. You know you're my first client. I want to make sure it's scalable before we invite others in."

Lauren was very tempted to roll her eyes, but too polite to do so. She allowed herself an internal *whatever!*

"Never mind," Hailey said. "You'll all be the first to know once it's official."

Carrie spoke in a sympathetic tone. "Sorry, Laur, but if Alex spelled it out like that for you, I would believe him."

"Yeah," Lauren mumbled.

"Josh says Alex never goes out anymore," Hailey said with great sympathy.

Lauren stared at Hailey. "Since when do you talk to Josh about stuff?" She didn't want anyone to feel sorry for Alex. He just needed time to heal.

"I asked him about Alex because I thought of inviting him tonight," Hailey said.

"Did you invite Josh?" Ally asked.

The women quieted. Dangerous territory there.

"Josh knows better than to mess with my plans," Hailey retorted.

"So he told you no," Ally said.

Hailey sucked in air.

"Josh isn't for me either," Lauren said, trying to make peace. "He's preoccupied with…other things." *Like Hailey.*

Hailey swerved suddenly, pulling into a spot on the street that had just become available. It was a couple of blocks away from the bar. Not too bad. They all got out.

"Let's roll, ladies," Hailey said. "And steer clear of Ethan."

11

————

Alex had to park several blocks away from Marcus's bar, The Burrow, and walked at a brisk pace. His dad had unexpectedly volunteered to babysit so he could hang with the guys. It felt good to get out again. He'd been out of the loop too long. Okay, it wasn't the guys he was pumped to see, it was Lauren. She'd be there and he didn't want her to have "sparks" with anyone but him.

Yup, he was going for it. And the moment he decided that, he remembered he was a man with needs, with a craving for the softness of a woman pressed against him, under him. Not just any woman. Lauren.

He felt *alive* as the bar came into view. Hands in the air at the top of the roller coaster alive.

He stepped inside to the usual Saturday night crowd. The bar to his right was packed. Booths for cozier eating were further back in the narrow long space. He scanned the bar and homed in immediately on Lauren. She sat sideways on a bar stool in a green halter top that tied at the neck and the middle of her back, the rest of her back completely bare. His gaze dropped lower to body-hugging black jeans and black heels with little bows on top. He was momentarily stunned at the transformation. It was easy to picture her in maternal mode, and, yes, the bikini had opened his eyes, but seeing her dressed so sexy on the prowl for a man made him want to pin her against the wall and kiss her. Stake his claim.

His gaze trailed to her long light brown hair glowing in the light of the bar and then her face, the curve of her gentle smile, the point of her chin. She leaned back and he recognized the man leaning forward with short dirty blond hair, giving Lauren his signature flirty smirk—Ethan.

"Ethan Case, back away from the bar," Alex barked like a cop and then swaggered toward him. Ethan was a cop, so he appreciated cop humor. His friend was three years older and had looked out for him growing up. Several heads turned to look at Alex and then turned back to the bar. That was New York City for you. Took a lot to hold people's interest.

"Alex!" Lauren squeaked.

Ethan broke into a rare smile, his sharp blue eyes lit with amusement. "So Viv finally gave you parole." He clapped a hand on Alex's shoulder. "Good to see you. I'll buy you a beer."

He thanked him and stood close to Lauren. "Hi."

Her green eyes were wide, looking up at him. "What're you doing here?"

He lifted one shoulder. "I wanted a night out. It's been a while." For more than just a night out.

"Oh, of course," she said sympathetically. "I didn't mean to…here, take my seat." She hopped off the bar stool, took her glass of wine, and squeezed past Ethan. "Enjoy your beer with Ethan."

"You don't have to…" Alex trailed off because she took off like a shot. Was it him or Ethan?

He watched as she met up with Hailey and friends standing close to the entrance. He recognized Carrie and Ally, both blondes; they'd been at his dad's house a few times when he was there with Viv. They were probably waiting for a few more friends. He'd thought they'd all be upstairs on the third floor, where Marcus had a private room for special guests with a fully stocked bar, pool table, and several round tables perfect for poker. Marcus wasn't tending bar, either. Maybe he was setting up the private room for later.

He took her seat and the bartender appeared to take his order. He sat sideways like Lauren had so he could keep an eye on any guys that might be flirting with her.

Ethan spoke under his breath. "Saved me a crash and burn. That one is skittish as a colt. Probably a virgin."

Alex ground his teeth. "Just because she didn't go for your moves doesn't mean something's wrong with her."

Ethan arched a brow.

Alex's beer arrived and he took a long swallow, still irritated with Ethan. "No way someone that looks like her is a virgin." He wasn't sure how old Lauren was, but she looked to be Mad's age. Way too old to be a virgin. Why was he so worked up about it? Maybe because he knew he wanted a lot more than a virgin was ready for. The beast had been awakened.

"Yeah? How's she look?" Ethan asked.

Alex's face heated. He glanced at Ethan, who brought his beer bottle to his mouth with a smirk. "Look for yourself," Alex muttered.

Ethan socked him on the shoulder.

"Shut up."

"You know why we're here tonight?" Ethan asked.

Alex took another sip of beer. "Yeah. Some kind of spark for Lauren thing."

"What?"

"Never mind."

"No, man, it's a singles mixer." Ethan turned and leaned an elbow on the bar, scanning the small group of single women with Hailey. "What do you think about me and Hailey?"

"Sure, if you don't mind high maintenance." He didn't know Hailey all that well, but the way she looked put together like a glossy picture in a magazine at every occasion, the way she organized and herded her friends, well, it all screamed high maintenance to him.

Ethan shuddered.

Alex's gaze returned to Lauren. Ben Wright, another of his honorary brothers with short light brown hair and blue eyes, was attempting to flirt with her, smiling his dimpled mischievous smile. Alex forced himself to wait and watch, not just barge in like a desperate guy. Lauren was blushing and shifting uneasily from foot to foot. Obviously she wasn't comfortable with Ben. And Marcus was out of the question. So that left Alex, since there was no way Lauren was going to hook up with some random guy at the bar. That wasn't her style. At least, he hoped it wasn't.

He turned to Ethan. "I'm going to call Ben off."

"Go for it," Ethan said. "Send him this way."

Alex grabbed his beer, went over and bumped Ben with his shoulder. "Hey."

Ben turned and grinned. "Hey, good game today." He meant their usual Saturday basketball game. Alex felt a little guilty because his dad had watched Viv this afternoon for the game and tonight too.

"I have to do something," Lauren announced and took off. Geez, now where was she going? He was beginning to suspect she was trying to avoid him.

He pulled Ben closer to the bar, out of hearing range of the ladies. "Are you seriously here to meet someone at Hailey's request?"

Ben spoke under his breath. "Her friends are hot."

"Yeah, but doesn't it feel kinda forced?"

"It's not a proposal. Why the hell not?" Ben glanced back at the women and his jaw dropped, his gaze caught on the door at a group of women who'd just arrived. "Who is that?"

"Which one?"

"Red hair."

"I don't know. One of Hailey's friends."

Hailey rushed to greet three more women, probably single. If tonight was for Lauren's benefit, Hailey sure brought a lot of competition. Marcus appeared from a side door marked staff and greeted the ladies. Marcus looked like a model, no lie, black close-cropped hair, dark eyes with thick lashes, tanned skin, classic chiseled cheekbones, sharp jawline, large bulked-up body. His nose had been broken, though, so he wasn't picture perfect. The ladies loved to touch his overly muscled arms. Marcus loved it too.

Lauren rejoined her friends with a smile and a little wave for Marcus. Somehow Marcus managed to flirt with Lauren, Carrie, and Ally all at the same time. He was a master at making each woman feel special. It shouldn't irritate him, really, Marcus wasn't singling anyone out, but it did.

"Come on," he said to Ben. "Ethan's down the other end of the bar."

They met up with Ethan, and Alex gave Ben his seat. He wouldn't be staying. He had to make his move, though he was so out of practice, and not used to a sweet woman like Lauren, he needed a few minutes to figure out a plan. He sipped his beer and kept an eye on Lauren smiling and talking more to her friends than Marcus. In his old life, it was so much easier. The places he went to in the city catered to free spirits, wild, edgy women comfortable with casual hookups. That was how he met Tammy, in a secret underground party that shifted around his Brooklyn neighborhood, except they'd connected, so similar that they'd hung on for a while. Things had started to fall apart four months in. Tammy was making noises about hitchhiking to San Francisco for a "new scene," which he was not cool with. Then they found out she was pregnant. He pushed Tammy from his mind. He needed to move on.

He was practically a different person now. His life was neatly divided into before Viv and after Viv. And after-Viv life required a woman like Lauren.

Lauren finished her wine and Marcus took the empty glass from her with a smile. She smiled back, pulled out her cell phone, and tapped on it. At least she wasn't taken in by Marcus's so-called charm.

His phone vibrated in his pocket. He checked the screen in case it was his dad. He smiled. It was Lauren. *Who's watching Viv?* He loved that she cared.

He quickly texted back. *My dad. You want to get out of here?*

She stiffened and looked around for him. He stepped away from the bar, closer to her, but not close enough to get sucked in with her friends. He crooked his finger and she walked right over.

"I thought you wanted to hang with your friends," she said.

"I saw them earlier for basketball."

She looked around stealthily. "I don't think I can leave. Hailey planned this entire night for me. Some of the guys brought her gifts."

He looked over and realized Hailey was holding a gift bag with some cards sticking out of it. "Why?"

She shook her head with a smile. "They think they're here for her birthday, but they know they're not, but she doesn't know that they know." She took a deep breath. "It's complicated. Do you want to go to her surprise party next month?"

"Sure."

"Great. I'll text you the details." She met his eyes with a warm smile. "It's good you're going out again. Josh says you haven't been."

"Should we make some kind of announcement? Soak it in, people! Alex Campbell left the house." He grinned.

She blushed and pushed her long hair over her ears. "So, anyway, I kind of have to stay and report on sparks or lack thereof."

He leaned close and spoke in a husky tone near her ear. "You feel any yet?"

Her blush stepped into the red zone. She looked away, her mouth opening and then closing.

"That's quite a blush," he teased. "Must've been some crazy sparks going on."

She laughed and shook her head. "No! Impossible."

"Why is it impossible?"

She put a hand on his arm, leaned close, and whispered, "I know way too much." She dropped her hand and met his eyes briefly before lowering them, studying the bows on the front of her shoes.

"Like what? You reading everyone's old-soul eyes?"

She shook her head. "I don't need to."

"So what's wrong with Ethan?"

She bit her plump lower lip. "I shouldn't repeat what I heard." She glanced at Ethan and then back to him, whispering, "It's private."

"He tell you something?" He couldn't imagine what it was. Ethan was downright boring as a cop nowadays. As a kid, he'd been tough with no respect for authority. Irony.

"No," Lauren whispered, blushing furiously. "Can we not talk about him?"

"Sure. What's wrong with Marcus?" He was enjoying hearing all about how his competition fared so poorly in her eyes. It wasn't usually the case.

She glanced back at Marcus now flirting with all of her friends. "I don't think he can pick just one."

"Maybe. Or maybe he just hasn't met the One."

Her head snapped back to him, green eyes wide. "Do you believe in the One?"

"No, I was joking."

"Oh. Why not?"

"Because it doesn't make sense. There's too many people in the world for there to be just one."

She lifted her chin. "I believe each of us has a soul mate."

"What about the spark?" he teased.

Her voice was firm and entirely sincere, her gaze steady on his. "You need the spark to get close enough for soul recognition."

He got a chill, even though he didn't believe a word of it. She believed it and it made it feel real. He swallowed and looked away, over her shoulder. That was when he noticed Ben checking out Lauren's ass. "What's wrong with Ben?" Oh fuck. He was coming over.

"Completely unsuitable," Lauren said.

He made eye contact with Ben and hitched his head in a gesture for him to back off. Ben kept right on coming.

"Come on, Ben's great," he said loud enough for Ben to hear. "Good job, good looking, great in bed, I hear." Ben grinned at that last part.

"He doesn't believe in marriage!" Lauren exclaimed.

Ben reversed course. Yup. He didn't. *So long, Ben.*

Alex bit back a smile and turned to Lauren. "Maybe he just didn't meet his soul mate yet."

She shook her head. "He's not ready. It's in his eyes."

"His old-soul eyes?" he asked with a laugh.

She looked away. "Now you're teasing."

"I just don't see how you can get all that from looking at someone's eyes."

She turned back to him and lifted her chin. "You don't have to believe me. I believe me."

"What do my eyes look like right now?" he challenged, letting her see the heat, the desire he was holding in check.

"Brown." She quickly looked away.

He wanted to touch her, to cup her face or stroke her bare shoulder, but he held back. Lauren was the kind of woman that needed to be eased into the physical. He knew that in his bones. "Anything else?"

She looked again, meeting his lusty eyes. Her eyes dilated and she licked her lips. She felt it, but would she acknowledge it?

"Old soul? Pain and sorrow?" He threw that out there in hopes she'd deny it and say what she really saw—pure hungry lust. The pain and sorrow she claimed to see was actually stabbing guilt.

He shifted closer, holding her gaze. "Lauren?"

"N-no," she stuttered. "Not that."

"Lauren!" Hailey waved her over. "Come on, we're going upstairs."

Lauren gave him an apologetic look. "I'll see you up there?"

"Yup."

She rejoined her friends. He got Ethan and Ben and they followed at a leisurely pace. Marcus's private room was exactly that, an intimate space with dark wood tones, soft lighting, and plenty of good liquor, perfect for meeting up with friends or a woman. He'd just been given a golden opportunity to make a move.

When he got there, Marcus was behind the bar, refreshing everyone's drinks. The ladies all favored white wine. There were seven women. Hailey introduced the three that had recently arrived as Missy (that was the redhead), Lexi, and Sabrina. The four guys, including him, got beers.

Ethan set up the balls for pool. "Who wants to play?"

The guys all did. The women declined. That was weird. Usually women loved to hang with Ethan.

Ethan put his hands on his hips and eyed the women hovering by the bar. "Come on. Two guys, two girls. Then we'll have the winners play the next two."

Hailey volunteered with a tone of bravado. "I'll play."

The women murmured to her and she lifted her chin and went to Ethan's side.

"Me too," Lauren said, crossing to Hailey's side in a show of support.

Alex headed to the pool table, saying, "I'm in."

Ethan gave Hailey one of his flirty smirks. "You any good?"

"I'm terrible," Hailey said.

"Me too," Lauren said.

"Then we'll have to teach you," Ethan said, shooting Alex a knowing look.

Alex jerked his chin. Teaching a woman to play pool was akin to foreplay and they both knew it. The worse they were at it, the better because then you had an excuse to lean over them from behind, guiding their hands around the stick. Damn, he was getting hot just thinking about it. He glanced away, working on cooling off. Marcus got a game of poker going while the four of them picked out cues from the rack on the wall.

And then they started to play. Ethan's first attempt at guiding Hailey ended with her jabbing him with the stick from behind hard enough to make him double over. He kept his distance after that, barking out orders to which Hailey reacted by playing worse and worse.

Lauren, on the other hand, was extremely amenable to instruction. From the very first, she looked to Alex for guidance, checking in with him for her next move on the table. She always took his instruction, lined up the shot, bent over the table and then looked back over her shoulder at him. "Like this?"

Whether or not she meant that as an invitation, it sure as hell felt like one and he took full advantage, guiding her from behind, his hands on hers, murmuring instructions in her ear. She blushed furiously, her entire body heating against his, but she did beautifully nonetheless, taking his direction.

And when she screwed up a shot, she apologized to him. He forgave her, of course.

And when she sank a shot, she jumped up and down and beamed at him. "Ah! Did you see that?"

He loved every minute of it.

And when they won, she threw her arms around him in an exuberant hug. He hugged her back and she slowly pulled away.

"Sorry," she said to his chest. "I got excited."

He grinned. "Me too."

Her head lifted, green eyes wide. Before he could say something suggestive, they were joined by the next team. Luckily, Ben and Missy were pool sharks and won in a quick victory. Lauren excused herself for the ladies' room and Hailey followed.

Alex went to watch his friends play cards. Ethan looked considerably happier at the card table, the chips piling up in front of him. Alex pulled out his cell. Nearly nine thirty. He texted his dad to see if he'd been able to get Viv to sleep. If she was giving him trouble, Alex would have to bail early and get her home to her own bed.

Sound asleep, his dad texted. *Come by in the morning.*

He relaxed. He had all night. A rare thing. Viv had only spent the night with his dad a couple of times when Alex had been sick and, even then, Alex had stayed in the spare room at his dad's house. That way Viv didn't miss him, but his dad could help take care of her. He hadn't minded not having time to himself. Viv needed him; he was there. But now, well, now he needed a little something for himself.

Lauren and Hailey appeared through the private entrance

in a heated discussion that only got louder as they moved closer.

"I'm just trying to help you!" Hailey exclaimed.

"And you have," Lauren said evenly. She turned and gave Hailey a hug.

When they pulled apart, Hailey said something too quiet for him to hear. Then they both headed for the bar.

He intercepted Lauren. "Everything okay?"

"Yes," she said in a low tone. "I think she's just a little frustrated with me because there's no sparks." She looked over at the guys and back to him. "It's not something you can manufacture, you know? It's either there or it isn't."

"So does that mean you can bail now? I could drive you home if you want."

"What time is it?"

"Late," he lied. "You definitely put in the appropriate amount of time to be polite."

She pursed her lips, trying not to smile. "Are you making fun of me again?"

He grinned. "Never."

"I need some kind of excuse."

"Tell her you felt a spark with me."

She blushed and pushed her hair behind her ears. "Alex."

"What?"

She lifted her gaze, looking at him under her lashes. "Did you feel a spark?"

"Big time."

Her eyes widened.

"Can we go now?" He held out his hand.

She stared at his hand for a long moment. He wanted to grab her hand and guide her right out the door, but restrained himself. She had to at least meet him halfway.

"Lauren!" Hailey called. "Marcus opened some champagne. Come on!"

Lauren gave him a small smile. "I love champagne."

"Then let's have some." He joined her at the bar, the only guy there. Carrie sat on Lauren's other side, followed by Ally and Hailey.

After Marcus poured the women their champagne, Alex asked, "What're we celebrating, ladies?"

"Forbidden romance," Carrie replied then burst out laughing.

Lauren rolled her eyes. "You're done." She took Carrie's glass of champagne from her and told Marcus, "She can't handle more than two glasses of wine."

Carrie pushed her black-rimmed glasses up. "That is not true."

"It is true," the women replied in near unison.

Carrie leaned around Lauren and poked Alex in the arm. "You're forbidden."

"Am I?" He exchanged a look with Marcus, who stepped right in.

Marcus leaned across the bar to Carrie. "You looking for a taste of the forbidden, darlin'?" he drawled.

"Yes," Carrie said with a bright smile. "But you're not forbidden." She cocked her head. "Hey, are you a unicorn?"

Marcus's lips twitched. "I'll be whatever you want, cutie."

"Lauren!" Carrie exclaimed, one hand cupping her mouth in a shout-whisper even though she was sitting right next to Lauren. "I found your unicorn!"

Hailey sighed dramatically. "Carrie, I told you he doesn't exist."

"What's she talking about?" Alex asked.

Lauren turned to him. "She's drunk. Don't listen to her."

Ally filled him in. "The gentle alpha. Turns out your brother Ty was the last one."

He puzzled over that. Gentle alpha? Ty was like a bull in a china shop. Boisterous, loud, over the top. Ty and gentle didn't go together.

"Not gentle!" Carrie said, slapping the bar top. "Sweet! A sweet alpha!"

Still didn't make sense.

"Can we get some coffee into her?" Lauren asked Marcus. "And food. Maybe some fries."

"You got it," Marcus said with a chuckle. He left to put the order in.

Alex spoke low in Lauren's ear. "Explain the unicorn concept."

She drank her champagne and kept on drinking until she finished it. Then she picked up Carrie's confiscated glass and took a sip.

He took a pull on his beer. "If you don't tell me, I'm sure Carrie will."

She remained quiet, also blushing. She gave him side-eye and sipped her champagne.

"You're looking for a sweet guy?" he guessed.

Still quiet. A long swallow of champagne.

He gave her hair a tug. "What's an alpha? You mean like a leader? Top dog?"

She let out a long sigh and answered in a low tone, staring straight ahead. "It's hard to explain. It's one of those you-know-it-when-you-see-it kind of things."

"Ah. Have you seen one?"

She slowly turned to him, giving him a once-over that said she appreciated his alpha maleness before whispering, "Yes."

"Yes," he echoed, hope and lust surging through him. Lust winning by a landslide. He stroked her hair back from her face, shifting to cradle her cheek. "I can be sweet too."

"I know." She leaned into his hand, her eyes closing. "You're intoxicating."

He stilled, stunned at the admission. She slowly opened her eyes hazy with lust, he hoped, and not alcohol. "Are you intoxicated?"

She smiled sweetly. "Just tipsy."

"Are they going to kiss?" Carrie's voice carried over to them.

Lauren stiffened and whirled toward Carrie, who said, "Sorry, go back to what you were doing and don't mind me!"

Carrie giggled, turned and whispered something to Ally.

Alex snagged Lauren's pinky finger with his and she slid her hand fully into his, tucked together under the bar.

Alex stayed quiet, enjoying being close to Lauren and hoping the women would drink and speak freely. He wanted to hear what Lauren had to say to her friends. No surprise, she was caring, concerned, and supportive, even when they said moronic things like "a vibrator is better than a man anyway." That was from Ally. Or plainly false, like Carrie, who kept insisting if she just had some champagne, she was sure the next man she met would be *the* man. Whatever the hell that meant. The man for what?

By the time the women had finished the second bottle of champagne, he knew way too much about Ally's lack of a sex life, which Carrie feared was catching. Hailey jumped in to reassure them, but when they turned the question around, wanting to know who Hailey had been with, Hailey immediately put the spotlight elsewhere.

"So, Alex," Hailey said with a knowing look, "what're you doing hanging out with us instead of the guys?"

"If you want me to go…" He shifted and Lauren squeezed his hand.

"You don't have to go," Lauren said. She shot Hailey a dark look.

Hailey turned to Ally and Carrie. "Do you think sketching someone is like flirting?"

Lauren turned bright red and stood. "Actually we're both going to go. Come on." She grabbed his arm and pulled.

"I'll take her home," he told the women. "Nice seeing you."

Hailey smiled smugly. He didn't care. He put a hand on the small of Lauren's back, loving the feel of satiny smooth skin that heated at his touch. He guided her to the card table, where they said their goodbyes. They headed for the door that led to the private staircase.

"I'm sorry about that," Lauren whispered a little loudly. "I mentioned that you sketched me, but I never said you were flirting."

"I was."

She stumbled and he caught her, keeping her upright. "Oh. Huh. That was before I told you how intoxicating you were."

He grinned. "Yeah. It was the bikini."

She beamed. "Thank you."

She started walking to the exit and he quickly caught up to her, opening the door for her. She brushed by him, her hand coming up to squeeze his shoulder. "You're my unicorn but...no, *no*, NO." She shook her head and then nodded once. "I can't have you."

He sucked in air. She could totally have him.

The moment the door closed behind them, he snagged her around the waist, turned and backed her into the wall of the stairwell. Her eyes were locked on his, her breath coming faster. *Easy. Slow it down.* She was sweet bordering on a complete innocent. Not a virgin, he was pretty sure, but so pure in spirit it was practically the same thing.

He let go of her waist and rested his palm on the wall next to her head. Close but not touching, heat radiating between them. Her cheeks and neck were flushed pink. God, she was sexy.

He lowered his head close enough to feel her breath fan over him. He waited, giving her time to stop him, but she didn't. Instead she tilted her face up to his and closed her eyes. He closed the gap, fitting his mouth over hers. Her lips were soft and yielding, exactly as he'd hoped. He slid his fingers under her hair, cupping the back of her neck, and deepened the kiss. She opened immediately and he swept his tongue inside. Sweet champagne and sexy woman. Lust like he'd never felt before surged through him. He pressed his body fully against hers, pinning her wrists against the wall over her head, kissing her like a starving man because he was. She melted against him, soft, pliant, hot. Raw carnal need had him grinding into her. She moaned into his mouth, arching her hips, meeting him. *Yes, yes, yes.*

He lifted his head, gazing at her for one hot moment, her lips wet, her breathing ragged. He released her wrists and cupped her jaw, brushing his thumb across her plump lower lip before kissing her again, his other hand slipping under her shirt, sliding up hot skin. No bra. He loosened the tie at her back with a quick tug and gained the room he needed to cup her breast, stroking the nipple into a hard peak. She arched into his hand with a moan. He kissed her long and deep, one hand holding her head, the other hand under her shirt, his fingers rolling and tugging her nipple. His own need magnified with her moans. It wasn't enough. He needed his mouth on more of her like right now. He broke the kiss, trying to catch his breath and slow things down long enough to get them somewhere more private.

"Alex," she whispered, "you're not ready for me."

"Maybe you're not ready for me," he countered, shifting to kiss the side of her neck, breathing in flowers, spice, and sweet Lauren. He let his teeth scrape against her and heard her sharp intake of breath, her fingers clutching his shirt.

He nipped and sucked the side of her neck, hungry for her, before moving to her ear to tell her the desperate truth. "It's been years since I've wanted anyone."

"You're ravenous." She said that like it was a bad thing.

He straightened, gazing into her eyes. "Yes, for you."

She grabbed his hands and held them. "You have too much baggage. You're not ready."

He stared at her. She was calling him out. Questioning his motives. So maybe he was acting on lust. So what? So was she.

"Lauren."

"I want a relationship."

He ran his hands slowly up her sides, under her shirt, stroking fever-hot skin. Her eyes dilated. He cupped her breasts, brushing his thumbs across the hard peaks. Her eyes closed, her head tipping back. "You want me."

"I can't have you," she said with so much longing he had to prove her wrong.

He kissed her. "Yes, you can. Do you like my mouth on you?" He brushed his lips across hers and then traced her lower lip with his tongue.

"Alex," she said on a sigh.

"My hands on you?" He slid his hands to the bare skin of her back, stroking down to cup her ass.

"Yes, but—"

He cut her off with a kiss and she held him close, her hands gripping his shoulders. When he finally let her up for air, she put her hand on his chest. "I won't compromise on what I want."

He narrowed his eyes. "Are you daring me to have a relationship?"

"Are you daring me to fuck you?" she asked softly.

12

Lauren swallowed as Alex's dark eyes heated to an edgy intensity that bordered on dangerous. His large hand came up to cup her jaw, surprisingly gentle as his thumb swept over her lower lip and then pressed on it.

"Sexy, dirty angel," he murmured before his mouth covered hers.

She lost herself in the kiss, her inhibitions down, her lust out of control. The kiss turned hard and hungry, his tongue thrusting inside. His hand gripped her hair; his other hand cupped her ass, holding her in place for the plundering kiss. She just hung on, her fingers clutching his shoulders, dimly aware this was what ravenous felt like, and she *loved* it. She arched into him, straining to get closer. He got the message, cupping the back of her knee and lifting her leg, opening her to him and grinding against her. She moaned, the kiss hot and wet and deep, on and on and on, the pressure building inside her. And then she was right there and he wasn't stopping. Her body jerked and then she flew, small cries escaping swallowed by his mouth.

He lifted his head, still holding her pressed tight against his hardness. She throbbed against him or maybe that was him against her. She moaned as an aftershock went through her.

His voice was rough and gravelly. "Did you just—"

"You were ravenous," she said in a shaky voice.

He released her leg. "I think you liked it okay."

She nodded once, unable to explain the fact that she had this firm line of no compromise for the relationship she wanted, that she knew he wasn't ready for, and then came apart in his arms anyway.

He turned her, redid the tie he'd loosened on her halter top, turned her back and laced his fingers with hers. "Come on."

She walked on shaky legs beside him down the stairs, through the bar, and outside. The night air was warm, the lights and noise of the city competing with the thoughts spinning through her brain. She had *not* been expecting that kiss. Or that orgasm. He'd surprised her, shocked her, overwhelmed her. The men she dated gave gentle kisses at the *end* of the night with no orgasm involved. Alex jumped in early, before she had time to think about it, catching her unprepared. He'd been aggressive, hungry, downright ravenous, as she'd predicted. Fresh heat rushed between her legs just thinking about it. He'd said Josh would chew her up and spit her out, but after that kiss, she feared that was exactly what Alex would do. Consume her and then drop her.

She glanced at his expression—still smoldering with intensity—his wide shoulders, his strong arms leading to large hands that had pinned her wrists against the wall. He hadn't hurt her, his grip was firm, not tight. She swallowed and looked straight ahead.

Any man that kissed like that, especially with a first kiss, was dangerous. Okay, yes, she liked it, but they weren't matching up on the right level. She was looking for a committed relationship. He was looking for hot rough sex.

She lifted her hair off her neck in a vain attempt to cool off. She suddenly wished she could talk to her friends and get their opinions, but they were nearly at his car, and how would she explain why she'd returned without him? "The kiss turned orgasmic and I needed to cool off" sounded ridiculous. Nothing was making any sense to her.

She wanted him was the problem. Wanted what she knew was a bad idea. She just had to wait for her body to catch up with her brain's excellent reasoning.

He stopped at the passenger side of the car and opened the door for her like a gentleman, gently shutting it behind her. She took a deep calming breath and tried to think of the right words to explain that while she enjoyed her orgasm very much, thank you, they probably shouldn't get naked any time soon on account of the mismatch between their expectations. Of course, she didn't quite know what his expectations were. She assumed hot sex.

She pressed her forehead against the window. She hadn't had sex in eight months. (And she hadn't come at all with that guy. Such a letdown.)

He got into the car, still quiet. She put on her seat belt, the click loud in the charged silence of the car. She jumped when he spoke for the first time since they'd left the bar.

"You okay?" he asked.

"Yes, I'm fine." Her voice came out too high. "How're you?"

"Fine." He put the key in the ignition, but didn't turn the car on. He studied her. "So, we good?"

"I'm fine. Maybe we should talk later when we're calmed down."

His gaze pinned hers. "About what?"

"The mismatch."

His mouth crooked to the side in a small sexy smirk of a smile. "Lauren, you orgasmed during our first kiss. I'm not seeing a mismatch."

She crossed her legs, heat flooding her at the reminder. "Yes, well, I'm pretty sure that was because you were ravenous."

His expression was intense just like before he'd kissed her to orgasm. "Maybe you're the one who's ravenous."

"Mmm," she said noncommittally to the windshield. It was hard to argue the point when her panties were soaked and her lips still tingled from his rough kisses.

He cupped her jaw and turned her toward him. His voice

was deep velvet that wrapped around her. "C'mere, kiss me again. I have a theory."

Her heart thudded against her chest. She couldn't move.

Their gazes locked.

He waited.

She waited.

Heat shimmered between them.

Part of her wanted to throw herself into his arms; part of her said to refuse him. She'd screwed up earlier, throwing her perfectly valid reason for resisting him out the window. She didn't want to do it again. It would be so easy to give in, to let the fire between them take over. But then what? She'd be the one burnt from the flames.

"Okay," he said quietly, dropping his hand and starting the car.

She sank back against her seat and let out a shaky breath. Alex pulled out of the lot and put on the radio to an edgy alternative station, the lyrics harsh, explicit, the beat fast. That was who he was, she told herself. She was soft rock; he was edgy alternative.

"What's up with Carrie and the forbidden?" he asked, a smile in his voice.

She was so relieved to get out of her own lusty head, she laughed. "It's silly. Just a fantasy romance thing. The kind of stuff we read in book club, but she went a little overboard."

"What else do you read in book club? Tell me your favorites."

She warmed to the topic. She loved romance, the life-affirming happy ever after. It filled her with hope and happiness. She blabbed on and on, telling him all her favorites and why. She was especially partial to the Fierce trilogy, as was everyone in book club, it was by Julia Marino, a former book club member (also turned into a movie). The hero had been a true alpha in every sense of the word. Of course, she left out the erotic scenes, instead sharing the hero's utter devotion to the heroine. She didn't want to make things awkward now that they were chatting like friends again.

She asked him about his work, his favorite projects, and

what medium he enjoyed the most. He loved sketching and digital painting best, especially full-color covers and illustrations for picture books. She was so happy to be back on safer ground, the ride home just flew by.

"So you're in Clover Park, right?" he asked once they crossed into Connecticut.

"Yes. The apartment complex by the edge of town bordering on Eastman."

"And you work there too. That's convenient."

"Yeah. I'm saving up for a house. Though I can't complain about the commute. When the weather's nice, I bike to work."

"I got that beat," he said. "I just roll out of bed, take ten steps, and I'm there."

She laughed. "True."

She gave him a few more directions and he parked in the lot in front of her building. "I'm just upstairs on the second floor," she said. Before she could thank him for the ride, he was already out the door, walking around to her side, and opening her door. The gentleman was back.

She stepped outside.

He shut the car door behind her. "I was raised to walk the woman to the door and make sure she gets in safe." He grinned. "You can blame my dad for beating gentlemanly manners into me."

She laughed and even to her ears it sounded nervous and high-pitched. The truth was she still wanted him and was very tempted to pull him inside her apartment. "Okay."

He put a hand on the small of her back, singeing her bare skin with his touch. They headed upstairs.

"You have a roommate?" he asked.

Her brain translated that to *I hope we can be alone*, making her knees wobble and her heart race. "Yes. Me and my two cats."

He flashed a smile. "Okay if I come in? It's my first Viv-free night and I'm not ready to turn in."

Translation: *let's fuck like animals.*

Her stomach did a few flips. "Probably not a good idea."

It's a great idea! her orgasm-loving parts screamed at her, basically all of her minus the tiny still-functioning part of her brain.

"Just to talk. Or we could watch a movie."

Translation: *I want you to feel comfortable before I fuck you.*

She tried very hard to think it through, her brain still sluggish with the lust running high between them. She must've been thinking too long because he spoke in a much gentler tone.

"Did I come on too strong before?"

She was quiet for a moment because he had, but she'd liked it. "It's okay, really. I was just surprised."

"I'm out of practice," he said flatly.

"Mmm-hmm," she said because she had no idea how to explain where she was at right now, both wanting him and trying very hard to resist him. They reached her apartment. "I'm pretty tired so…" She let him fill in the blank and turned from him, facing the door and pulling out her key. "Good night."

"Lauren." His voice was low and deep, weakening her resolve. "Give me another chance to do this right."

She swallowed, seriously torn.

She slowly turned to face him. His expression was clear in the light by her front door—a dark hunger, *ravenous*. She shivered. "See you on Monday."

She whirled and dropped her keys. He scooped them up, unlocked the door for her, placed the keys back in her hand, and held the door open. "See you Monday," he said.

She rushed inside and leaned back against the door, feeling like she'd just run a marathon, breathing hard, shaky, and weak. She slowly sank to the floor. She did the right thing. She didn't want to be a late night booty call. She wanted to feel special. His words rang through her head, *give me another chance to do this right.*

She hadn't given him a chance.

It was either the smartest or stupidest thing she'd ever done in her life.

~

Lauren got through the week working for Alex with boundaries firmly in place. She took care of Viv at his house every morning while he worked in his studio, they all had lunch together, and she took Viv out in the afternoons. No problem at all. Except not. Because things had changed between them, an awareness and tension in the air. Sometimes she'd catch an unguarded look in Alex's eyes—pure carnal hunger. Her body got the message, flushing with heat, damp between the legs. And that was just from a look. She wasn't sure how much longer she could resist him. Part of her said just go for it, put them both out of their misery, but then the more rational part said to be smart about Alex. He wasn't there yet. Maybe he never would be.

Hailey texted multiple times that week, urging Lauren to go on another date from the online service this coming weekend. But Lauren was too conflicted over Alex to go back to the original plan. She felt so stuck—not ready to go forward with more blind dates, not sure if there was a way forward with Alex. At least not one that didn't involve her tender heart getting crushed.

Fortunately, her weekend plans fell into place easily on Saturday morning. She'd texted Carrie about spending the afternoon at Grand Lake in Clover Park. And she was excited to go. The lake was surrounded by trees with a nice beach perfect for relaxing on the sand. Not five minutes later, Mr. Campbell, Joe, she reminded herself, called and invited her to a family barbecue on Sunday. She was satisfied with that. She'd get some relaxing time and she'd get some time to observe Alex in his natural habitat, get to know him a little better and feel out the situation. It wasn't so easy to have an adult conversation with Alex when Viv was around. She figured a family barbecue would provide plenty of adults to entertain Viv.

Saturday afternoon Lauren found Carrie already set up on the sand, relaxing on a beach lounger, wearing a modest sky blue one-piece bathing suit and a large floppy hat that nearly met the huge sunglasses that fit over her glasses. Her bright blond hair fell in soft layers just past her jaw, one lock stuck to the thick layer of sunscreen on her cheek. Carrie slathered herself in sunscreen because her pale skin was prone to sunburn. She was, as usual on their beach days, enjoying a Yoo-hoo chocolate drink. A cooler sat near her feet.

"Hey, girlie," Lauren said, unfurling her extra-large beach towel next to her friend's chair.

"Hey!" Carrie exclaimed. "I'd hug you, but I'm slippery with sunscreen." She gave her an air kiss and pulled the hair away from her sticky cheek. "Yoo-hoo?"

Lauren stashed her sunglasses in her purse, took off her T-shirt and shorts, and sat on the towel in her usual bikini. "No, thanks. Maybe later." She slid her sunglasses back on and stretched out her legs, leaning back on her elbows.

"Sunscreen?" Carrie offered.

"I'm going to soak in some rays first." She tilted her head up to the sun, relaxing in the warmth.

"So how's things?" Carrie asked.

"Things are good."

"Any more sketching happening over at Casa Campbell?"

She'd kept the carnal kiss to herself all week because she wasn't sure what to do about it, but she couldn't keep it in any longer. She sat up to whisper, "He kissed me *ravenously*."

Carrie shot straight up in her seat. "Omigod! I'm so jealous! Good for you!"

"You're jealous?"

Carrie grabbed Lauren's arm. "Are you kidding me? The forbidden romance! Tell me everything." She flopped back in her lounger and took a long chug of Yoo-hoo.

"Um, okay. It's not forbidden."

"He's your boss," Carrie said with great enthusiasm.

Lauren grabbed a hair band from her purse and pulled her hair up. "It's just a temp summer job. There's nothing forbidden, trust me."

"So how was it?"

Orgasmic.

Lauren took a deep breath before admitting, "Over-whelming."

"Yeah?" Carrie said eagerly.

"Yeah." She sat cross-legged and closed her eyes, listening to the happy sounds of children playing, the soft lapping of the water on shore, the slight rustle of a breeze through the surrounding trees. Carrie interrupted her Zen moment.

"Anything else?" Carrie whispered. "What position did you do? Did you sixty-nine?"

Lauren's eyes flew open. "Geez, Carrie! I said he kissed me not fucked me." She normally didn't speak so crudely without a few drinks in her, but Carrie went there first.

Carrie raised her sunglasses and peered at her with wide blue eyes through her black-framed glasses. "Sorry, I got excited."

She nudged Carrie's shoulder and then had to wipe the sunscreen off her fingers on the back of her neck. "It's fine. Now I'm not sure what to do." She lowered her voice. "He's been celibate for two years."

Carrie dropped her sunglasses back in place. "That's an effing long time."

"It is, but then what, you know?" Lauren confided in a whisper. "I'm just not sure he's into me, like, as a person, not just as a convenient…fuck." And it wasn't like Alex had tried to seduce her, he'd even checked to be sure she was okay after their kiss, which was sweet. The problem was she couldn't stop thinking about how much erotic promise that one kiss held. Scorching passion that had swept her off her feet in a way she'd always dreamed would happen and never did.

Carrie nodded sagely. "I get it. Like, oh, there's the nanny I see all the time, let's hit that."

"Exactly!" People didn't appreciate what came easy to them. She flushed, her own thoughts striking her as much dirtier than usual. Came easy, came hard, it was all so much to miss out on.

"I'd still go for it," Carrie said. "He's hot for you, you're hot for him, wham-bam, thank you, sir!" She saluted.

Lauren shook her head. "It's more complicated because he's a dad and he's grieving Tammy."

"Yeah, that was terrible what happened."

Lauren sighed. "The timing is bad. This was supposed to be my summer to find Mr. Right. Hailey's been working her ass off to find someone for me. I wish I could meet Alex in the future once his head's on straight, his eyes are clear, and his heart is open."

"Too late. You already met him and like him. Plus if you met Mr. Right this summer, then meeting Alex in the future is moot."

"You're right. I just wish things were—" she waved her hand around, searching for the right word "—I don't know, simpler. I turned down one of Hailey's setup dates this weekend because I can't decide what to do about Alex."

Carrie took another slug of Yoo-hoo. She handed the bottle to Lauren to hold while she pulled out a small bag of potato chips from her cooler, offering some to Lauren. She shook her head and Carrie took one for herself.

"I'll see him tomorrow," Lauren confided. "His dad invited me to a family barbecue. I thought it might help to get to know him a little better."

"Yeah, maybe his brothers will tell you all his embarrassing stories."

"I don't want to embarrass him. I just want to get to know him in a different way."

They were quiet for a few moments. Lauren started fretting again. What if she got to know Alex, fell hard for him (she was already leaning that way), and then they weren't on the same page. What if it was a hopeless cause?

Carrie lifted her drink. "I swear on this Yoo-hoo I'll have a fling with the next bad boy I meet."

Clearly all those forbidden romances had addled Carrie's brain. She was usually so, well, demure. Not uptight, but definitely not this blatant about wanting to get her some. "You don't want a bad boy in real life. You want someone that will treat you nice."

Carrie flashed a smile. "Like Alex."

"He's not that nice," she admitted. Alex could be rough and aggressive, not the kind of nice mild-mannered guy she was used to. "But he's not a bad boy either. He's a responsible parent."

Carrie grabbed her arm. "What'd he do?" she asked with a note of alarm.

Lauren squeezed her friend's hand, loving that Carrie was so supportive and caring. "Nothing bad. He's just a little rough around the edges."

"I want that," Carrie said in a low voice. "Just use me up, wring me out, limp noodle, goodbye!"

"What is with you lately?" Lauren asked. "You're starting to worry me."

Carrie chomped on a chip. "My eyes are finally open. I had no idea how repressed Edward was." That was her ex. She leaned close and whispered, "Do you know he never went down on me? Six years!"

"Sorry," Lauren said sympathetically. She'd bet good money the reverse wasn't true. Edward sounded like a selfish loser, but she kept that to herself. Carrie was already upset enough with what she felt she'd missed out on.

Carrie took some more chips, her hand rustling around in the bag. "That's number one on my bad-boy list. I've got all these things I've never tried."

"How many things are on the list?"

"So far three, but I just started it last night. I'm going to add at least ten more. Lucky thirteen! Then the next bad boy I meet, I'll hand over the list and wait to be ravished."

Lauren laughed. "I don't think bad boys follow lists."

"Oh." Carrie's shoulders drooped. "Really?"

"I don't know. I'm just guessing. I would think they'd rebel against that kind of direction."

"Hmm," Carrie said around a potato chip. "No offense, but you're a woman. I need to ask a guy if it would work."

"Don't do that."

"Why not?"

"Because it's inappropriate," Lauren said patiently. "Text me the list and I'll give you my thoughts. It'll be just between us." Honestly, it was the only way to save Carrie from herself. The road to bad boys was littered with good girls.

"How's that going to help me out with a bad boy?" Carrie asked.

"It'll get it out of your system so you don't embarrass yourself showing it to a guy. If, no, *when* you meet the right guy, he'll want to please you and give you everything you deserve. And if he needs some direction, then whisper what you want in the middle of the action and see what happens. Okay?"

Carrie shook her head and ate some more chips. "I'm so glad I checked in with you, Laur, that could've been super embarrassing."

"No problem," Lauren said. She reclined on her towel, soaking in the sun, her body warm and relaxed. She'd nearly drifted off when Carrie startled her.

"Ack!" And then, "Oh no, oh no, oh no."

Lauren sat up. "What's wrong?"

"I just texted my bedroom list to my neighbor Larry! He's right next to you in my contacts! He's eighty! I'm his in-case-of-emergency person!"

Lauren cracked up. "You might've just caused an emergency—heart attack."

Carrie texted furiously, her thumbs flying. "One word for you, Laur, karma."

She promptly shut up. She leaned over and pulled her cell from her purse. A text from Alex. It was a picture of Viv, her hand on a sheep, a big grin on her face. The caption said: *She wanted you to see.*

Her heart squeezed. She already loved Viv so much, such an amazing little girl. She quickly texted: *Viv, that is so awesome! Give the sheep a pat from me.*

Alex: *She wants me to get you here right now. She has no sense of time. We're at the Bronx Zoo. Wish you were here.*

She suddenly wished she was there too, but the Bronx Zoo was more than an hour away.

Alex: *Don't worry about it. We're leaving soon.*

She felt like she'd missed out.

Lauren: *Have fun!*

Just when she thought she'd gotten herself settled down, she was all worked up again. She didn't want to miss out on these important moments with Viv. But she had no right. That wasn't where she and Alex were at. They weren't a family. She was going to miss out on Viv stuff for a while, maybe forever. Her heart sank.

Karma was a sneaky bitch.

13

Alex arrived at his dad's house, the same three-bedroom colonial he'd grown up in, and followed Viv around to the backyard. The hard part of his day was over. He could even have a beer and kick back. His dad and brothers and sister would play with Viv, giving him a break. Bonus, now that Ty had married Charlotte, she'd be there and Viv always had a blast playing with Charlotte. He hated to admit it, because he tried to be everything for Viv, but it was clear to him Viv was looking for a mother figure in her life. She gravitated to women, especially those with long hair like Charlotte or Lauren.

He rounded the corner of the house and halted abruptly.

"Thuper!" Viv exclaimed, running toward Lauren.

Lauren bent down and opened her arms. "Princess Kei-Kei!" Viv flew into Lauren's arms, who lifted her and gave her a big hug.

He swallowed over the lump in his throat and slowly approached, the sights and sounds of the family gathering fading into the background. Viv was chattering like an excited chipmunk, catching Lauren up after their one-day separation. It sounded like zoo talk. Lauren exclaimed excitedly, matching Viv's enthusiasm.

Viv finally wound down and turned, probably looking for him. Lauren spotted him and set her down.

He closed the distance and Viv snagged his hand. Lauren was dressed casually in a light blue tank top, denim shorts, and sneakers. Her long hair was down, her skin sunkissed. Beautiful. Sexy. Irresistible.

"Hi," she said with a smile. "Sounds like the Bronx Zoo was a hit."

Viv yanked his hand, jumping around while holding it.

"Yeah," he said. "I, uh, didn't know you'd be here."

"Oh!" She blushed and looked around before pointing to his dad. "Joe invited me yesterday. He says I'm on the list for barbecues and parties now." She laughed. "I guess because of Viv. I would like to be included in her life."

"Ball!" Viv hollered, pulling away and running toward the shed, where his dad kept the sports equipment.

He glanced over his shoulder and saw Viv was by herself, nearly at the shed. He pointed over at her. "I should—"

"Yes." Lauren rocked on her heels. "Hope it's okay I'm here. Maybe I should've given you a heads-up? I mean, in case—"

"It's fine." He smiled. "I'm happy to see you."

She clasped her hands together and then crossed her arms. Awkward and nervous as all get out. Things had been weird since their kiss last Saturday. Lauren had put the brakes on and he'd tried to respect that, but there was no getting around the attraction. It was a living, breathing thing between them. Worse, for him, anyway, he knew the sounds she made when she came. Had heard as much as felt them against his mouth. That stuck with a guy.

"Okay, then!" she said and laughed.

He pointed to where Viv was fighting with the shed door. "I really should—"

"Yes!" She put her hands on her hips and then dropped them to her sides. "Ha! Of course."

He went after Viv, a little worried over how nervous Lauren seemed around him. He wished for a do-over with her. She wasn't like the women he usually hooked up with and he'd obviously made her uncomfortable. On the other hand, his kiss had never made a woman come before. Maybe she was embarrassed over that, though she shouldn't be. It was sexy as hell.

"Daddy!" Viv hollered, slapping the shed door with her palm. "Please!"

He reached Viv. "What do you want? Baseball, basketball, or football?" He knew his dad had toddler-sized versions for Viv.

"Ball!"

"Which one?"

She banged on the shed door. "Ball."

"Please. Ball, please."

"Please, Daddy! Please!" Her brown eyes were wide and beseeching.

He shook his head and opened the door. She darted inside and he quickly picked her up. "What do you want?"

She pointed at the football. He snagged it and put the helmet on her. "Bat!" she exclaimed, trying to dive out of his arms after it.

"Oh, so we're just getting everything? Okay, wait here." He put her outside on the grass, snagged all the toddler stuff and set it at her feet.

"Thuper!" she hollered, trying to gather everything in her little arms at once. "Grandpop! Uncle Josh! Aunt Mad! Aunt Charlotte!" she called, though her speech still wasn't that clear. *Gwandpop, Unk Josh*...he knew her sounds.

He turned. "Everyone! Viv would like to see you."

Everyone gathered around Viv, who beamed, her helmet askew. Most of his siblings were there—Josh, Ty, Logan, and Mad—along with a few of his honorary brothers, Ethan and Ben.

"You bellowed?" Josh said dryly.

"Play!" Viv exclaimed.

Soon they were playing an exciting (for Viv) game of tee-ball. Though the game was pretty slow for the rest of them. He couldn't help but notice Lauren in the outfield, talking to two couples—Charlotte and Ty (married) and Mad and Park (engaged). He knew she was friends with Charlotte and Mad. She seemed a little left out, trying to make conversation and then waiting for whatever affectionate moment had just occurred to pass before getting a response.

He joined them, even though he was supposed to be playing third base. After greeting everyone, he turned to Lauren. "You want to help me bring out some cold drinks?"

She pushed her hair behind her ears. "Sure."

He tried to slip quietly away, but Viv noticed. "Daddy!" She took off her helmet and dropped it on the ground like she needed to be sure he knew it was her.

"I'll be right back," he said. "I'm getting some drinks. You want a juice box?"

She nodded, pushed her helmet a distance away and took another swing at the ball that took the tee down with it.

"Run!" he hollered. She took off.

"Woo-hoo!" Lauren yelled. "Keep going! Home run!"

They exchanged a smile. She blushed and looked away. He opened the back door and gestured for her to go ahead. He admired the curve of her ass, since she couldn't see, and kept going to the refrigerator, where he found a couple of six-packs of beer and an eight-pack of toddler fruit punch.

"Beer or juice box?" he asked her.

"Hmm, tough decision," she said with a smile. "What do you think?"

"The fruit punch is shit. Ninety-four percent water."

"Then I'll take a beer."

He took out one for both of them, snagged the bottle opener, and popped the caps. He handed her one and then raised his bottle in a toast. They clinked bottles. "To you, the best nanny ever."

"Thank you, thank you." She made a small curtsy.

"You've heard that one before, haven't you?" he asked.

"Every time," she said with a laugh.

He needed better words. Something that said he wanted a second chance with her. Something that said it was cool with him that she came apart in his arms. Something that said he liked her without revealing the sharp intensity of his lust. It kept him up at night. He had needs, long-neglected needs. He wasn't sure which was stronger—lust or like—all he knew was that he needed more.

He glanced over at her slouched awkwardly against the counter, sipping her beer and playing with a lock of her hair.

"You seem nervous around me," he said. "You don't need to be. At all."

She straightened abruptly. "I'm fine." She rubbed the end of her nose. "Why? Am I being awkward?"

Yes. "No."

She sipped her beer.

He crossed to her and set his beer on the counter. Then he took hers, set it next to his, and leaned down to her ear. "I'm cool with what happened during our kiss. Don't be embarrassed."

"I'm not," she squeaked.

He straightened to give her a skeptical look.

She blushed and spoke to his chest. "That's *never* happened to me before."

He grinned. "Me either."

Her eyes flashed. "You're enjoying this, aren't you?"

He took her hand and squeezed it gently. "I'm not trying to make you uncomfortable. The opposite. I can't stop thinking about you."

"Oh."

"If you still want to put the brakes on, I'll respect that, but I'm hoping you'll give me a second chance to do things right. Would you like to have dinner with me?"

Her brows shot up. "Like a date?"

He smiled. "Yes, exactly like a date."

She smiled sweetly, her voice soft. "I'd like that very much." She hugged him, squeezing him around the middle. All that softness got to him, he felt desire stirring and it was not gentle. He could get through a simple dinner date without trying for more. Right? Except he'd never done the whole dating thing.

He cupped the back of her neck and whispered in her ear, "This dating thing is new for me, so I'm going to follow your lead. Only thing that's going to happen between us is what you initiate."

He released her and stepped back. She stared at him.

"We good?" he asked.

She nodded and then she beamed. "I guess we should get everyone's drinks. They're probably wondering what's taking so long."

"Sure." He retrieved a juice box for Viv and handed it to her before grabbing the two six-packs.

She gathered their opened beers from the counter and took a step toward the door.

"Wait." He wasn't sure if he'd get another opportunity to get her alone today. "Thanks for giving me a second chance."

She smiled her sweet smile. "Thanks for asking for one."

She sailed out the door.

He stood there for a moment as an unusual feeling came over him. Nerves. He'd been granted a second chance and he knew he couldn't screw it up.

14

———

Lauren was ridiculously nervous for her date with Alex. It wasn't like she didn't see him practically every day. It wasn't like she'd have to screen for weirdo potential or struggle through small talk. It was just that it felt different. Momentous. Real.

She even dressed up in a brand-new teal blue halter dress with embroidered flowers. Of course she spent forever on her hair and makeup, though she wasn't sure why. Over the past three weeks, he'd seen her in a ponytail, no makeup, and plain old T-shirt and shorts.

He showed up on time. She wouldn't have faulted him if he was late since he had to drop off Viv at his dad's house, but she was happy not to have any extra time to get worked up.

"You look beautiful," he said in the deep velvet voice that made her insides dance. His dark eyes were so warm and tender. For her. Her heart stuttered, overwhelmed by that look in his eyes.

"You too." He wore a white button-down shirt and gray pants, clean-shaven with that fresh-from-the-shower scent she loved.

"Ready?" he asked.

She suddenly realized she was just standing in her doorway, staring at him. "Yes." She laughed and locked the door behind her before joining him.

They walked side by side to his car, neither of them speaking. Was he as nervous as she was?

He opened the passenger-side door for her and gently shut it behind her. Then he got into the driver's seat, turned the ignition, and pulled out of the lot.

"I'm looking forward to Chinese," she said, desperate to break the silence. They'd already talked about going to a nice Chinese restaurant in Eastman.

"Good."

Another long silence.

"Is this weird, or is it just me?" she asked.

He laughed. "It's probably me. I'm working on being an ideal date and no clue if I'm pulling it off."

"You're doing great. I told you I find you intoxicating."

His smile lit up his gorgeous face. "So you did, angel."

She relaxed immediately. He was irresistible. If she was the one he felt warm and tender for, the only one he'd wanted to go on a date with in years, then maybe she should see where things went. Who was she kidding? She'd been hot for him ever since their kiss—two weeks ago—and he'd done nothing but look at her since then. Hot looks, but still. Didn't she owe it to herself to experience passion? If it was backed up by tenderness, surely it would lead in the right direction. "How long do you have before you have to get Viv?"

"I said I'd pick her up at nine."

She smiled to herself.

"Why?" he asked.

She shook her head. He gave her a speculative look but didn't push.

Dinner was much more relaxed. The food was excellent— they shared two courses and an appetizer of her favorite fried pork dumplings. Alex asked her tons of questions, wanting to know about her job, her travels, her hobbies. She filled him in and asked the same. Turned out they'd both backpacked across Europe, though at different times. Alex had always worked freelance with his graphic design and was now glad he had because it gave him the flexibility he needed to be there for Viv. She loved that about him. The minute they finished dinner, she invited him back to her place for a drink.

Once there, Alex sat on her sofa and she sat next to him. Now she wasn't sure what to do. She'd thought inviting him in was a green light to a hot makeout session. He wasn't even trying to hold her hand.

"Where's your roommates?" he asked.

"Huh?"

"Your cats?"

"Oh. They sleep on my bed mostly. They don't come out for company."

She blew out a breath. Should she just launch herself at him or ask him to kiss her? Why did he have to be a gentleman and only act on her initiative? She'd never seduced a man in her life.

"Nice place," he said. "I like the colors."

She glanced around distractedly. She liked cool pastels with warm accents of jewel tones. Her sofa was a pale gray, the pillows emerald and ruby. The coffee table and end tables were smooth dark wood and held unscented candles of different sizes. She liked cozy. But right now she didn't want cozy and comfortable.

She took a deep breath and turned to him. "Alex?"

"Yeah?"

"Are you hungry?" she blurted.

"We just ate."

She put a hand to her forehead and closed her eyes. "I meant thirsty."

"Sure."

"Me too." She went to the refrigerator and pulled out a bottle of chardonnay. She poured them both a glass and returned to the living room.

He took a sip and set it on the coffee table. She took a greedy swallow, needing some liquid courage to make a move. She glanced at him and he smiled.

"What time is it?" she asked way too loud.

He checked his cell. "Seven forty-five."

They had an hour. He'd need at least fifteen minutes to get to his dad's house. She didn't have time to flounder around.

"I don't want you to be late," she said and took another swallow of wine.

"I'm good. Viv's doing a lot better since that one molar came in."

"Yes, that must've been a relief for her."

"For both of us," he said with a laugh. "Now that she's sleeping better and just dealing with one teething molar, she's starting to show signs of being her old sunshine self."

She stared at his hands, at the long tapered fingers. Should she just put them on her? Or maybe she should put her hands on him. But where to start? She drained her wine.

He watched her set the empty glass on the coffee table with a clank. "I can't thank you enough for helping us over that speed bump with the medicine. We couldn't have done it without you."

She scooted closer, lifted a hand and couldn't decide where to put it. His cheek? His shoulder? His crotch? Her hand felt weird, tingly and shaky, exposed with confused intent. She stared at his mouth and realized he was talking. "What?"

He took her hand hovering in the vicinity of his head and held it in a warm, firm clasp. He gave her a small smile and his eyes were so very warm on hers. "I said you're a miracle worker."

"Oh."

"How're my old-soul eyes looking now?"

"So much better," she breathed, lost in the warm and tender look. "More warmth, a lot less pain. So you've had time to deal with the heavier stuff?"

"All I did was let the light of Lauren into my life."

"Oh, Alex..." She lifted her other hand and slid her fingers through the rough cut of his hair and then curled them around the nape of his neck. He stayed stock-still, watching her. She slowly closed the distance and placed a soft kiss on his warm lips. She pulled back and met his eyes. Warm, so warm.

"Again, please," he said.

She kissed him again, more firmly this time, reveling in the heat, venturing to taste. His hand still held hers, the rest of him still. She pulled back to check in with him again, surprised he was so, well, restrained.

His dark eyes were hot on hers. She could feel the tension in him, like he was working hard to keep passion in check. To let her take the lead. But she liked his passion, craved it.

"You know how you're new at dating?" she whispered.

He gave her a rueful smile. "Yeah."

"I'm a little new at seduction."

He cupped her face with one hand and stroked his thumb over her bottom lip, pressing on it. "I'm open to whatever you want."

She kissed him again and somehow kept kissing him as she straddled his lap. Maybe she did have some seductress moves. Her dress shifted to hip level. He spread his legs, opening her on top of a hard bulge she felt through the thin barrier of her panties. His hands slid up her bare thighs to her hips, where they stayed. Her turn. She wrapped her arms around his neck and kissed him with wild abandon. He groaned, his tongue delving deep, his hands moving now, one hand cupping her bottom, the other sliding over the damp panel of her panties. And then the kiss changed, his mouth hard and demanding as his fingers slipped under the panties to stroke her intimately. She was lost in sensation, no longer in control, no longer caring.

His mouth trailed to her neck, biting and sucking, sharp sensations penetrating the hazy pleasure of his skillful fingers. She rocked her hips mindlessly, moaning softly and then louder and louder until his mouth covered hers, his long fingers sliding inside her, his thumb pressing in exactly the right spot. Her body jolted and then his thumb was moving, working her as his fingers thrust. Everything in her tightened and then exploded, her harsh cry swallowed by his mouth.

He broke the kiss and she gasped for breath, heart pounding. His hand slowly slid from between her legs and another tremor of pleasure made her moan.

He wrapped his arms around her, burrowing into her neck. "Lauren," he said gruffly.

She relaxed against him, his hand stroking her back. Finally she lifted her head and looked at him. His expression was intense. She kissed him again and spoke against his lips. "I want you."

He groaned and framed her face with his hands. "Tell me exactly what you want from me."

"I want you inside me," she whispered.

He closed his eyes, whispering, "Yes," like she'd answered his prayers. Then he wrapped his arms around her. "Hang on."

She did, and then he was lifting her, walking to the bedroom. The cats leapt off the bed the moment they crossed the threshold and raced out of the room. Alex pulled back the covers and gently laid her down on the bed. He immediately reached under her dress and slid her panties down and off.

He sat next to her, smoothing his hands down her legs from upper thigh to ankles, bringing warm tingles everywhere he touched. "Take off your dress," he said.

She lifted her hips, got the dress out from under her, sat up and took it off. She hadn't worn a bra since the dress was lined and backless.

"You too," she said. He was still fully dressed.

He kicked off his shoes and joined her, kissing her and rolling her under him. She gripped his shoulders, but then she lost her grip as he shifted lower, leaving stinging biting kisses down the column of her throat, making her gasp. And then he captured her breast, cupping it with one hand, lowering his head and suckling, her insides clenching in response. He released her breast slowly, letting his teeth scrape against her nipple, jolting her before giving the other breast the same treatment. He confused her body, tender and then rough, and she couldn't anticipate. He shifted lower, continuing in his confusing way with his hands and mouth, making her jolt and gasp and sigh.

"Legs over my shoulders," he said, shifting between her legs and dropping a kiss on her sex. She tensed, not sure if she was ready for that kind of hold. She'd be at his mercy. His fingers slid up and down her center, opening her to his view. And then he simply waited.

She closed her eyes, swallowed hard, and did what he asked. She was rewarded with a rough tongue and hungry mouth.

"Fuck!" she cried, bucking under him.

He growled, she felt every vibration against her sensitive center, and then he dove back in, hungry, greedy. Her back arched, hips lifted, and his shoulders pushed her open more. She panted, overwhelmed and completely out of control, keening with primal sounds she barely recognized as her own. Oh, God. She couldn't catch her breath. Her fingers tangled in his hair, tugging, trying to pull him away. His fingers thrust inside her, momentarily distracting her from his relentless mouth. She dimly registered this was what passion felt like and then her mind shut down, her body moving to his rhythm, taking what he gave, hard jolts of pleasure, deep pressure, so good, so good, and then it hit, the orgasm ripping through her, making her body bow and her neck arch. Alex stayed with her, pushing her through a dark, pulsing pleasure that went on an on until she went limp.

She felt him shift away. She couldn't move, couldn't speak, couldn't even open her eyes. She heard the creak of the bed and then clothes hitting the floor. The rustle of a condom wrapper.

Then he was on top of her, his hand reaching down to guide himself inside. She expected a hard thrust, but he pushed in slowly, inch by inch, stretching her.

He shifted so his arms were braced on either side of her. His mouth grazed her ear. "You're so tight."

"It's been a while," she admitted. "I'm okay; you don't have to go slow." She gasped as he thrust fully inside her.

"Wrap your legs around me," he ordered. "I don't want to bang you into the headboard."

Her eyes widened, but she did as he said. And then he fucked her fast and hard and deep and she just hung on, clutching his shoulders, feeling the muscles flexing with his powerful thrusts. She wished she could look into his eyes. His were closed, his head to the side of hers, his breath ragged and harsh by her ear. She craved that intimacy but was too far gone to explain it.

He whispered in her ear, "Tip your hips up for me. I wanna go deep."

She thought he already was, but she did as he said, and the next thrust sent a shockwave of pleasure through her. He groaned and pumped faster and faster. Her nails dug into his shoulders as she raced to a climax that hit with a jolt; her body rocked with it, electric sensation radiating from her core, shooting through her limbs. Alex thrust deep with a low groan for his release, rocking into her, and then stilled.

She hugged him with her arms and legs, feeling all kinds of soft and tender toward him. He chose her after denying himself for so long. That meant something.

Finally, long moments later, he withdrew, collapsing to the bed beside her, lying on his back. He was smiling. She smiled too, scooting closer and rolling to her side to wrap an arm around him.

He shifted to cup the back of her neck and kissed her soundly. "That was amazing." He flopped back on the mattress.

A little voice in her head nudged her, *now what?* She stared at him lying there, eyes closed, sated. She craved some words, a little tenderness after the intensity of, well, *everything*. "How's dating me so far?" she asked playfully.

He chuckled low and deep. "Fantastic."

"I've never had multiple orgasms before," she informed him.

He groaned and kissed her again. "You're killing me. I wish I could stay. It's been too long and I've got a lot stored up."

She sighed. "I wish you could stay too."

He shifted to check the radio alarm clock on her nightstand. "Shit. I gotta go."

Disappointment washed through her, even though she knew he had a valid reason. "Sure," she said softly.

He kissed her again. "Angel."

He got up and headed to the bathroom, probably to take care of the condom.

She shivered and pulled the blankets up to her chin.

He returned and quickly dressed. "Maybe you could stop by tonight. I'll text you as soon as Viv's asleep. You have the key."

"Like a booty call?"

"Come on, don't be like that." He sat on the side of the bed and put his shoes on. "We had a good time."

A good time. That was all it was. She'd mistaken heat for tenderness.

He leaned over and kissed her. "Stop by, okay?"

She felt wrung out, well used, not well loved. "I'm going to sleep." Her voice came out small.

He gave her a long look. "Okay. Sleep well. I know I will."

He left and she flopped back on the bed, arms spread wide. She couldn't work up a good mad, though some part of her wished she could. She still felt too good, sparkling, tingling along every nerve ending. At least they did have a spark, even if they hadn't gotten close enough for soul recognition. Some part of her still hoped they would.

15

____

The next morning Lauren decided to go for a long bike ride, destination Ludbury House. That was the mansion in Clover Park where Hailey worked as a wedding planner. Or if she wasn't there, she'd go to Hailey's apartment a few blocks away. Either way, Lauren needed to talk to her ally in the Make Love Bloom (TM) plan and call it off. She didn't want to be in love with Alex, but she was leaning that way even knowing the risk to her heart. Maybe Hailey could help give her some clarity.

She pulled her bike off the rack, mounted it, and was immediately reminded of all her late night activities with Alex. Damn, she was sore. It had been a good eight months since she'd had sex and Alex was more than she was used to in every way. She smiled to herself. He was her unicorn, the sweet alpha she'd been secretly hoping for and never finding. Most of the men she'd been with were sweet. Not timid, but not alpha either. And definitely not large. She got off the bike and locked it on the rack.

A brisk walk would be good. It took her a half hour, and by the time she got to Ludbury House, she was hot, tired, and cranky. It started bugging her to be unsure about Alex. She'd found what she was looking for yet felt strangely unsatisfied. She stopped on the front sidewalk to admire Ludbury House

—a sprawling two-and-a-half-story white clapboard mansion with white columns and a gorgeous wraparound porch. Even as many times as she'd passed by the mansion, it still gave her a wistful sigh, imagining her own wedding here.

She opened the heavy wooden front door and found Hailey in the back ballroom, sitting at a small table with a couple in one of her wedding planner appointments.

Hailey promised to meet her at Garner's for a quick break in an hour. So here Lauren was at Garner's. She headed for the empty bar, where Josh was slicing limes, and took a seat. It was nearly eleven on a Sunday. The only other people here were eating brunch in the dining area.

"Hey, Lauren, you're here early," Josh said with a charming smile. She studied him for a moment. His dark brown hair was shaggy, his jaw sported a couple days' growth, and his gray T-shirt stretched tight across a broad chest and shoulders. He was a bit of a badass despite the charming smiles. She wondered if this was what Alex looked like before Viv. Add in some piercings and she was sure she would've been too intimidated to ever flirt with Alex. She was like the opposite of a badass. She was a goodass. Wait, that sounded weird—

"You okay?" Josh asked, sliding the sliced limes into a plastic bin. He met her eyes and waited.

She focused on his chest because his old-soul eyes full of pain unsettled her.

"You want something to drink?" Josh asked.

She met his dark brown eyes, the buried pain there squeezing her heart. She wanted to hug him. "Just water, thanks."

"Coming right up."

She stared at the bar top, having a weird out-of-body experience, mixing the two brothers with their similar pain and similar looks. It was Alex she needed to confront and comfort, not Josh. She couldn't even imagine kissing Josh. He would probably grin after like he'd been teasing all along. No, he only teased Hailey like that. What was she going to do about Alex? Was he thinking of her? Did he care about her?

Or was he just hoping for more time in the sheets? Why did she sleep with him so quickly? She should've waited until she knew where she stood. It wasn't like he'd tried to seduce her last night. That had been all her, inviting him in, hovering her hand near his head.

No way around it—she was a seductress.

She dropped her head in her hands and a glass of ice water appeared in front of her.

"You want me to get Mad for you?" Josh asked, gesturing over to the dining area, where Mad was waitressing. That was his younger sister, a friend of Lauren's, but not the first she'd confide in, given A) Alex was her big brother, so Lauren couldn't share the intimate details and, even if she could, B) Mad was abrasive and blunt. The morning after required someone gentle and understanding. Carrie immediately came to mind, though the way Carrie had been so gung ho for forbidden romance and all that jazz lately, her judgment was questionable.

She straightened and sipped the ice water. "No, I'm okay. I'm supposed to meet Hailey here in an hour."

"You want something to eat?" Josh asked.

She could definitely eat. She suddenly craved red meat. "I'll take a burger and fries. Thanks."

"You got it," he said and punched in the order on a computer.

Feeling a lot better, she decided to lay the groundwork for Hailey and Josh peace. "Josh, can I tell you a secret about Hailey?"

He leaned across the bar. "I'm all ears."

"If you focus on outsweeting her—"

"Outsweet?"

"Yes, if you're extra sweet, sweeter than even Hailey could think of being, you'd bring her to her knees."

He straightened, a devilish gleam in his eyes. Then he frowned. "That won't work. I was extra nice to her like you said, gave her a free drink—"

"And she reciprocated that niceness."

"She paid me back double the price, thumbing her nose at

me." He scowled. "It's like she won't let me buy her a damn drink. Sorry, but I don't think I can be much nicer or sweet, whatever you want to call it, than that."

"You could, I don't know, offer to buy her a book. She loves books."

He arched a brow. "What kind of book?"

"Maybe you could talk to her about her favorites, see if there's a new one coming out by an author she likes, or maybe find a first edition of a classic."

He shook his head. "I dunno. Being nice and sweet and all might work for some guys, but I'm bored out of my skull. I think I gotta razz her a little more. Keep things interesting."

It was like they enjoyed fighting. How was she ever going to get them close enough to recognize the obvious spark? Then she thought of her spark with Alex and deflated. A spark didn't always lead to soul recognition. Sometimes it just led to confusion and aching uncertainty.

She sighed. "If you're sure that's the way to go."

"She likes it or she wouldn't keep coming back for more," Josh said. "As a matter of fact, I think she finds the nice me boring." He shrugged. "Who could blame her?"

She sipped her water. "I would like it."

"Yeah?"

"Yes."

"How's Alex treating you?"

Heat crept up her neck. "Nice."

Josh tapped the bar. "Good. He needs you too much to be anything but. You're amazing with Viv. You should've seen him before you arrived on the scene. Total wreck."

She shook her head, smiling. "I'm just experienced with kids," she said modestly.

"She talks about you all the time. Says thuper in a lot of sentences."

"I told her to call me Super L." Instead of mommy, she added silently.

"Ah, and she shortened it to super. I'm so grateful to you. We all are."

"Thanks. Glad to help." She couldn't manage a smile, so she took a long drink of water.

Josh went on. "Alex is like a new man. Saw him early this morning, he brought Viv in for pancakes, and he was just beaming happy. He says it's all because of you."

She choked on her water and coughed furiously.

Josh waited until she calmed down before saying, "He's sleeping better; Viv's sleeping better. Just one molar to go, and he's in the clear."

"Until the next phase," she said with a small cough. "Three is the year of defiance."

"Hopefully you'll be around to give him a little advice now and then."

"Sure." Hopefully, maybe, if, if, if.

Josh left and returned a short time later with her early lunch. She dug in; everything tasted so good. After lunch, she stopped to chat with Mad on her break, and returned to the bar to find Hailey sitting there with a tall glass of pink lemonade. Hailey was in a super cute white off-the-shoulder dress with a layered flounce trimmed in crochet appliqué with a layered skirt. The waist cinched in between the two flouncy layers, emphasizing her narrow waist. Lauren had to admit Hailey still looked the part of a beauty queen. She hadn't gotten a good look at her outfit earlier when Hailey was sitting with her clients, binders stacked all around her.

"Look what Josh made me!" Hailey exclaimed with a big beaming smile. "It's a Hailey special. Strawberry blonde like my hair." She lifted a lock of her long hair.

Lauren caught Josh's eye and he winked. "Awesome," she said.

Hailey slurped some lemonade before saying, "So are you ready for another Make Love Bloom date?"

Josh rolled his eyes and headed back toward the kitchen.

"I'm paying you triple for this!" Hailey called.

Josh turned, scowled, and waved a dismissive hand, grumbling under his breath, before continuing into the kitchen.

"So?" Hailey asked brightly.

"I think I'm done with Make Love Bloom (TM), though I thank you very much for your help."

Hailey grinned. "Are you with Alex now? I saw the spark between you two."

"We went out last night."

Hailey elbowed her. "Yeah, and?"

"And it was good."

Hailey nodded, slurped more lemonade, and pressed her fingers to her forehead. "Brain freeze. Ow, ow, ow." She glared at the kitchen door. "I bet that was Josh's real motive in giving me ice-cold lemonade on a hot day."

Lauren shook her head. These two were impossible. "So I guess I'm done with online dating and all that. I want to see where things go with Alex."

"Aww, Lauren, you found your unicorn, didn't you?" She pressed her hand to her forehead, wincing.

"Yes and no." She blew out a breath. "I'm not sure he's quite where I'm at."

"This is no problem at all. You found your unicorn, just keep going."

Lauren gritted her teeth. Hailey made it all sound so simple, but what real experience did she have? As far as she knew, Hailey hadn't had any serious relationships.

The devil made her do it. She saw Josh walking through the kitchen door, heading their way, so she whispered to Hailey, "Josh said any woman who was extra sweet to him would bring him *to his knees*. He told me that in strict confidence. It's his Achilles' heel." That might've been taking it too far, but Hailey gobbled it up.

Hailey's eyes widened. "Really?"

"Yup."

Josh was behind the bar now, still a distance away.

Luckily, Hailey's whispers always carried like a shout of exultation. "What I wouldn't give to bring Josh to his knees!"

Josh ambled over to them, dark intent in every step, his eyes locked on Hailey. He stopped in front of Hailey, slapped his palms on the bar and got in her face. "You're the one that's going to be on your knees, princess."

Hailey flushed pink from cheeks to chest, her eyes widening and then narrowing into a glare.

They had an impressive staredown—not one blink.

Lauren's work here was done. Her phone dinged with a text and she snagged it off the bar.

Alex: *Come over tonight after Viv's asleep.*

He was very persistent. She texted back *see you on Monday* with a smiley face so he'd know she wasn't mad. They needed to talk and showing up there late at night sent the wrong message. It wasn't like she expected a commitment. At least not so soon. But she needed…something…some inkling that he had real feelings because she was having way too many soft and tender thoughts.

"Come on, Lauren, back to my place for a debriefing," Hailey said, tugging Lauren's arm.

Lauren quickly paid in cash and followed, hoping talking about it would help things become clearer.

When they stepped outside, Hailey stopped on the sidewalk. "Sorry. I do need to get back to work. I just needed an excuse to bail on the staring contest without losing. Call me later if you want to talk, okay?"

"Sure," Lauren said.

Hailey walked briskly down the block back to Ludbury House.

Lauren turned in the opposite direction and walked at a much slower pace back home, her mind a muddle. Could she resist Alex long enough for a good talk? It sounded simple, but with Alex, nothing was that simple. He was a triple threat —sexy, ravenous, and irresistible. And she was long overdue for passion. But was that enough?

16

Alex opened the door to Lauren on Monday morning and hungrily took her in from her long light brown hair framing an angelic face to luscious breasts in a black tank top with black shorts and those long tanned legs. He had to get her alone again, hopefully tonight.

"Morning," he said gruffly. The beast was out of his cage and he was hungry for more.

"Morning," Lauren said softly.

Viv launched herself at Lauren's legs, hugging her tight. "Thuper!"

"Princess Kei-Kei!" Lauren picked up Viv, giving her a hug.

Alex watched the exchange and found himself smiling. He loved that Viv was crazy about Lauren and vice versa.

"Dolly!" Viv hollered, pointing to her room. Lauren set her down and Viv ran back to her room. He'd bought Viv a new Dolly yesterday—same exact doll, hence the same name, but with hair.

Lauren went to follow, but he stopped her, pulling her in for a hug. She wrapped her arms around his waist and hugged him back. She couldn't help it. She was a hugger.

He whispered in her ear, "I read your favorite books last night. The Fierce trilogy."

She jerked back, her hand on her throat, her green eyes wide. "You did not."

He pulled her hand away from her throat and replaced it with his. Her pulse beat rapidly under his fingers, her skin heating to his touch. "I skipped to the good parts." He felt her swallow.

Yup. He had her number. And would be taking every opportunity to act on it. He'd been worried about being too aggressive with her, keeping himself in check with great effort, but then when he read her fantasy, what really turned her on, he realized he didn't have to hold back at all. She just had to admit what she secretly craved—dirty talking, no-holds-barred sex with a man who's comfortable taking charge. This was going to be fun.

He gave her a slow knowing smile, stroking his fingers down her throat. Her lips parted, her eyes heating.

"Alex," she whispered in a breathy voice that made him lean in, "I do like those books, but I've never done that stuff in real life. I need to feel comfortable."

He shifted to her ear. "You found the right guy for all your fantasies. I'll get you there and you'll like it."

She sucked in an audible breath.

"Dolly!" a small voice exclaimed. They both turned to find Viv holding her new doll by the hair.

"What a beautiful new Dolly!" Lauren exclaimed. Her voice wobbled and was a little loud. Viv didn't notice, but he sure did.

"Tonight," he told Lauren.

"We'll talk later," she threw over her shoulder and joined Viv for their morning fun.

He went to his studio, energized and ready for work. He threw himself into his project, putting the finishing touches on the fantasy book covers. He'd gotten an extension on the due date. He skipped lunch he was so immersed in the project finally coming together. He emerged from his studio late that afternoon when Lauren pulled into the driveway. She frequently took Viv out in the afternoon to the playground, the Spray Bay, or to visit his dad. And she always texted a picture of Viv enjoying herself when they were there and then texted again when they were heading back. He couldn't have imagined a better caretaker for Viv—responsible, caring, affectionate. She genuinely seemed to enjoy being with Viv, who was a bundle of energy and not easy to keep out of trouble.

He met them in the driveway and peeked into the backseat. Viv was sleeping. She frequently napped in the car, especially after a day of outdoor activity.

Lauren got out to get her. "She made another new friend on the playground. A little boy named Liam."

"Awesome. I'm going to let her nap. I'll carry her in and then you—" he dropped his voice to a husky register "—come with me."

She froze. "Alex, we need to talk."

"Sure, we can talk." After, he added silently. Sue him, he was ready to explode with his long-neglected needs.

Lauren shot him a dubious look. "It's important. We both probably have stuff to say."

"Or do."

Her eyes flashed.

He bit back a smile. Lauren was finally comfortable enough with him to drop the angel act. Sure, she was nice, but that wasn't all she was. After reading the erotic part of her favorite erotic romance books, he suspected she had a lot of fiery passion bottled up. And he was the lucky man who got to pop the cork.

He opened the car door. "Let me get her settled first and then we'll have some quiet alone time."

"To talk," Lauren insisted.

He ignored that. He carefully, oh so carefully, got Viv out of the booster seat, nudged the car door closed with his hip, and carried her toward the house, careful not to jostle her. Lauren opened the door with her key, holding it open for them. The *moment* he stepped in the house, Viv woke up. "Daddy!"

He sighed. "Hey, pumpkin." He looked to Lauren, who was trying not to laugh. "I'll text you about later."

Lauren grinned, seeming pleased his nefarious plans had been thwarted. "Only if you promise we'll talk."

"We will," he said. *After.*

Lauren eyed him suspiciously. It was like she could read his dirty mind. Well, he had given her a big hint.

He smirked. "Come on, it's the only time we can talk without little ears."

Viv put her hands on his cheeks and squeezed. "Talk, talk," she mimicked.

"See?" he said through squeezed cheeks.

Lauren laughed. "Come on, Miss Vivian, let's get your diaper changed."

He set Viv down, who ran down the hallway toward her room. "I can change her."

"I got it," Lauren said. "That's why you pay me the big bucks."

He chuckled. "You're worth more than I could ever pay."

She looked at him under her lashes. "You do have a way with words."

"I've got a lot more stored up. Words that'll make you blush and moan."

"Shh." She blushed bright pink.

He cupped her warm cheek. "You are quite the blusher. Don't worry, she can't hear."

"Alex." A reluctant smile tugged at her lips.

He held her chin. "Come on, give me the full wattage."

She shook her head, laughing.

"There it is," he said with a smile. She was so beautiful, so sexy.

Viv reappeared naked from the waist down. "Mommy, pee!"

He and Lauren exchanged a look of shock. He wasn't sure which part was more shocking, the mommy or the pee. Lauren had been so careful to correct Viv, telling her to call her Super L. Viv hadn't said it since that first time three weeks ago.

Lauren recovered first and focused on the important part. "Well, let's see."

They all trooped to the bathroom, where Viv proudly pointed at her potty. He peeked over. The tiniest drop of pee in there. Not even enough to trigger the potty song that was supposed to happen when she peed. Did that even count? Where was the rest of it?

"Wow!" Lauren exclaimed. "What a big girl you are! Good job! Now let's flush and wash hands. That's what everybody does."

"Good job, Viv," he added belatedly. He was still new at all this potty-training stuff. Though come to think of it, he hadn't even realized Lauren had begun training her.

Viv followed Lauren eagerly, helping her flush the drop of pee and then washing her hands and drying them. Anyone looking at them—so in synch, with similar coloring—would think they were mother and daughter.

His eyes watered. There was no way he could ever let Lauren go. Viv needed her.

~

Lauren had just finished a quiet dinner at home that night when her phone dinged with a text. She picked it up. Alex.

How do I keep up the potty training? She won't go again.

That was the weird thing. Lauren hadn't even started training Viv yet. She'd bought her the cute panties with pink ruffles last Friday, made a big deal out of washing them and putting them in her drawer for when she was ready to be a big girl, and then her plan to begin today flew out the window when Alex informed her he'd read her favorite erotic romance trilogy in a husky voice that said he had some ideas. She gave herself a moment to get over the hot flash of lust that memory sparked before texting back.

Make a chart, put a sticker on it every time she goes, and give her an M&M.

Alex: *What kind of chart? Monthly? Daily?*

Lauren: *Just draw some rows for the stickers. She doesn't know days, weeks, months yet.*

Alex: *True. I don't have stickers. You better come over.*

She smiled. She did have that stuff, but she knew he also had an ulterior motive. *I'll bring some later. Text me when Viv's asleep. I'd really like to talk.*

Three hours later, Lauren was yawning and thinking about going to bed. She checked her cell one last time. Alex had texted five minutes ago. *She's asleep. Come over and wear a dress.*

She ignored the request. *On my way.* She grabbed her purse, about to tuck her phone inside when it dinged again.

No panties.

She glared at the screen. *If you're not going to take this seriously, forget it. :(*

I'm serious. Promise.

Then I will see you with panties on.

She shook her head and headed out the door, determined to have that talk and figure out where she stood before she got in too deep. When she got there, she decided to let herself in with the key so the doorbell wouldn't wake Viv. She pushed the door open and Alex was standing there, a dark hunger in his eyes.

"Hi," he said in the deep velvet voice her body now recognized as seduction. Heat surged through her as he pulled her inside and quietly shut the door behind her.

"Hi," she managed.

"I'll take that," he said, taking her purse and setting it on the table where he kept his keys.

She took a deep breath, surprised to find she was trembling slightly. She straightened. There was nothing to be nervous about, she told herself. They were simply going to talk. Get everything out in the open.

Alex closed the distance between them alarmingly fast. Her breath caught, registering his intent, and then all coherent thought deserted her as his mouth crashed over hers, his tongue thrusting inside. He pinned her against the door, wrists over her head, his leg wedging between hers. She was liquid heat, her heartbeat thrumming in time to the pulse between her legs. His mouth was ravenous, hard and demanding, and she reveled in it, her hips moving restlessly against him, needy in a way she'd never been before.

He released her suddenly. She blinked, disoriented as he turned her, bending her over and pinning her hands against the door under his. His voice, low and deep, rumbled in her ear. "Spread 'em."

"Are you a cop?" she asked, light-headed with the quick turn of events. This wasn't in the Fierce trilogy, though he'd only read the sex scenes. The hero was a dominating alpha who always took the heroine, a shy librarian, from behind. The similarities were as clear as the pulse pounding in her ears.

He nudged her legs apart with his leg and then cupped her breasts with both hands. "I might be. What're you hiding under these clothes? Feels like a killer body."

A laugh escaped before she gasped, his hands stroking straight from her breasts down her stomach and between her legs.

"I feel like I'm being frisked," she said, breathless.

"Yup. You're giving me some trouble. That's why I had to bend you over the hood of my car." He pulled her shorts down and off.

Oh, fuck. He was going to do her right here out in the open. "Alex," she protested, though not too loud because the last thing she wanted was a two-year-old witness to debauchery.

He yanked her panties off and then slid his palms slowly up the inside of her legs. She held her breath, both needing his touch and needing to get somewhere private fast. "Where's the dress, huh?" he asked, his fingers stopping just short of pleasure central. "This is a crime."

She straightened in disappointment, turning to face him. He pulled off her shirt, bra went flying, and then his mouth covered hers, his hands stroking her bare back. He finally let her up for air, took off his shirt in one quick move, turned her back to the door and bent her over. His chest heated her back as he leaned down to bite her earlobe and tug. Liquid heat pooled between her legs.

"Alex, please." She didn't even know what she was asking—she just knew she needed what only he could give.

He groaned, his hands roaming, seeming to be every-where at once, igniting her. "I love to hear you beg."

She looked at him over her shoulder. He still wore shorts with an impressive bulge. "You take me to your bedroom right now," she ordered.

He grinned and slid his long fingers to her center, parting her to stroke intimately before thrusting his fingers inside her. Her knees buckled. "Lauren," he growled, stroking her on the inside, "tell me what you want. What you crave."

She couldn't catch her breath.

His fingers withdrew and then stroked her bottom lip with one finger, pushing past her teeth and inside. She tasted herself, an erotic unusual sensation for her. She sucked his finger and he groaned. He pulled her up, grabbed all their clothes in a surprisingly considerate move, took her by the hand, and led her to his bedroom.

He shut and locked the door, dropping the clothes on the end of the bed. Hiding the evidence, she realized, in case Viv woke. She swallowed hard as he turned to her with a preda-tory look.

"I'm going to give you everything you secretly desire," he said in a gravelly voice, the words scraping against her insides.

Her mouth went dry. He crossed to her, his arm snaking around her waist as he slowly backed her into the far wall, his eyes dark and ravenous. She was dimly aware they were as far from Viv's room as they could get and could only hope she could keep the noise level down.

He entwined his fingers with hers and pinned hers against the wall. He stared at her mouth. "Say it."

"Kiss me."

A ghost of a smile crossed his features before he took her

mouth in a passionate kiss, hard and demanding and thorough. She felt possessed, claimed, his. She throbbed and lifted her hips, silently asking for what she needed. It was all she could do. He possessed her mouth, her hands pinned by his, the hard planes of his body pressing against her softness. He trailed open-mouthed kisses along the side of her neck, his teeth scraping against her, leaving an electric charge of pleasure in his wake. And then lower, his mouth continuing to her collarbone as he slowly lowered their grasped hands to her sides.

"Alex," she said breathlessly, "I want to touch you."

He released her hands, kneeling in front of her.

"Oh, God," was as far as she got before he cupped her breast and sucked, pushing her nipple to the roof of his mouth. She slid her fingers into his hair and held him to her, her insides tightening, aching for him to fill her. He released her breast, his teeth scraping against her sensitive nipple, jolting her. Before she could get out a word, he'd captured the other breast, drawing it deep into his mouth. Her fingers loosened in his hair, a soft whimper escaping.

His hand cupped her between the legs suddenly and she gasped. His fingers were wicked and demanding and amazing. His mouth continued suckling her breast, a direct line of pleasure to her sex. She panted, moving to his rhythm, overwhelmed, the pressure building and building. Oh, God. She was going to—she slapped a hand over her mouth, trying to keep quiet through what promised to be a hard climax, when he suddenly released her, standing and pressing his body against her. She whimpered, achy and needy.

His hand cupped the back of her neck firmly. His dark eyes gleaming. "Let me hear the words. Say it."

"I want you."

He bit her lower lip and then sucked. "Want me to what?"

"Fuck me."

"Yes," he muttered before his mouth took hers roughly. He grabbed her hand and pushed it between her legs. "Touch yourself and tell me how you want me to fuck you."

She glared at him. "I can touch myself anytime. I want you to do it."

He grinned and moved his fingers over hers, making her touch herself. "You do that a lot, angel?"

She moaned and he stilled both their hands. "Yes. I haven't had sex in eight months before you."

He groaned. "You are making me so fucking hot. Keep touching yourself." He yanked down his shorts and boxer briefs, kicking them off.

She did, revving up fast as she stared at his thick erection. No wonder she was sore after the last round. Her fingers stilled, watching him stride to the nightstand, rip open a condom, and roll it on. She moved to join him and he quickly closed the distance between them.

"Nope," he said, backing her up. "Right here. Against the wall. Just like in your favorite book."

"They fucked in a lot of places."

He swore. "I am loving hearing fuck come out of that angelic mouth." His mouth covered hers as he pressed her against the wall. She clung to his shoulders, her nails digging in, needing a lot more from him. He cupped the back of her knee, lifting her leg, opening her to him. *Yes! Finally.* He pressed at her entrance and she arched to meet him.

He stilled and stared at her mouth. "Tell me all the places they fucked, all the ways. I want all the filthy details."

She was so done talking about fiction. She reached around, grabbed his ass and pulled him tight against her, reminding him how hot and wet she was. She whispered the filthy words from the book, words she knew he was dying to hear come out of her mouth. She'd barely gotten started when she yelped as he suddenly turned her to the wall and bent her over in one quick move.

He covered her with his body, his hand on her mouth as he spoke fiercely in her ear. "You have to keep quiet or you'll wake Viv. Put your palms flat on the wall."

She did and he took her in one swift thrust. She cried out, the sound muffled by his hand. He thrust again, his voice deep velvet. "Now I'm going to fuck you hard and deep." He took his hand off her mouth. "Keep the volume down."

"Do it," she practically growled.

He gripped her hips and gave her what she needed. Hard, pounding thrusts that filled her, excited her, his breath harsh by her ear. She'd never truly been fucked before Alex, their bodies slick with sweat, everything dropping away to a haze of primal heart-pounding need. And then his hand reached around, his fingers delving between her legs, and she bit back a cry, trying to keep quiet. Soft whimpers escaped as he overwhelmed her, thrusting deep, stroking over and over until she broke. He continued to stroke her, making her shudder and moan helplessly under him, the intensity too much as he slowly pumped into her and she realized he wasn't going to stop. He wanted her to come again and she was way too raw and too far gone. Her breath hitched in a moment of alarm. He filled her, held her captive, controlled her completely.

His voice was low and deep. "Let go. Don't fight it."

She tensed as he pushed deep, stroking her faster, and then she was lost in sensation. His voice, gruff and rasping in her ear, told her in explicit detail all the ways he wanted to take her. Her body jerked and then she broke violently, the sounds of her ecstasy suddenly contained by his hand over her mouth. Finally he released his hold on her mouth, grabbing her hips with both hands and pumping deep over and over until he let go, his mouth pressing against her neck. She felt as much as heard the low groan he was trying to contain vibrating against her neck. A long moment passed where they both caught their breath. Her heart was still pounding, her head slightly woozy.

He withdrew and she straightened, her legs trembling. She grabbed his arm for balance. He pulled her to the bed, yanking back the covers for her. She collapsed face-first into a pillow, completely boneless.

She vaguely remembered they were supposed to talk, but she was beyond speech. She drifted, sleep pulling at her. She wished he'd turn out the lights but couldn't formulate the request. He was moving around the room and she wanted to tell him to settle down and sleep already.

Slowly she became aware he'd joined her in the bed, coaxing her with his deep voice and warm hands.

~

Alex took one look at Lauren's soft supple body, completely limp and relaxed, the best possible state for having his way, and felt his cock stirring back to life. He trailed his fingers down her spine, making her shiver. He continued down her smooth back, sliding both hands down her sides and the curve of her hips and then cupping her ass, aching for more. She didn't stir. He'd thought way too much about being with her again. Especially after reading what she was into.

He shifted, lifting her hair and gently kissing the nape of her neck. She sighed. He kissed across her shoulder and back up her neck to the soft spot just under her ear. It occurred to him that he wanted her to stay in his bed permanently. This thing between them worked. And Viv would have the mother she needed.

"Imagine if you didn't have to go home," he whispered, knowing she was too wiped out to move. She had to listen.

"What do you mean?" she asked softly.

He pressed his advantage, she was so soft and agreeable right now. He slid his hands across her shoulders and down her back. "I mean if you lived here permanently."

Her eyes were closed, enjoying his touch. "We've only been…whatever for three weeks."

He nipped the side of her neck. "Say it."

"Lusting, craving, fucking. Pick one."

He got harder. "Yes to all three. But it's more than that, right?" He rolled her over and she moved as easily as a rag doll. He slid his palm up her inner thigh and nudged her leg to the side. She opened her legs and reached for him. He climbed on top and she wrapped her arms and legs around him like a hug. He should probably get another condom, but he felt too good to move away from what his body craved.

"Mmm," she said, a satisfied sleepy smile on her face.

He kissed that smile. "Viv loves you. We work well together in and out of bed…we should get married."

Her eyes flew open. "What?" She dropped her arms and legs from him. "What?" she repeated, blinking like she was confused or something.

"That's what you want, right? A committed relationship. I'll give it to you."

"You can't even look at me when we fuck."

"I'm looking at you now."

She huffed. "I'm getting the feeling you haven't had much intimacy in relationships."

"Not much relationships either. Does it really matter?"

She pushed at his chest. "I can't talk like this. Get off."

"Why?" He was enjoying this position and hoping for more once he got the marriage thing out of the way.

"Your body muddles my brain. I seriously can't think."

He grinned, happy to hear that, and shifted to lie next to her. He propped up on an elbow and splayed his hand low on her flat belly. She pushed his hand off and rolled to her side, propped up on her elbow, facing him.

"How long were you with Tammy before you found out she was pregnant?" she asked.

"Four months."

"And how long were your relationships before her? Anyone serious?"

"Nothing ever lasted more than a couple months. I don't get why that matters. I don't care how long you were with someone. All that matters is here and now."

"I'm just trying to understand how you can propose marriage after three weeks."

He stroked her hair back over her shoulder. "Easy, we fit."

She groaned, rolled to her back, and covered her face with her hands.

"What's that mean?"

She dropped her hands. "Do you love me, Alex?"

"What kind of question is that?" he asked, stalling for

time. He couldn't say the words. He wasn't in love, but what they had was better, compatibility, a mom for Viv.

"A legitimate one," she snapped.

"For someone who just proposed marriage?" he asked like he was offended.

Maybe he'd brought it up too soon, but it all fit in place in his mind. She remained quiet and he decided to distract her. "C'mere, sit up." He sat up too. He hadn't taken her in that position yet and thought she'd probably like it. Bonus, he'd get credit for intimacy facing each other.

She scrambled up to a sitting position. "I don't take marriage lightly."

He debated moving her into his lap or just telling her to get there. He reached for her and she crossed her arms. "What's more serious than a proposal?" he asked.

"Love!"

He went on the offense. "Do you love me?"

She looked away. "I'm trying not to, but I'm leaning in that direction."

He couldn't help his wide smile. "Okay, so you're leaning, that's good. We both love Viv. She needs a mom—"

"See?" she cried. "This is what I was afraid of. You want me for her."

"I want you for me too. Plenty of women threw themselves at me before I met you and I had zero interest." Fuck it. He pulled her into his lap, settling her long legs around him and pulling her close for an erotic naked hug. As always she hugged him back, her arms around his torso, her head resting on his shoulder. "But then you came along and I wanted you like I've never wanted anyone before."

He stroked her back, trying to enjoy the hug and not push for the hard fucking he craved like his next breath. If he wanted her more every time they fucked, that would make marriage easy.

She pulled back to look at him. "If you had met me before Viv, would you have wanted me?"

He kissed her, avoiding the question. She yielded immediately. This was what he couldn't get enough of, the soft surrender, the open vulnerability even when he was pushing her out of her comfort zone. He broke the kiss, sliding his hand under her hair to cup the back of her neck, giving it a squeeze before admitting, "Before Viv, I liked wild free spirits like me, but I've changed since she came into my life and what I want changed too. Now I like women with the face of an angel—" he brought up his other hand, brushing his thumb across her lower lip "—and the body for sin."

She jerked her head away.

He cupped her face with both hands, turning her back to him. "And a good heart. A mother's heart."

Her eyes welled up. "This isn't going to work out."

"Why not? Everything fits."

She tried to pull away, but he kept her close. "Lauren, I need you. In so many ways, in and out of bed."

She took a deep shuddering breath. "I know you checked all the boxes and think it all makes sense, but it's...it's not happening. I can't marry you. Not like this."

"Lauren."

"Please," she said softly to his chest.

He loosened his hold and she climbed off his lap.

"Need and love are not the same thing," she said quietly.

That hit him like a shock of cold water. It sounded so final. Even worse, she got out of bed and reached for her clothes.

He watched numbly. She needed the words, the right words, but he had nothing. He'd given up his old careless ways, given up all relationships but one, the important one, Viv.

He didn't have it in him to give any more than that. And he knew for damn certain he didn't deserve her love. But they could have something better, more stable, for Viv's sake.

He watched her dress, at a loss as to how to make her stay.

She turned to him, completely dressed, her hair still mussed from their tangle, whisker burn on her neck. "Look, I'll still help with Viv, but this part—" she pointed to the bed and then met his eyes, her chin lifting "—this *fucking* part is over."

She left, quietly shutting the door behind her. He waited,

stupidly hoping she'd have second thoughts and return. She wanted him as much as he wanted her. She'd admitted she hadn't been with anyone for months before him.

The front door quietly closed too.

He flopped back on the mattress and promptly hit his head on the headboard. "Dammit!" He held his smarting head.

A toddler cry went up from the next room.

The angel had left and he was back in hell.

17

———————

Alex knew he needed Lauren as a nanny, but being with her every day and not *being* with her was torture. Pure torture. He never should've slept with the nanny. Or at least he should've waited until the end of the summer when he didn't have to have her in his house every day. What the hell was he supposed to do? It had only been three days and he didn't know how he was going to get through the next seven weeks.

Yesterday just before Lauren left for a long Fourth of July weekend off, he even caved and asked her if she was going to more singles events with Hailey this weekend. Her answering snarl told him all he needed to know. They were both hurting with the cool distance after being as close as two people could get.

Clearly he'd royally fucked up.

It didn't help that Viv babbled about "Thuper" when she missed Lauren, which felt like all the time. Viv wanted him to tell Lauren stuff during her time off, but since he and Lauren were on rocky ground, he only pretended to.

He dressed Viv in a red T-shirt with fireworks on it, put her hair up in pigtails, and headed to his dad's place. His dad always had a cookout for the Fourth of July. Later they'd go to nearby Clover Park for the fireworks. Call him overprotective, but he had a small set of headphones to shield Viv from the noise.

He supposed it spoke to his desperation that he hoped his longtime bachelor dad might have a clue what he should do to fix things. He figured, since his dad spent a lot of time with Lauren, it was at least a slim possibility he could be helpful.

Luckily when he got to his dad's house, Josh was manning the grill, not his dad. Logan, Ty and his wife, Charlotte, were there too.

"Hi, Viv! Don't you look festive with that fireworks shirt?" Charlotte asked.

Viv held out the bottom of her T-shirt, showing off the fireworks.

"You know what would go perfectly with your shirt?" Charlotte asked, reaching into her large purse.

Viv shook her head so hard her pigtails smacked her in the face.

"A fireworks barrette!" She held up a sparkly red barrette with short red, white, and blue ribbons hanging down from it. Perfect for a little girl.

"Yes!" Viv hollered, running over to Charlotte and turning her back to her the way she did when Alex did her hair in the bathroom mirror. "Thank you!"

Charlotte clipped it to Viv's hair above one pigtail and took a picture with her cell phone, showing Viv.

Viv turned to him. "Daddy! Thuper."

He pulled out his cell and dutifully snapped the picture he knew Viv wanted him to share with Lauren. "You look awesome. Like a superstrong fireworks girl." He made sure she thought of herself more as strong than cute, even though she was extremely cute. He wanted her to be a kickass girl who took shit from nobody. Like his sister, Mad.

"Thuper!" Viv insisted.

"I know, I know." He wasn't enough anymore. Everything had to be shown to him and Lauren. He sent the picture to his dad instead of Lauren. He looked over at Viv, who was patiently waiting. "She says awesome."

Viv beamed and his heart sank. He had to come up with

some way to keep Lauren in their life. He couldn't disappoint his little girl.

"Where's Dad?" he asked his brothers.

"Inside cutting up a fruit salad," Logan said. "I brought it from the supermarket, already sliced, but he's cutting it all to toddler-sized pieces. He's even cutting the grapes in half."

Alex smiled. His dad looked out for Viv and would definitely want to help Alex snag the best mom for her. "Can you all keep an eye on her while I talk to Dad?"

"Sounds serious," Josh said.

"It is." He turned to Viv. "Ask Uncle Logan to play basketball with you."

"Ball!" Viv said, pointing toward the side of the house with the basketball net.

"Basketball," Logan said, scooping her up and holding her on top of his shoulder. Viv squealed in delight.

"Hold up, I want in on this too," Ty boomed.

"Me too," Charlotte said.

"You just watch," Ty said to Charlotte. "Let's keep you nice and still." Charlotte was three months pregnant and Ty was vigilant in keeping her from too much activity. With good reason. Charlotte was at risk for a number of scary pregnancy complications due to a previous health condition. So far Charlotte was perfectly fine, but after what happened with Tammy, Alex couldn't blame Ty for his concern.

Charlotte rolled her eyes and they all headed around the house to the driveway. The toddler-size basketball net was always set up in front of the regular net.

He went inside where his dad was carefully chopping grapes. "Hey, Dad."

His dad put the knife down. "Oh, hey, I didn't know you were here. Where's Viv?"

"Playing basketball with the guys."

"She's going to be an athlete," he said with a big smile. "She's a Campbell all right." His dad got them all into sports as soon as they could hold a ball.

"I guess she did take after my side a bit."

His dad went back to chopping grapes. "A lot. You had

light brown hair at her age too. Same eyes, cheeks, ears, *attitude.*"

He shoved a hand in his hair. "Sometimes all I see when I look at her is Tammy. Especially the bow in her top lip and the cleft in her chin."

His dad paused and then went back to chopping. "You haven't mentioned Tammy by name in a while. Viv been asking about her mom again?" Somehow not having to look his dad in the eye made it easier for Alex to talk about Tammy.

He got out two glasses. "No, Viv hasn't talked much about her mom since Lauren started taking care of her." He went to the sink and filled them with water. "It's just that Viv has become so attached to Lauren and I can't help but think she wants a mom. And then I think about Tammy and all Viv's missing out on not having her."

His dad gestured to the kitchen table. Alex took a seat, passing his dad his drink. They often sat at the table growing up, talking over a drink. They were quiet for a few minutes, but it wasn't uncomfortable. His dad was good at handling sticky situations. Alex didn't know if it was from being a cop or just from dealing with all of his kids and the troubled kids he mentored through the Police Athletic League. Many of those kids had become like family—Park, Ethan, Marcus, Zack, and Ben. His dad had so much love to give and Alex couldn't help but wonder where all that came from. After all, Alex's mom had dumped his dad years ago when Alex was only five years old. Just up and walked out on her kids, never to return. His dad had been a single dad, holding it together for six kids plus his honorary brothers. Alex could barely hold it together as a single dad to one kid.

His dad broke the silence. "I know you sometimes wish Tammy was here to be Viv's mom." He paused and then asked gently, "Do you think she would have loved Viv the way you do?"

He stared, surprised at the question. "You think she wouldn't have?"

His dad's lips formed a flat line. "I don't know. I just

wonder if Viv missed out on as much as you seem to think she did."

Alex took a long drink of water and stared at the glass. "Tammy was indifferent," he admitted. "She called the baby a parasite." He lifted his head. "I'd hoped after Viv was born, the maternal instinct would kick in."

"Not everyone has that maternal instinct. Especially not to the degree Lauren has it. She's exceptional."

His heart kicked hard at the mention of Lauren, even though he was trying to talk about her in a roundabout way. "I guess."

"I mean look at your own mom."

He clenched his jaw. "Heartless bitch."

His dad started. "Hey now. Your mom wasn't completely heartless. She loved you in her way. It just wasn't the way you might want a mom to love you." He took a drink of water and shook his head. "I'm sorry. I wish things had been different for you kids."

"It's not your fault."

His dad nodded. "Thanks." He met Alex's eyes with a sympathetic look. "I didn't know Tammy all that well, but I gotta say I didn't see a lot of love from her in your direction either."

Alex let out a long breath. "I know. I think she was planning on dumping me; she kept talking about hitchhiking to California, knowing I didn't want to leave the city. I convinced her to stay until the baby was born." And then she died, never seeing her daughter. The guilt pressed down on him again, making it hard to breathe.

His dad clapped a hand on his shoulder. "I've told you this before and I'm telling you again, what happened with Tammy wasn't your fault. Until you can forgive yourself—"

"How can I ever forgive myself for robbing Viv of her mom?" he exclaimed.

His dad squeezed his shoulder before dropping his hand and letting out a long sigh. "I hate to say it, but you have mother issues. Your mom left, Viv's mom left, through no fault of her own—"

He interrupted, the old bitter self-recrimination returning. "My fault. I got her pregnant; I convinced her to have the baby."

His dad pinned him with a hard look. "Again, it takes two for both of those things. The fact is you saved a life—Viv's. And Tammy's death, though tragic, was nobody's fault. Not yours. Not Viv's. Not the doctor's. Random bad luck." Tammy had to be put under general anesthesia quickly for the C-section because Viv's heart rate had dropped. Then Tammy had a bad reaction to the anesthesia, her heart stopping. They tried to revive her. And failed.

He swallowed hard.

"Alex?"

"Yeah."

His dad waited until he met his eyes before saying, "Please hear me. When you can stop blaming yourself for what happened with Tammy, then you can move on and have a good life for both you and Viv."

That good life couldn't happen without Lauren. They needed her. "Lauren is perfect for Viv."

"What about for you? Is Lauren the person that'll make you happy?"

He stared at the table. "She's too good for me."

His dad slapped the table, startling Alex. "Then you be too good for her. You can put some effort in, right? Wine her, dine her, make her feel special."

His dinner with Lauren had ended in bed. Somehow sex had muddled things between them. Now that he thought about it, most of his past relationships had been based on sex. He had to figure out a better way to connect with Lauren. Fast.

"I have off until Monday," his dad said. "I'll babysit every night Thursday through Sunday and then every Saturday night until the end of summer. You think that'll give you a head start?"

He gave his dad a small smile. "So I should date the woman I want to marry?"

"Marry?" his dad exclaimed.

He lifted his palms. "I asked her. I thought it all made sense. We both love Viv. We're compatible."

"But she said no, I'm guessing."

He dipped his head. "She said no." She wanted him to love her. If anyone deserved love, it was Lauren, yet something held him back.

"It's harder for you now," his dad said quietly. "To love someone, I mean, after losing Tammy the way you did."

He stared at his dad for a moment, the truth of that statement sinking in. He'd thought he'd moved on, but he was still stuck there in the grief and loss and guilt. The birth, Tammy open on the table, blood everywhere, the monitors blaring, doctors and nurses shouting, the baby crying. He closed his eyes and tried to push down the memories. Tammy's black rose from her last artwork formed in his mind. He still looked at her work daily, especially the work from when she was pregnant. A series of bleak pictures—lone objects, abandoned lots—finishing with the black rose in an empty lot. How could she feel alone when he was right there with her? When she was carrying their baby? The black rose meant death and mourning. Did she leave that clue for him? A goodbye because she was leaving him and Viv? Why a black rose?

His dad squeezed his shoulder. "Have you been to the cemetery since the funeral?"

He shuddered. "No."

"You need to find a way to say goodbye. To let her go and be at peace with what happened."

He swallowed, his throat tight, his chest aching. There was no way in hell he was going to the cemetery. He was never reliving that funeral again. He'd barely made it through the first time, guilt so heavy he could barely drag in air. He never wanted to set foot in a hospital for the same reason.

"I'll go with you if you want," his dad offered.

Alex finished his water and stood. "Thanks but no."

"Okay," he said quietly.

Alex looked out the kitchen window, not really seeing anything, back in that dark place of self-recrimination. Guilt stabbed at him. Viv had lost so much. Tammy had lost everything.

"Don't worry," his dad said, "I've been putting in a good word for you every time Lauren comes to visit."

He froze and slowly turned. "What're you telling her?"

"I *might* have shared some baby pictures."

"Dad!"

"And some original signed kindergarten art. You showed very early signs of talent."

He groaned. "Anything else?"

"I trash-talked Ethan, Ben, and Marcus so she wouldn't date them at Hailey's singles mixer."

"Dad!"

His dad winced. "I might've mentioned Ethan was a sex addict."

Alex did a double take.

"Too far?"

He laughed despite himself. Ethan was *not* a sex addict. He was a flirt, but very choosy about who he was with. Now at least Alex knew why all the women were steering clear of Ethan at that singles mixer. "You didn't just scare off Lauren with that one. All the women avoided Ethan that night and probably in the future too. Women talk, especially these women."

"Damn." His dad rubbed his forehead. "Try to help one son and you gotta go fix something with the other. I figured you needed it more. Okay, I know what I need to do."

Alex shook his head, though now that he thought about it, all that trash talk had worked out nicely for him. Lauren had been doing her best to avoid the other guys' advances, giving him the opportunity to make a move. "No more. I'm on my own now."

"Great. She'll be here in an hour."

He stared at him in shock. He hadn't had any time to prepare for seeing Lauren. He hadn't figured it all out yet.

He worked for an even tone, since his dad had tried to be helpful earlier. "You invited her over again without telling me?"

"Maybe you should ask yourself why she didn't tell you."

"I have no idea. What does it mean?"

His dad stood. "Maybe she wanted to surprise you. Maybe she just wants to get to know you without you proposing marriage. Geez, Alex, I can't believe you proposed marriage so soon. Not that I don't love that girl, sweet as they come." He shook his head, smiling at the thought of Lauren, it seemed. "You need to treat her extra special. Like a queen."

"Like a queen," he echoed, not at all sure how to do that.

His dad picked up the bowl of fruit salad and a serving spoon before heading for the back door. He stopped and called over his shoulder, "You'll figure it out."

Alex followed him outside. Everyone was there. Viv must've got tired of basketball. He did a quick survey of the guys, trying to figure out which one of them might be helpful in the whole nailing-down-a-relationship thing. He held onto a thin hope that, even though he didn't entirely have his shit together, Lauren wouldn't quit on him just yet. He couldn't lose her so soon. Josh didn't do relationships. At least not any that Alex knew about. Park and Mad were here now, but damn, it had been so easy for Park. Mad had worshipped him since she was a kid. All he had to do was return the favor. Logan had one serious relationship in college and had never quite gotten over it. That was a sore subject. So that left Ty. Exuberant over-the-top Ty. Ah, hell. What did Alex have to lose?

Alex had only taken a few steps when Ty met up with him apparently on his way out. "You need anything at the store?" Ty asked. "I'm going on a veggie run. I want to make Charlotte a kale smoothie."

Alex fought his gag reflex at the thought. "I'll go with you. Give me a minute."

He met up with his dad, asking him to keep an eye on Viv, kissed Viv goodbye, and then joined Ty at his new minivan. Ty spent the first several minutes of the drive extolling the safety features of the car in excruciating detail.

"Wow," Alex muttered.

"I know she's not much to look at, but she's number one in safety from the Insurance Institute for Highway Safety."

"So important for a family."

Ty flashed a smile. "You get it."

It was only a short drive to the supermarket, so Alex didn't waste any time getting right to the point. "How'd you get Charlotte from dating to a wedding?"

"Easy," Ty said with a grin, "knocked her up."

This was true. Also, not helpful. Alex was definitely not going that careless route again. The thought of Lauren pregnant and possibly dying made him break out in a sweat. He took a few deep breaths.

"Okay, let's back it up," Alex said. "How'd you get her from pissed off to all over you?" Alex remembered the first time Ty asked Charlotte out. They'd all been there at Garner's. She'd turned him down cold, still pissed over something Ty had done the first time they met. Alex didn't know all the details only that Charlotte had been pissed.

"Why?" Ty asked. "You making a move on someone?"

"Lauren."

"She's a sweetheart. Good for you. And Viv loves her already."

"I know. I already screwed up twice with her. I obviously need dating one-oh-one."

"Third time's a charm," Ty quipped.

"What did you do? Flowers? Candy?"

Ty flashed a smile. "Let's see, I asked her to dinner, performed a stripper-style dance, took her on a sunset dinner cruise on a yacht...you know how that ended."

"Yeah." Ty somehow got the yacht stuck in the mud and they had to wait hours for high tide with no dinner at all. The local police had to rescue them.

Ty went on. "Yeah, so, after that, I made my intentions clear and she was mine, all mine."

Alex thought about that. He couldn't see how any of that applied to him, not even the dancing. He could only do a slow shuffle and a jumping *Princess Kei-Kei and the Elves* dance. Dammit. How did other single dads manage a social life? He had no one to ask.

"Why so glum?" Ty asked.

"I dunno."

"Look, in the end, it doesn't matter what you do."

"It doesn't?"

"Nah. Just go full steam ahead with good intentions. That's something I told Char right up front. I always have good intentions even if it doesn't come out the right way. Women are very forgiving if you're sincere. Lauren especially strikes me as the forgiving type."

"You think asking her to dinner is enough?"

"Absolutely. Be sincere, let her know you're really into her."

"How do I do that?"

Ty reached over, grabbed Alex's chin and moved his jaw up and down like a ventriloquist dummy. "I'm really into you, Lauren."

Alex slapped his hand away. "Idiot."

"It really is that easy. Use your words."

Alex rolled his eyes. He'd already done that, stupidly blurting a marriage proposal. Too much, too fast. But he couldn't shake the feeling he was running out of time. Like it was urgent that he secure Lauren as a mom for Viv. Fuck. His dad was right. He did have mom issues. And Tammy issues. No wonder Lauren pushed him away. He was a mess.

After a quick trip to the produce section of the supermarket for a ton of green leafy vegetables, they headed back home. Alex had a lot tumbling through his head—Lauren, his talk with his dad, his talk with Ty. Halfway home, he told Ty, "Dad says I have mom issues."

"Ha! Don't we all? Having your mom bail when you're just a little kid will do that for you." Ty had been six.

"So how'd you get past it? I mean, you seem so happy now."

"I am. I just decided there was nothing I could do about it. She made her choice. We have family around us. Lots of family and the guys." He paused. "You probably know this already, since you have Viv, but having a family of your own is like a second chance to experience the whole family thing."

"Yeah, but Viv doesn't have a mom, so it's not like a real family."

"Sure it is. You think because we just had Dad that we weren't a real family?"

He sucked in a breath. He'd never thought about it like that. "No, you're right. Dad made it a real family."

"Damn straight. But what I meant about having a second chance at the family thing is you get to experience the joy of being a kid right along with Viv and give her everything you would have wanted."

He stilled. That was exactly the problem. He saw himself in Viv, motherless, and wanted to give her what he wanted so badly as a kid—a mom. But Viv had never known her mom. Not like him and his brothers and sister. He knew and lost his mom. It hurt. Neither situation was ideal for him or Viv, but Viv only ever knew him as her main parent. Was it possible that Viv didn't long for a mom at all? No, it couldn't be. Everyone needed a mom. Right?

Ty went on. "I can't wait for our baby—" He stopped himself and pointed to the sky. "No early deliveries, stork."

He tuned out as Ty launched into all the requirements for good prenatal nutrition. Alex threw in a few murmured *uh-huhs*, but was otherwise quiet, reeling over the realization that he'd projected his own longing for a mom on Viv. He still wasn't sure what it all meant. What did Viv really need?

Ty parked in front of their dad's house. Alex stepped out of the car and chills ran down his spine. Viv was wailing, loud sobs interrupted by, "Daddy! Daddy! I want Daddy!"

His adrenaline surged and he ran full speed to the back-yard. He found his dad holding Viv in a chair. Lauren was there, kneeling at Viv's side, trying to comfort her.

"Viv," he said, but she didn't hear him or see him.

Her eyes were scrunched tight as she let out another long wail. "Daddy!"

"She only wanted you," Lauren said.

He scooped up Viv. "I'm here. Daddy's here." He tucked

her against his chest and rubbed her back. The sobs were terrible, but she didn't sound like she was in serious pain. "What happened?" he asked his dad.

His dad stood and indicated Viv's temple, which had a bright red spot. No swelling. "She whacked herself with the bat by accident during tee-ball." It was a plastic bat.

Alex's heart slowed as Viv quieted to sniffling sobs. It hit him that she needed him. Not Lauren. Him. He gave Viv a little squeeze and then pulled back to inspect the red spot again. "No blood," he told her. "You're okay."

She popped a thumb in her mouth and settled on his chest. Content.

Why was he trying to force the mom thing? Viv was content with him.

He was enough.

He dropped a kiss on top of Viv's head. They were enough. They were a real family.

18

———————

Lauren's heart squeezed seeing the tight bond Alex and Viv had. It made her love him even more. She wished it weren't true, but there it was, somewhere along the way she'd fallen for Alex. Probably the first time she saw him dance with his little girl. She sighed and shifted to stand with her friends Charlotte and Mad. They were watching Ty and Logan, who seemed to be competing for maximum number of push-ups. Park was keeping score. Josh and Joe were at the grill.

Lauren's gaze drifted back to Alex. He was sitting in a chair with Viv now, talking to her in a low soothing tone and Viv looked like she was nearly asleep, exhausted after all her tears.

"That is so damn sweet," Charlotte said, looking at Alex and Viv.

"It is," Mad said. "He's always been so good with her."

"He asked me to marry him," Lauren whispered.

"What?" Mad and Charlotte exclaimed in near unison.

Lauren's eyes stung and she blinked rapidly, trying to hold off tears. "He wants me to be Viv's mom."

It had only been three days since their massive hookup-breakup event. She never thought she'd be looking at her first marriage proposal and hurting over it. It was the way he did it. So casually, like some kind of contract almost. Like, you be Viv's mom because we're *compatible*. Not love, compatibility. But now the pain in Alex's eyes was so much worse, like maybe he was hurting over her and Tammy, trying to bring Lauren close to take the place of the other. Her stomach churned. She never wanted to add to Alex's pain.

Charlotte's brown eyes were wide. "What did you say?"

"I said no." Lauren took a deep quavering breath. "He doesn't love me."

"Moron," Mad muttered. Then at Lauren's surprised look, added, "Not you. Him. You want me to knock some sense into him?"

"No!" Lauren exclaimed. Several heads turned in their direction. "I'm telling you this in confidence. Please don't say anything to anyone."

"I can tell Park, though, right?" Mad asked. "That's the significant-other rule. You can tell them stuff and it doesn't count as secret spilling."

"No!" Lauren snapped.

Charlotte looked away.

Lauren sighed. They'd both probably spill to their guys, which was bad, bad, bad. Obviously it would get back to Alex. "This group is too connected."

"Sorry," Mad said. "It's not my fault you all keep falling for my brothers. No one said they were good at relationships or romance or whatever." Mad turned to Charlotte. "Why'd you fall for Ty anyway? You used to hate him."

Charlotte rubbed a hand over her tiny baby bump. "I never *hated* him. He just pissed me off once. But now he's sweet and tender. How could I not fall for him?"

At that moment, Ty boomed, "Next time, young pup!" before putting his palm on Logan's face and giving him a shove.

Logan slapped his hand away.

Ty grinned and wiggled his fingers, egging him on. "You wanna go a round with me?"

Logan stalked off to talk to Josh.

"Are you going to keep working for Alex?" Mad asked Lauren. "I can imagine things got awkward after you turned down his proposal."

"Yes, of course. I said I would." No matter how difficult it was on a personal level, she knew he needed her. And she loved spending the day with Viv. She almost hadn't come today, figuring a long weekend away from Alex would help, but she couldn't turn down Joe's warm invitation. They'd become friends.

"You're too damn accommodating," Mad said. "Make it hard on him. Make him work for it."

Charlotte shook her head. "Not at the expense of a child. Lauren's doing the right thing." She put an arm around Lauren's shoulder and squeezed. "You're a sweetheart."

"That's me," Lauren said with a sigh.

"So let me get this straight," Mad said. "You've been working for him for what, three, four weeks—"

"Three and a half," Lauren said.

Mad gave her a strange look. "Three and a half, okay. And then, out of the blue, he proposes marriage."

Charlotte lowered her voice. "Duh, Mad."

"What?" Mad asked.

Charlotte gestured to Lauren. "Obviously she's sleeping with him. Men don't propose for no reason."

Mad stared at her expectantly. Lauren blushed furiously.

"Huh." Mad cocked her head, studying Lauren. "Interesting."

Charlotte elbowed Mad. "Stop embarrassing her."

Lauren's gaze drifted back to Alex and Viv. She longed to join them, to be part of their little family, but finally had to acknowledge that in refusing Alex, she'd closed that door. Her eyes stung and she quickly tuned back in to her friends.

~

Alex didn't take his dad up on his offer to babysit over the long Fourth of July weekend. Instead he spent the next three days with Viv and his nights alone. Not exactly alone—with Tammy. He knew he had to stop looking at her art every day. He needed to let her go. And the only way he could think of was to give her to Viv. Tammy gave him Viv. He would give Viv Tammy. He'd create his gift now and give it to Viv when she was old enough to understand.

The first night, after Viv fell asleep, he gathered all the pictures he had stored on his computer of Tammy from the beginning of their relationship to nine months pregnant. Thirteen months of memories. He supposed in the long view it wasn't much, but his life had changed so profoundly because of her it felt like more. He uploaded them to a photo website, where he ordered a hardcover photo book for Viv, the images printed in high resolution on the pages. Tammy looked so young. She'd only been twenty-five when she died. He'd been twenty-eight.

With that accomplished, he copied the original pictures to a flash drive, set it on the desk, and then clicked over to delete the pictures from his computer. His adrenaline kicked in, full-out sweat and shaking fingers. No. Not yet. He left the pictures on his computer and went to bed.

The next night he did some deep breathing and gave himself a pep talk. He wasn't erasing Tammy, he was merely creating something new. Something tangible that Viv could hang onto forever. He opened the art folder he looked at daily, though it never made him feel better. Just the opposite. He uploaded all of her artwork to the photo website and considered what to make from them. There was too much here for another photo book. He quickly decided to only focus on the art she'd created once they knew she was pregnant. Twenty-six pieces in all, not a lot because she'd been tired from the pregnancy and not able to stay up late often to create. He rubbed his aching chest—another thing taken from Tammy. He told himself it was normal for her to be fatigued from pregnancy and not his fault, but it was hard to push away the old guilt.

He found himself going through the nine months of art

again and again. He arranged them all in order on the large computer screen and stared, trying to understand one last time. His gaze shifted as it always did to the last piece she'd created—the black rose. The pressure on his chest returned, heavy like a hand pressing down. He couldn't get a full breath. This piece haunted him. If he could just figure out why she'd created it, what it really meant, he could let it go.

He Googled "black rose," as he'd done before. It meant death and mourning, which he knew. Since he'd promised himself he would stop looking at it every day, he kept going, clicking through every search result, desperate for a different meaning. Several minutes later, he found something. Some people said the black rose was the symbol of antiauthoritarianism, others said it represented a journey into unexplored territory. Both of those fit Tammy. She was antiauthority, defiant to the bone. She was also about to explore new territory as a mom. Could that be it?

He suddenly felt immensely tired. He'd never know the answers to his questions, so how could he let it go? He stood and dragged himself to bed.

The third night was Sunday night, so no more fucking around, he had to get back to his own work and stop torturing himself with Tammy's stuff. He decided to make a photo book of her pregnancy photos with the art she'd created during each month. He hoped it would be something Viv would treasure, seeing herself grow along with her mother's work. Some part of him hoped it would bring clarity. He was a visual person and needed to fit the pieces together. He worked slowly deep into the night, arranging the art on the page in a way that made it flow one piece to the next, one stage to the next. He finally finished and stared at the last two-page spread: Tammy nine months pregnant on one side, the black rose on the other. The contrast was so striking—life and death. He left the black rose on a page by itself and shifted the nine months pregnant picture for last. He stared at her huge belly and the picture got blurry, his eyes watering, knowing it was Viv in there. Tammy looked radiant, full-on smiling at the camera. At him. It was St. Patrick's Day and he'd just given her a plate of four cupcakes with green sugar clovers on vanilla icing from her favorite bakery. She had a bit of Irish in her and had bemoaned the fact she couldn't do her usual bar crawl. He'd tried to make it fun for her with the cupcakes.

He wiped his eyes and quickly typed "St. Patrick's Day" and "black rose" into the Google search box. He sucked in a breath and clicked on an article from *Rolling Stone* about how Thin Lizzy's "Black Rose" was the perfect St. Patrick's Day song.

He dropped his head in his hands and broke down in tears. Jesus. All this time he'd thought terrible things—she expected death, she was saying goodbye, she hated the baby. It was just a song. A fucking song. She'd probably been listening to it while she created this last piece. She hadn't been looking toward death. It had caught her by surprise just as it had caught him.

A long while later he wiped his tears and sat there, spent. She hadn't hated the baby and, by extension, him. She'd gone through a lot to have Viv. Morning sickness, swollen fingers and ankles, heartburn, sleepless nights, aching back, he heard it all. And then the labor. She'd wanted a natural birth, as she'd said in her snarky way, "So I'll remember not to do it again." But maybe she wanted to truly experience all of it because she was embracing the journey.

For the first time, he felt some peace. The article had a link to the song. He hit play—ripping guitars morphed to Celtic melodies and soft keyboard and back to rock. The lyrics and tune both hard and, at times, tender. This was Tammy—hard shell covering the tender underbelly. He finally got her. He didn't need to keep looking at her art every day for answers. He knew deep down everything he needed to know. Tammy loved him. Tammy loved Viv.

Tammy's journey ended, but it lived on in a way through Viv. He added a title to the photo book: Viv and Mom's Journey.

More tears leaked out and then it seemed he was done. His eyes were gritty, his limbs loose, the pressure on his chest gone. He ordered the photo book, transferred all of her art to the flash drive, checked that everything was on there—pictures of her, all of her art—and finally deleted all the Tammy stuff from his computer. He let out a long breath, stood, gripped the flash drive in his hand, and sent a silent prayer of thanks to Tammy for Viv, added a quick sorry that she hadn't lived to see her, and finally finished with goodbye.

"Goodbye," he said again, out loud this time because he hadn't at the funeral. He'd been in shock.

He turned and crossed to his room, where he stashed the flash drive in the fireproof box on the top shelf of his closet along with Viv's birth certificate and other important papers.

It was nearly dawn. No use trying to sleep. Viv would be up soon. He went to her room and sat on the side of her bed, gazing down at her. She slept on her back, arms flung wide. He gazed at the bow in her top lip, at the cleft in her chin, which he knew were from Tammy, then to her light brown hair and her ears, which he knew were from him. His eyes welled again, but this time they were happy tears because his little girl was the most precious gift he'd ever been given.

The sun rose while he sat there, the new day bringing new hope. He heard his name a short while later.

"Daddy?"

He brushed her hair back. His little sunshine. "Right here."

She sat up and hugged him. He lifted her and kissed her chubby cheek. "Love you, Viv."

"Love you, Daddy."

He stood with Viv in his arms. "Let's get ready for our day."

~

Lauren showed up for work at Alex's house on Monday morning not at all sure the reception she was going to get. He hadn't gotten in touch over the long holiday weekend, not even a text, and had been distant when she'd said goodbye at his family's Fourth of July barbeque. She rang the bell, and the moment the door opened, her heart squeezed. He looked rumpled like he'd been up all night, his jaw had at least a few days' growth, his eyes were bleary and a little puffy. Had he been crying? Or did he have another rough night with Viv?

"Alex, are you okay?"

"Yeah," he said quietly. "Tired, but okay."

She hugged him. "Is Viv okay?"

His arms wrapped tight around her. "She's good."

"Thuper! Watch me!"

Alex pulled away and turned. They both watched Viv on the floor with Dolly on her back, attempting to do push-ups like her dad. She couldn't quite manage one without Dolly sliding off her back. Then she'd grab her doll, put her back in place, and try again.

"Look at you, superstrong girl," Alex said. He crossed to her and held Dolly on her back for her. "I got Dolly. Let's hear you count off."

Viv did her toddler form of a push-up, her butt going high in the air. "One, two, three!" she counted for the first one. "Five, seven, eight!" She counted for the second. "Nine, ten!" She did a third one and collapsed to the floor.

"Wow!" Lauren exclaimed. "You're going to be fit just like your daddy."

Viv stood and beamed.

"Let's see some sit-ups," Alex said, getting out the mat for her.

"Princess Kei-Kei!" Viv hollered.

Alex smiled and started the music. Soon Viv was busy doing the whole routine with Dolly that Alex usually did with her.

He took Lauren's hand and guided her farther away where they could still see Viv, but the music wasn't as loud.

"You look exhausted," Lauren said. "You want to nap while I watch her?"

"I will but not yet. I was up all night. I made a photo book of Tammy's artwork with pictures of her for Viv."

"That's really nice. I'm sure she'll appreciate that when she gets older." She squeezed his hand and gave him a sympathetic look. "That must've been difficult for you."

He nodded. "It was. But good too. I found some peace with it."

"I'm glad."

They were both quiet for a moment, watching Viv lift Dolly over her head like a barbell. She glanced at Alex to find him smiling. "Guess she was paying attention," he said.

"Sure, she experienced it."

He turned to her. "I used to look at Tammy's art every day on my computer. Every damn day searching for answers. Last night I deleted all of it. I said goodbye."

Her eyes widened in alarm. "You deleted it? That seems—"

"No, it's okay. I made it into a photo book and saved it in a different place. I'm just trying to say I'm moving on. And I hope that means I can move forward with you." He gazed into her eyes. His dark eyes were so tired, so bleary, but also at peace. In fact, his whole demeanor had changed from on edge to completely relaxed.

She swallowed over the lump in her throat and hugged him again. Not because she felt sympathy for him. Because she needed to feel his strong arms around her. She'd missed him since their fallout last week. "I'd like that too," she whispered.

His hand cupped the back of her head and she felt him let out a long breath. "Good."

She knocked into him as Viv joined their hug, launching herself at Lauren's legs. "Group hug," she said with a laugh.

"What happened to dance party?" Alex asked, looking down at Viv.

"Hug, hug!" Viv hollered.

Lauren bent down and scooped her up, handing her to Alex. Viv turned and wrapped an arm around Lauren's neck too. She smiled, kissed Viv on the cheek and turned to Alex, who was smiling through tears. And then tears were leaking out of her eyes too because she knew he was all there—body, heart, and soul.

The happy elves song blared on, Viv wiggled to get down, and they let her go back to her dance party.

And then they were kissing and crying happy tears and nothing had ever felt so right.

19

———

And so began what Lauren liked to think of as Alex's formal courtship. Every afternoon when she returned to his house after her outing with Viv, Alex gave her a single red rose. She put it in a large glass and left it by his kitchen window so she could admire it. She spent most of her time at his house anyway. By Friday afternoon, she had four roses in full bloom, opening their petals to the sun.

"Would you like to have dinner with me tomorrow night?" Alex asked.

She smiled to herself and turned from the roses to gaze into his eyes, feeling his sincerity down to her toes. She soaked in the moment. They'd been out together before and even went to Hailey's surprise birthday party together last night, but this felt different, like their first real date since Alex opened his heart again. "Yes," she said and beamed at him.

He smiled back, the joy lighting up his handsome face.

"Yes!" Viv mimicked, grabbing Alex's leg.

Alex looked down at Viv, cupping her head with one hand. "You're going to visit Grandpop tomorrow and have pizza. Me and Lauren are going to a restaurant that's just for grown-ups."

Viv accepted this in typical style, jumping up and down and hollering, "Pizza!"

The next night Alex showed up at her doorstep with another rose.

She pulled him inside her apartment with her, the rose still clutched in her hand. "Alex?"

"Yeah?"

She smiled and said in a teasing voice, "I'm starting to feel like you made a reward chart for me, but instead of a gold star, I get a rose each day I'm with you."

He gazed back at her, his dark eyes warm and tender. "It's not a reward chart." His voice was gruff with emotion. "I'm trying to make love bloom."

"Are you teasing?" she whispered.

He shook his head, completely sincere. "I love you, Lauren."

"I love you too!"

She dropped the flower, threw her arms around his neck, and kissed him passionately.

Next thing she knew he had her pinned against the wall, his mouth sealed to hers, his hard planes against her softness. Which was exactly where she wanted to be.

Tonight was the night. Their two-month anniversary and Alex was going to propose. Lauren counted it as two months (since their first kiss) and he agreed because, though there'd been some separations, Lauren had loved him through it all. He still couldn't believe he'd gotten so lucky to find the person for both him and Viv. And, damn, he'd almost lost Lauren in the process of opening his heart again. His own fear of dealing with the pain had held him back, but he did it, and, ultimately, he came out the other side feeling good. Actually, better than good. He felt fully alive and so full of love he thought his heart would burst with it. Like ridiculous levels— dancing under the stars, singing to the rooftops about his love for Lauren.

But first he needed to do something important for Viv. He let her watch some Saturday morning cartoons while he got everything ready. He'd framed a picture of Tammy, the one where she was nine months pregnant with St. Patrick's Day cupcakes that had finally given him the answers he sought. Now he hung it in the hallway that led to the bedrooms. Then he hung a picture of their little family, him and Viv last Christmas, next to it.

When Viv's show ended, something about puppies, he turned off the TV and scooped her up. "I've got something special to show you." He carried her over to the picture and pointed. "That's your mommy."

Viv stared, brown eyes wide.

"And that's you in her tummy. Later when you were born, I was so happy. I love you, baby."

Viv scowled. "Not a baby. Big girl." She was out of diapers—huge kudos to Lauren for making that happen—and damn proud of her big-girl status.

"Big girl. I love you, Viv."

"Love you, Daddy." Viv touched the picture. "Sleeping forever?"

"Yes. Sleeping forever in heaven."

"Wake up!"

"No," he said gently. "She's with the angels now. But we can say hi sometimes. Hi, Mommy."

"Hi."

"Or we can tell her stuff whenever we want. Like guess what? I made a new friend named Kaitlin."

"Thuper."

"Sure. You can tell her about Super L." He moved to the next picture. "And this is our family. You and me."

"Yes. Hungry."

And that was a two-year-old in a nutshell. Great! Next?

He took her to the kitchen. "I know you're a smart girl with a lot more words in there. Say, I'm hungry. May I please have a snack?"

She hugged him tight around the neck. "Please, Daddy! Please!"

"May I have a snack, please?"

She let go of his neck and looked him in the eye. "Yes!"

"Say may I have a snack, please?"

"May I have a snack, puh-leze!" she demanded.

"Say it nicer, please. May I have a snack, please?"

Viv huffed and looked to the ceiling. That was Tammy right there. Defiant streak a mile wide, though Tammy had some legit reasons to rebel. He waited patiently.

"May I have a snack, please, Daddy?" Viv asked in the sweetest of tones, toddler lisp and all.

"Yes, you can. Raisins or yogurt?"

"Yogurt!"

He set her down. "You get the napkins. I'll get the yogurt."

They had a good day together just the two of them. But he hoped with everything in him that tonight Lauren would say yes and always be with them.

That night after he dropped off Viv at his dad's house, he picked up Lauren at her apartment. They were going to dinner, where he planned to propose, and then heading to Garner's for his honorary brother Zach's welcome-back party.

She answered the door in her cute teal sundress with a sweet seductive smile on her face. He handed her a dozen red roses. "Thank you," she said. "I'm not wearing panties."

He kept a straight face and stepped inside with her. "Frankly, Lauren, I'm shocked."

She frowned. "Really, you are?"

"Here I was about to declare my love with utmost sincerity and you try to turn it into a dirty—" he backed her into the door and pinned her there, pressing his body against all her softness and lowering his head to brush his lips against hers "—a dirty *lusty* thing."

She sighed, wrapping her arms around his neck.

He pulled back just enough to meet her eyes. "I love you with everything I am. I've never felt like this before with anyone."

"I love you too. So very much."

And then he couldn't help himself, he turned it into a dirty lusty thing too. He dropped to his knees and licked his lips.

She stared at him, lust in her eyes, which was exactly what he wanted.

"Lauren, will you marry me?"

She blinked. "What?"

He pulled the diamond ring from his pocket and offered it to her. It was a simple gold band with a round diamond. Classic, elegant, and beautiful. Like Lauren.

Her jaw dropped. He liked the shock and awe effect and really hoped it meant she was on board.

He spoke from the heart, the words raw, his voice rough through the tightness in his throat. "I know me and Viv will be okay just us. You'd be a bonus. You don't have to be a substitute for anyone. But I really love you and Viv really loves you and I'm just hoping—"

"Yes!"

He let out a whoop and slid the ring on her finger. Lauren dropped to her knees and hugged him. He wrapped his arms around her and kissed her hair, overwhelmed with emotion, his eyes tearing up.

Lauren pulled back and looked at him, tears spilling out of her eyes. "I know I could never substitute for Viv's mom, but I love you and I love Viv. I'd love to share in her life and yours."

He cupped her face with both hands. "Ours. Now it's ours. For the rest of our lives."

She nodded, tears still leaking out. He brushed away her tears and kissed her. And then he needed more, so he stood, pulling her with him to the bedroom. Dinner forgotten.

Once there, he peeled off her dress and admired her for a long moment. "So beautiful."

She tugged at his shirt and he yanked it off. They slammed together, mouths hungry, hands greedy for skin on skin. He pulled away long enough to get them both undressed, condom on, and they tumbled into the bed. He rolled on top of her, bracing himself above her and looked down into her green eyes hazy with lust and love. He entwined his fingers with hers, pressing them into the mattress as he slowly thrust inside her. She lifted her hips to meet him, her legs wrapping high around his waist. Tight. Hot. Wet. Perfection.

He kept his eyes open, gazing into hers as he made love to her, climbing higher and higher, her soft sounds urging him on. And then he felt it—that soul connection. It zinged through him in a flash of recognition. She was his. He was hers.

He brushed his lips against hers. "I feel it."

She smiled. "Me too. Body, heart, and soul."

"Yes."

And then there were no more words. He tried to take it slow, but Lauren urged him on with her dirty words and tight hot body arching up to meet him, clenching around him. He took her on a heart-pounding exhilarating ride that had them both shouting in exultation and then collapsing.

He rolled to his side and wrapped his arms around her in a hug. She hugged him back as always. As close as two people could get.

20

Lauren dressed, freshened her makeup, and brushed out her hair, hoping she didn't look too much like a woman who'd just been well fucked. They still had to get over to Zach's welcome-back party at Garner's. She stepped into the bedroom, where Alex was still lying in bed, naked, his hands clasped behind his head.

"Why aren't you dressed?" she asked.

He crooked his finger at her.

She shook her head and eased a step back.

He sat up. "Don't make me come get you."

A tingle of anticipation raced down her spine. "We're going to be late." *Come get me.*

His feet hit the floor. "Engaged people are always late."

"They are not." She backed toward the door. "It's rude," she added. *Come get me.*

He stood, a predatory gleam in his eye and, down below, a rapidly rising erection. She stared for a moment, shocked he was ready for round two so fast. He lurched toward her suddenly and she jumped, a squeak escaping. Then she turned and ran around the other side of the bed to give him more room to chase.

He caught her easily, wrapping his arms around her waist from behind. "Not done with you yet, beautiful." He kissed along her neck and she tilted her head to give him better access. "Unfortunately, we have a party to get to. I can't miss it. Zach hasn't been home in years." He started walking toward the bathroom, one arm around her waist, her back plastered to his front. "Shower sex, then coffee, and we're on our way."

"Okay, but it has to be a fierce alpha wall banger of a fuck. No time for the sweet stuff."

"Yes, angel."

By the time they made it to Garner's, the party was in full swing. She and Alex first went to welcome back Zach, a tall lean man in his thirties with thick dark brown hair and a beard. He was reserved and surprisingly quiet given how boisterous all the guys were with him.

A short while later, Lauren got her second wind after some hot appetizers, surrounded by her friends again. Carrie was all made up and beautiful in a cute purple V-neck wrap dress that clung to her curves. And no glasses! Her delicate features were suddenly in full view with big blue eyes and a cute button nose.

"Did you get contacts?" Lauren asked.

"Yup," Carrie said. "New dress too. I'm all set." She scanned the room full of single men.

Lauren tamped down the urge to warn her away from certain men she had dirt on and instead said, "You look beautiful."

"Thanks! You too!" Carrie did a double take and grabbed Lauren's hand. "Omigod! Did you get engaged?"

Alex slid an arm around Lauren's shoulders and grinned. "Sure did."

Lauren beamed. "I'm so happy."

"You're glowing!" Hailey exclaimed. "Congratulations to you both!"

All the women exclaimed over her happy glow and congratulated them.

"Thank you," Lauren said, turning to gaze at Alex. "He made love bloom."

Her friends awwed, except Mad, who stuck her finger down her throat in a gagging motion.

"Looks like my plan worked!" Hailey declared. "Who's next for my Make Love Bloom service?"

"It's legit," Alex said with a straight face. "Trademark and everything."

Lauren nodded solemnly. She and Alex grinned like lovesick fools at each other.

Surprisingly, nobody volunteered for Hailey's service. Hailey narrowed her eyes and speculatively studied each of the single women, who shifted uneasily.

Ethan came over to greet Alex, heard the happy news, and congratulated them both.

"Looks like Viv let you out on good behavior," Ethan said with a wink. "Enjoy the freedom." Cop humor. He hitched a thumb over to the bar, where some of the guys were toasting Zach. "He's finally back from no man's land."

"No man's land," Carrie said under her breath, her eyes gleaming. Then she added, "Wait, do you mean jail?"

Ethan stared at her, seeming surprised at the question. "No."

"But he's bad?" Carrie pressed, her voice rising in excitement.

"Understatement," Ethan said, exchanging a look with Alex.

"Uh, Carrie—" Lauren started, putting her hand on Carrie's arm to hold her back. Her friend had sworn to get herself a bad boy despite Lauren's repeated warnings against it.

Ethan went on. "He's got a history, but don't we all?"

Carrie squeed.

"He straightened out," Alex said.

Ethan lifted a shoulder. "More or less."

Carrie pulled free of Lauren and made a beeline for Zach, saying something to him that made him look at her speculatively before a slow smile spread across his handsome features.

Lauren turned to Alex. "Should I go over there?"
Alex kissed her temple. "She's in good hands."
Lauren sighed. "That's what I'm afraid of."

"When two people love each other a whole lot, they want to be very close."

Alex shot Lauren a dark look for quietly laughing at his explanation of marriage to Viv. He was aware it was beginning to sound like a birds and the bees talk. He was also keenly aware that tomorrow was move-in day for Lauren and all her stuff at his house. It was the end of August and he wanted her settled before she started the new school year. They planned to marry in October. He would've been fine with a quickie wedding at the courthouse, but Lauren had other ideas—the kind of wedding she'd been dreaming of since she was a little girl—so they'd be married in October at Ludbury House with Hailey as both wedding coordinator and maid of honor. All he cared about was Lauren's happiness. And Viv's. His heart squeezed painfully, throat tight, eyes stinging. It was impossible to contain the deep well of emotion once he opened to it, and he wouldn't have it any other way for his two favorite people in the world.

Viv nodded solemnly from her perch on the sofa, seeming aware a life-changing announcement was in the works. Her pigtails were crooked, her red T-shirt was on inside out (she'd insisted on dressing herself this morning), and her blue leggings had one side up and one side down. Her socks were white with grass stains on the bottom from a previous run through the backyard. He'd given up trying to keep her socks white. But damn, he'd never forget how precious she looked on this momentous occasion.

He and Lauren stood together in front of Viv, mostly because Lauren had a present hiding behind her back. He put an arm around Lauren. "I love Lauren very much."

"Thuper," Viv said.

"Yes, Thuper," Alex said. "I mean Super."

Lauren jumped in. "And I love your daddy very much too. We're getting married."

Viv cocked her head. "Mawwied?"

"Yes," Alex said. "That means we promise to love each other forever. And love you too."

"I love you, Viv," Lauren said with a big smile.

"I love you too," Alex told Viv over the lump in his throat.

Viv nodded and busied herself pulling off her sock.

Lauren went on. "We're going to be a family. I'll live here with you and take care of you. You can call me Super L or Mommy, whichever one you like best."

Viv tossed the sock behind her. It hit the big picture window and fell behind the sofa. Alex restrained himself from stopping Viv's sock tossing because Lauren was approaching Viv with the present.

"I got you a present for being my new daughter," Lauren said, sitting next to Viv with a large flat box with bright red paper and a gold bow.

Viv yanked the other sock off, dropped it, and accepted the gift. "Thank you!"

Lauren smiled. "You're welcome. Go ahead and—"

Viv didn't need any encouragement. She ripped the paper to shreds. What a mess. Lauren helped her lift the top off the box and pull out the tiara and dress.

Viv's jaw dropped, brown eyes wide. "Princess Kei-Kei!" she hollered.

The dress was hideous and all Lauren's idea. It was pink satin on top with puffy sleeves, huge neon green bows on the shoulders and waist, with a pink tutu covered in a pattern of ugly neon green elves (they looked more like trolls). It came with a silver rhinestone tiara with a picture of Kei-Kei and the head elf in the center.

He watched as Lauren helped Viv put the dress on over her T-shirt and leggings. Then she added the tiara. Viv went to the open area of the living room and did a few twirls, letting the dress puff out.

"Fabulous!" Lauren declared.

"Daddy!"

"Fantastic," he said with as much enthusiasm as he could. He hoped this outfit was strictly for home. He really didn't want to take her out in it or to her new preschool next month.

"Dance party!" Viv hollered, jumping up and down.

"Not yet," he said. "I have a present for you to give to Lauren. Come on."

He led the way to his studio. Over the past few weeks, he'd had Lauren pose with Viv so he could sketch them. Not easy with a squirmy giggling two-year-old, but over the course of several sessions he'd finally captured their likeness. Alex did a self-portrait, putting himself into it too, turning it into a digital painting that he had printed in high resolution onto a canvas. He'd tied a fat red ribbon around the top and made a bow.

"Help me carry it," he told Viv. They each took a side, though it wasn't heavy. He just wanted her to be part of it.

By the time they got to the living room, Viv ran out of patience, dropped her side and raced to Lauren, climbing up next to her on the sofa. "Present!"

Alex handed it to Lauren. "An early wedding present from both of us."

"Oh, Alex! I love it!" Lauren exclaimed, sliding off the bow. She turned to Viv, who was leaning into her side. "Thank you so much for this beautiful painting! Who is this family?"

"Family!" Viv exclaimed happily, pointing at each of them. "Mommy, Daddy, Viv."

"That's right," Alex told her.

"Two mommies!" Viv exclaimed.

Lauren beamed. "What a smart girl you are." She tapped Viv on the nose. "And so lucky to have two mommies."

"Well, not at the same time," Alex muttered. He could see having to explain that scenario soon, as Viv would likely blab to all her new friends at preschool. He'd cross that bridge when they came to it.

Lauren must've really loved the portrait because a week later she'd had the image transferred to a blanket, a pair of matching mugs, and a keychain. He figured it would probably be on their Christmas cards too.

Of course, the original hung in the hallway next to the other family pictures—Tammy, Alex and Viv, and the three of them. All of Viv's different families. One day in the not too distant future, she'd have a brother or sister—that was the plan after his and Lauren's one-year anniversary. He'd already warned Lauren that, while he was happy to be a dad, he was probably going to be an overprotective (mildly) irritating husband throughout her pregnancy because of what had happened with Tammy and fully expected to pass out during the birth. Lauren assured him she expected nothing less of her sweet alpha and declared it endearing. She also assured him she'd have a support person at the birth for both of them. Her complete acceptance and understanding touched him deeply. She was his soul mate, the one person perfect for him, that he never believed existed. He still couldn't believe he got so lucky to find her.

Two months later, they married.

Lauren was the most beautiful bride he'd ever seen in a white gown that looked like something you'd see on a princess.

His other princess wore her Kei-Kei and the elves dress. Naturally.

Dear Readers,

　　What will it take to get Josh and Hailey from two boxers in a ring to friends? Maybe a sneaky jab right to the heart. If only their defenses were down long enough! For now, Hailey is too busy looking out for good girl, Carrie, who's hell-bent on finding herself a bad boy for a fling. Next up is Carrie and Zach's story, *Bad Boy Done Wrong*, book 5 in the Happy Endings Book Club series. Join the club and get your happy ending!

Bad Boy Done Wrong

　　Good girl nurse Carrie Young only has to catch one glimpse of bad boy Zach Harrison with his wild hair, full beard, and hooded eyes to know he's exactly what she needs to get over all those wasted years with a repressed and controlling ex. Full seduction ahead!

　　Only the next morning, her bad boy doesn't disappear after having his wicked way with her and he's making her breakfast! WTF (What the fudge)! Did she do the bad boy thing all wrong?

　　Zach's no dummy. He knows a good thing when it falls into his lap. And if that means pretending to be a bad boy, he's game. No harm in a little role play, he figures. Besides, his work as an anthropologist will soon take him overseas. He's destined to be a lone wolf forever—near the action, not embroiled in it—great for his career *and* for ruining relation-ships. In the meantime, there's one naughty girl in need of a bad boy and he aims to please.

Sign up for my newsletter and never miss a new release! kyliegilmore.com/newsletter

ALSO BY KYLIE GILMORE

Unleashed Romance <<steamy romcoms with dogs!

Fetching (Book 1)

Dashing (Book 2)

Sporting (Book 3)

Toying (Book 4)

Blazing (Book 5)

Chasing (Book 6)

Daring (Book 7)

Leading (Book 8)

Racing (Book 9)

Loving (Book 10)

The Clover Park Series <<brothers who put family first!

The Opposite of Wild (Book 1)

Daisy Does It All (Book 2)

Bad Taste in Men (Book 3)

Kissing Santa (Book 4)

Restless Harmony (Book 5)

Not My Romeo (Book 6)

Rev Me Up (Book 7)

An Ambitious Engagement (Book 8)

Clutch Player (Book 9)

A Tempting Friendship (Book 10)

Clover Park Bride: Nico and Lily's Wedding

A Valentine's Day Gift (Book 11)

Maggie Meets Her Match (Book 12)

The Clover Park STUDS series <<hawt geeks who unleash into studs!

Almost Over It (Book 1)

Almost Married (Book 2)

Almost Fate (Book 3)

Almost in Love (Book 4)

Almost Romance (Book 5)

Almost Hitched (Book 6)

Happy Endings Book Club Series <<the Campbell family and a romance book club collide!

Hidden Hollywood (Book 1)

Inviting Trouble (Book 2)

So Revealing (Book 3)

Formal Arrangement (Book 4)

Bad Boy Done Wrong (Book 5)

Mess With Me (Book 6)

Resisting Fate (Book 7)

Chance of Romance (Book 8)

Wicked Flirt (Book 9)

An Inconvenient Plan (Book 10)

A Happy Endings Wedding (Book 11)

The Rourkes Series <<swoonworthy princes and kickass princesses!

Royal Catch (Book 1)

Royal Hottie (Book 2)

Royal Darling (Book 3)

Royal Charmer (Book 4)

Royal Player (Book 5)

Royal Shark (Book 6)

Rogue Prince (Book 7)

Rogue Gentleman (Book 8)

Rogue Rascal (Book 9)

Rogue Angel (Book 10)

Rogue Devil (Book 11)

Rogue Beast (Book 12)

**Check out my website for the most up-to-date list of my books:
kyliegilmore.com/books**

ABOUT THE AUTHOR

Kylie Gilmore is the *USA Today* bestselling author of the Unleashed Romance series, the Rourkes series, the Happy Endings Book Club series, the Clover Park series, and the Clover Park STUDS series. She writes humorous romance that makes you laugh, cry, and reach for a cold glass of water.

Kylie lives in New York with her family, two cats, and a nutso dog. When she's not writing, reading hot romance, or dutifully taking notes at writing conferences, you can find her flexing her muscles all the way to the high cabinet for her secret chocolate stash.

Sign up for Kylie's Newsletter and get a FREE book! kyliegilmore.com/newsletter

For text alerts on Kylie's new releases, text KYLIE to the number (888) 707-3025. (US only)

For more fun stuff check out Kylie's website https://www.kyliegilmore.com.

Thanks for reading *Formal Arrangement*. I hope you enjoyed it. Would you like to know about new releases? You can sign up for my new release email list at kyliegilmore.com/newsletter. I promise not to clog your inbox! Only new release info, sales, and some fun giveaways.

I love to hear from readers! You can find me at:
kyliegilmore.com
Instagram.com/kyliegilmore
Facebook.com/KylieGilmoreToo
Twitter @KylieGilmoreToo

If you liked Alex and Lauren's story, please leave a review on your favorite retailer's website or Goodreads. Thank you.

9 781942 238300